Madoc, Prince of America

A young prince, an outcast since his birth due to the jealousy of his powerful father, returns home to reconciliation and romance. But his happiness is short-lived, as the struggle for power amongst his family soon drives him away once more. Prince Madoc, minstrel, shipbuilder and navigator, shakes the dust of his native Wales from his feet and crosses the Western Ocean in a tiny vessel, to discover and settle a new land beyond the setting sun.

This is a novel based on the famous legend of Madoc, bastard son of the King of North Wales in the twelfth century. It has intrigued men's minds since a Flemish minstrel first wrote about it within fifty years of the extraordinary voyage. The story was scorned during the last few centuries as being mere Tudor propaganda, but recent historical researches have shown that there is good evidence that Prince Madoc actually reached the mainland of North America over three hundred years before the voyages of Columbus.

Bernard Knight

Madoc, Prince of America

ROBERT HALE LIMITED

LONDON

ST. MARTIN'S PRESS, INC.

NEW YORK

©Bernard Knight 1977
First published in Great Britain 1977
First published in the United States of America 1977

St. Martin's Press Inc.
175 Fifth Avenue
New York, N.Y. 10010.

Library of Congress Catalog Card Number 76-4653

Library of Congress Cataloging in Publication Data

Knight, Bernard.
  Madoc, prince of America.
   1. Madog ab Owain Gwynedd, 1150–1180? 2. America – Discovery
and exploration – Welsh. 3. Explorers – Wales – Biography. I. Title.
E109.W4M334   973.1'4'0924 [B]   76–4653

Robert Hale Limited
Clerkenwell House
Clerkenwell Green
London ECIR OHT

ISBN 0 7091 5868 8

Printed in Great Britain by
Clarke, Doble & Brendon Ltd,
Plymouth

AUTHOR'S NOTE

The truth behind the legend of Madoc has been hotly debated and disputed since Tudor times, as it was held to be merely English propaganda against the Spanish claims in the New World.

Throughout succeeding centuries, innumerable claims to contact with the "Welsh Indians" in North America have kept the dispute alive, even to the extent of an expedition being promoted amongst London Welshmen to explore the upper Missouri for their lost compatriots.

During the last century, a controversial National Eisteddfod essay added fuel to the fire of controversy, but in 1967, the definitive historical treatment of the subject was published by Richard Deacon, whose researches have greatly restored credence to the legend.

It is largely upon Richard Deacon's book that this novel is based and the author gratefully acknowledges his debt to Mr. Deacon's *Madoc and the Discovery of America,* as well as to personal communications.

Further thanks are due to the staff of the Cardiff Central Library, the British Museum, Mr. A. N. Stimson, Deputy Head of the Department of Navigation at the National Maritime Museum and to Mr. B. W. Bathe, of the Department of Water Transport of the Science Museum, South Kensington, for their assistance in providing material which, it is hoped, has added all possible authenticity to this story.

ONE

MAY 1160

The youth reined his horse at the top of the rise and waited for the old man to come plodding up behind him. Though his impatience was tempered by his respect for the other's reputation, he found it hard to conceal his impatience with the ungainly way the older man was draped side-saddle over the docile mare.

For his part, Gwalchmai, court bard to Owain Gwynedd, Prince of North Wales, heartily wished that he had made the journey on his own two feet. He was discovering that Irish horses were no more comfortable than the Welsh variety.

Gripping the long-suffering mare's mane tightly with one hand, Gwalchmai lumbered up to his guide, who sat across his own steed with an easy assurance.

Below, the wide curve of grey-blue sea that formed Dublin Bay, funnelled into the tidal channel of the River Liffey. The huts of Dublin itself were way up-river, but immediately below them were ship-yards that straggled untidily along the northern bank.

Rising smoke from a dozen fires showed where the midday meals were being prepared. The youth pointed down the slope to the river bank.

"He could be anywhere along there, sire. We shall have to ask for him." The old bard suffered the jolts of the mare as she picked her way through the rough grass and rabbit-holes of the scrub-covered land, long since robbed of trees to supply the boat-builders down below. There were no sizeable trees for as far as the eye could reach.

For several hundred years now, ever since the Northmen had erupted from their Scandinavian homes, these shores had provided the timbers for generations of the dragon-prowed ships and the less terrifying trading vessels that had succeeded them. Now timber had to be brought from Caledonia, Wales and the lush woodlands around the Severn Sea.

As they neared the Liffey, the sound of axe and adze on this vital wood came drifting up to them. Soon Gwalchmai could see ships in various stages of completion along the bank of the river. All flat-bottomed, their keels were laid on rollers well above the high-water mark. When finished, they were hauled to the water's edge and slid into the calmness of the Liffey, then towed to staithes nearby. Here the single stubby mast was fitted and the square leather-banded sail rigged.

The two Welshmen soon reached the edge of the yards, where the grass gave way to beaten mud and wood-shavings. A confusion of piled timber and waste wood stood around a few ramshackle huts, where tools were kept and meals eaten in bad weather. Further along were some larger, though equally wretched buildings, where women cooked and children played in the muddy squalor.

Idwal, the old man's guide, called out to a slatternly woman who was throwing corn to some dishevelled chickens, using words which Gwalchmai recognised as a curious mixture of Irish and Norse.

The woman shrugged and waved her hand vaguely towards the nearest boat being built. The Welsh boy moved on.

"Where might Madoc the minstrel be, friend?" Idwal asked several men passing by and each pointed towards the inland end of the boat-yards.

Here a noticeably larger ship was under construction. Gwalchmai could see a dozen men busy on the last stages of planking the sides, driving both iron nails and wooden pegs through into the oak ribs. Further up the bank, some women and even children were feeding scrap wood onto several fires that kept large cauldrons belching forth steam. Two figures were holding the end of a long plank in the vapour, warping it so that it could be forced into position along the curve of the bow. One of the figures was a tall, fair-haired young man, whom Idwal recognised.

"Hey, Madoc! I've brought a visitor for you," he yelled.

The fair youth waved back in recognition. Apparently the plank must have had enough steam, for the other man began hurrying towards the ship with it, leaving Madoc free to greet his visitors. In a moment he was standing expectantly at the side of Gwalchmai's horse. He recognised the old man as a bard by his flowing robes dyed in multi-coloured stripes and by the round cap above the pigtail of grey hair. The youth made a quick small bow and looked enquiringly at Idwal.

"This is a bard from your father's court, Madoc. He arrived at Clochran yesterday." The guide shifted his eyes to Gwalchmai. "This is the one you seek, sire. This is Madoc of the Ships." He grinned as he spoke and Madoc smiled with him, his blue eyes twinkling as he playfully grabbed at Idwal's leg. Gwalchmai again sighed inwardly at the full realisation of the generation gap between him and these young lads, the inheritors of his present world.

"I am Gwalchmai ap Meilyr, Madoc," he said gravely, "one of the Royal Bards of Prince Owain of Gwynedd. I have come especially to seek you, from your father's lands."

"The Prince has sent me a message, sir?"

Gwalchmai shook his head, a little sadly. "No, Madoc ab Owain . . . not your father. I come secretly from your mother."

The young man's face paled, then reddened in a blotchy livid pattern, so great was his confusion. "My mother, sir . . . but I never knew her name . . . nor even if she still lived."

Gwalchmai looked away from the boy, to the bustle, noise and squalor of the shipyard. "This is no place to talk of such things. We must go back to Clochran and I will give you my news in more tranquil surroundings."

Madoc, bewildered, bowed his head to the bard. "I will go and borrow a horse . . . I have been living here these past few days, helping with the big ship."

He dashed away towards the crude buildings and Idwal kicked his horse across to Gwalchmai's side.

"We will start back, sir. The sooner we are out of this stinking place, the better."

Gwalchmai pondered on the lad he had just met, a royal son of the Prince of North Wales. "Does he really live in that pig-sty of a place for days on end?"

Idwal nodded vigorously. "For weeks, sometimes. He is in love with ships and all manner of things to do with the sea. Though our cousin Merfyn of Clochran is always generous with hospitality, Madoc spends more and more of his time away from there. Sometimes, he actually goes to sea with the ship-masters. Last year, he was away for three months, when he went to Brittany

11

and France on a trading vessel. And this year, he went in a Viking *knarr* up to some islands in the far north of Caledonia."

Gwalchmai shook his head. "Vikings! Yes, of course Madoc has Norse blood in his veins, as well as Welsh. His great-grandmother was a Viking princess, who married his great-grandfather, Cynan ap Iago, when he was also in exile in Dublin. Strange how history repeats itself."

The thud of hooves on the turf came up behind them.

"Here he comes now,' said Idwal, "in a great haste to learn more. I know that for years, the thought of his mother has plagued him."

The bard risked a backward glance as he hung onto his horse's neck. "A fine lad. I wonder what he will make of my news."

After the evening meal was over, Merfyn, Lord of Clochran, led his guest to a small chamber off the wooden hall.

"Much as we would like to have the honour of your songs this night, Gwalchmai ap Meilyr, I think the fatigues of your journey and your need to talk privately with our beloved Madoc, must come first." Diplomatically, Merfyn withdrew and Gwalchmai beckoned Madoc near.

Gwalchmai saw the young man's open face gazing at him expectantly. Madoc was indeed a handsome youth, with a high brow, a longish face, but most of all an expression of calmness, almost innocence that rarely left it. Anger, greed and hatred would be strangers on a face like that—it was more the countenance that he had seen on hermits and saints, living apart from the troubles and temptations of civilisation.

"You have always known that you were a bastard son of Owain ap Gruffydd, the Prince they call Owain Gwynedd?" he began.

Madoc nodded, his blue Nordic eyes fixed on the bard's face. "I have lived here in Clochran ever since I can remember. Always, people have called me Madoc ab Owain Gwynedd and given me some respect for being the son of a great prince."

Gwalchmai smiled, almost cynically. "Yet exiled kin of princes, be they bastard or not, can be had by the sackful in Ireland, eh? Royal blood does not place gold in the purse!"

Madoc shook his head, puzzled. "No, but I care not about those. I have been happy with my friends and my ships, though sometimes I feel the call to live in the land of my birth."

12

"Your birth . . . what have they told you about that?"

"Nothing . . . some have said that my mother died in labour, others that she was but some servant or concubine of my father's, unknown by name. I feel somehow that they were wrong, but maybe that was wishful thinking."

Gwalchmai sighed. This boy had been deprived of his mother, denied by his father and exiled from his homeland, all in his short lifetime. Yet, Madoc had fallen on better times than many royal by-blows, having been fortunate in being adopted into the household of Merfyn who ran a little island of Welshness in the Dublin countryside.

"I know who your mother is, Madoc. I was in her company less than four days ago when she pleaded that I came to you with her message."

Madoc's expression almost glowed up at him.

"Who is my mother, sir . . . please?"

Gwalchmai looked down at him gravely. "She is Brenda, daughter of Hywel, Lord of Carno. Brenda, your father's favourite mistress these many years."

Amazement, then sheer elation chased themselves across Madoc's face. Suddenly he grasped Gwalchmai's hand in an impulsive gesture of gratitude. "Brenda . . . then I am a full brother to Riryd. Oh, God, Riryd, my real brother . . . my full, real brother."

Gwalchmai shrugged to himself. He had crossed the choppy Irish Sea and sat on a blasted horse for league after league to bring the news of a mother to Madoc and now the boy had gone into raptures because he had discovered that one of his nineteen half-brothers was also his full brother!

"Sit down, boy," he snapped, rather testily. "What is so important about Riryd?"

"He is my closest friend, as well as being a blood relative, sir. We share a love of ships and the sea . . . though he is seven years my senior, we are almost as twins. I knew that we must be especially close," he said fiercely, with a return of some of his excitement.

"Where is Riryd now?"

"Gone with a Cornish trading ship to Brittany. . . . I could have gone too, but this big vessel is near completion and I wanted to be at the launching." He brushed a hand across his face.

13

"But my mother, please . . . what of her? What is she like . . . is she well . . . what message did she send me?"

"Wait . . . wait! Firstly, she wants to see you, that is the main reason for my visit. Secondly, no one is to know of this matter for the time being until she can sound out your father's reaction to news of your return to Gwynedd."

Madoc's smooth brow creased. "Why should that be, sire? Why have I always needed to remain here in Ireland, banished and unrecognised? Riryd, son of the same parents, has been to Prince Owain's court and acknowledges our mother openly."

Gwalchmai sighed. "It's a long story, Madoc . . . a long story."

TWO

JUNE 1160

Madoc crouched alongside Gwalchmai as the little boat clawed its way along the last stage of their voyage.

The old bard was almost as bad a sailor as he was a horseman for he groaned for most of the two days' journey from Dublin to North Wales.

It was not a planked ship, but an Irish *curragh,* made of tarred skins stretched over a flimsy framework. As the three scrawny Irishmen who made up the crew fought the little boat across the ebbing tide towards Deganwy, it lifted and slapped sickeningly on the choppy waters. They were painfully edging across the broad stretch of shallow sea between the island of Môn—or Anglesey, as it was becoming known since the Norseman's arrival—and the great hook of the Orme peninsula—another recent Viking name. The waters here funnelled down into the narrow northern entry of the Menai Straits and on their right, the great mountains of Eryri* loomed in the summer mists.

Madoc stared thoughtfully at the massive bulwarks of Gwynedd towering into the clouds. It was behind that central core of Eryri that they were bound : there that Madoc had been born—in the little castle of Dolwyddelan, one of the strongholds of the Princes of Gwynedd.

"Gwalchmai, where does my royal father spend most of his time now—in Dolwyddelan or Aberffraw?"

The bard painfully swallowed the welling saliva that accompanied his nausea. "Uh . . . mainly in Môn, my son . . . though he comes quite often to Dolwyddelan . . . Oh, Christ, will this journey last for ever?"

Yet two hours later, when they had their feet on the solid ground at the port of Deganwy, Gwalchmai rapidly came back to life. They lodged for the night at an inn looking across the estuary of the Conwy river. Though Gwalchmai, as a royal bard,

* Snowdonia.

15

could have claimed lodging in the castle of Dinas Conwy, he preferred to keep clear of any establishments belonging to Owain Gwynedd until the reaction of that fiery prince to the reappearance of yet another of his bastards could be gauged.

Next morning, they set out early on two hired horses. Noon saw them sixteen miles up the broad vale of Conwy, to the point where the little Lledr river came down a side valley from the southern peaks of Eryri.

By late afternoon, they were at Dolwyddelan. Madoc had been getting more and more restless as he neared his birthplace, which he had left long before he could remember any events of his childhood. In fact, he had no idea how old he had been when he left the castle. He asked Gwalchmai, just before they turned the last bend into the pleasantly wooded valley.

"How old, boy? About three weeks. It would have been three hours if the prince had got to know the truth earlier." He refused to be drawn further and they rode in silence up the quiet vale towards the castle of Dolwyddelan.

It stood on a spur on their right hand, high above the meadows of the valley. The old road, originally Roman, came from Ardudwy in the west and climbed behind the castle on the barren southern slopes of Moel Siabod, one of the southern outliers of Eryri. This road cut away from them over the hills, to join the Vale of Conwy downstream from the confluence of the Lledr.

They came to a little stream that tumbled down through rocks and sodden turf from the castle to the meadows. A path led up towards the old road and the entrance to the fortress. Madoc looked with curiosity and some misgivings at the royal building now silhouetted against the reddening western sky. It was here that he had been delivered into the world—by all accounts, a world that had not been particularly excited about his arrival.

After nineteen years, he was to meet his mother again—and hope not to meet his father. Gwalchmai had made sure in Deganwy that Prince Owain ap Gwynedd was safely housed in Anglesey at his major court of Aberffaw. Though the bard hoped to engineer Madoc's acceptance at the court of Gwynedd, the time was not yet ripe for such an abrupt disclosure.

So the bard's consternation was acute when he heard Madoc exclaim as he pointed back along the old road across the hills.

"A cavalcade, Gwalchmai . . . who can be coming?"

The older man picked up the hem of his robe and hurried to the youth's side. Shielding his eyes, he squinted across the rough uplands towards the Vale of Conwy. The sun glittered off the pennants and spear-heads of a procession winding its way along the road, still three miles distant.

Gwalchmai groaned. "It can be no one else but Owain Fawr!"

"But you said he was safe in Môn! They told you this morning at the port," protested Madoc, a sudden feeling of terror gripping him.

"Then they told me wrong!" snapped the bard, anxiety fraying his temper. He whirled around and dragged his horse towards the castle, which loomed high over their heads. "Quickly, let us get you tucked away at once . . . it will be the better part of an hour before they reach the gates. We must see whether your mother feels that you can safely be hidden away."

They hurried the last few hundred paces to the castle, which perched on a great rocky hump amidst marshy ground. A long pool acted as an incomplete moat on the side facing them. A rough wooden bridge, merely a few crude planks, stretched across it and on the other side, rough steps were hewn into the rock to climb to the narrow gateway.

"I had imagined Dolwyddelan to be all in stone," murmured Madoc, as he followed on the heels of Gwalchmai.

"It will be soon, boy . . . the keep has been re-fashioned in masonry already . . . your father intends to do the same with the West Tower and the curtain walls before long . . . apeing the Normans, I call it!"

It was more a fortified tower than a castle, only the new stone keep having any air of dignity about it. This was two storeys high and had a gabled roof. The rest of the castle was composed of a wooden stockade diverging from each side of the keep, which stood on the apex of the crag overlooking the Lledr valley. The palisade enclosed the whole rugged platform of rock and a lower, wider wooden tower formed the remainder of the structure at the opposite angle. The whole place was not more than forty paces across in any direction—its cramped quarters were emphasised by the straggling collection of huts and shacks that clustered around the foot of the crag and housed the more lowly members of the Dolwyddelan household.

These were times of peace, at least here, right in the heart of

Owain Gwynedd's kingdom and the security on the gate was a mere token. The castellan and his staff were too concerned with the distant sight of the Prince approaching to bother with the familiar figure of Gwalchmai the bard and some young man he had picked up in his travels.

The pair passed unheeded among the busy folk in the small courtyard as they made their way towards the flight of steps that led up to the entrance of the keep. The only door was a dozen feet above the ground, to make defence easier, the basement being entered only through a trap-door in the floor of the hall. Above this was a single large bed-chamber, together with a few tiny closets cut in the thickness of the walls.

At the great studded door into the hall, Gwalchmai stopped an agitated maid-servant and asked after the Lady Brenda.

"In her chamber, *Pencerdd*,"* she said hurriedly, "getting herself ready for the lord's appearance."

Gwalchmai groaned. Turning back, he swung the bemused Madoc around and went back down to the courtyard. "Lady Brenda lives in the West Tower . . . I had thought to find her in the hall."

Madoc looked at him in puzzlement. "Why does not my mother stay in the main bed-chamber up there, then?"

Gwalchmai nudged him sharply with his elbow, as they passed through the thronged yard. "Keep your voice down, boy . . . no one is to know who you are until we see how the land lies. You are Merfyn, an apprentice bard from Aberdaron, understand."

Madoc nodded reluctantly.

"But why is she skulking in this old wooden house, when a new stone keep lies within arm's reach?" he persisted, in a lower tone.

"Boy, your life in that wild bog of Ireland has made you innocent—or simple," hissed Gwalchmai. "Look, your royal father has a wife . . . albeit a union cursed by the priests of Rome. Even he must pay lip service to convention."

They plunged into the gloom of the West Tower, a grand name for a structure that looked like a high barn with massive oaken walls. The ground floor was a combined kitchen and eating hall for the lesser folk of Dolwyddelan, but a stair at one side led to an upper floor divided into three chambers, the largest of which

* Chief bard.

18

was that of Brenda, favourite concubine of Owain Gwynedd for so many years.

As in the rest of the castle, all was bustle and preparation, the permanent retainers scurrying around to get the place ready for an extra two score people. They climbed the stairs and came to a low door at the end of the short corridor above.

The bard tapped, his ear close to the jamb. As soon as he was bidden, he pushed the door open and gestured for Madoc to follow.

Madoc's eyes rapidly sensed a big curtained bed and sombre tapestries hanging from the walls. Even before his gaze dropped to the woman standing expectantly in the centre of the room, his mind seized on the probability that that bed was where he had been both conceived and born.

He looked at the figure waiting to greet him. Without a doubt, this was his mother. It was in her face and her eyes as she came across the room, hands outstretched. She had borne a number of sons—and insignificant daughters—to Owain Gwynedd, but here was one who had been taken from her almost at birth.

On his part, he suddenly found his blue eyes unaccountably full of tears. Blinking them back indignantly, he darted forward, intending to kneel before Brenda, but somehow the formal gesture seemed to crumble on the way and he found his face crushed into her waist and his arms gripping her mantle below the armpits.

For a moment, no one spoke, the mother's cheek pressed into his hair, the boy struggling to regain his manly composure.

It was Gwalchmai who broke the silence, with a warning.

"Lady, Owain Fawr is within sight. You must say what you wish to be done."

Brenda looked up at the old bard over her son's head. "How long?" she asked.

"Half an hour . . . the cavalcade is but a mile away by now."

She put her hand on Madoc's head. "Five minutes . . . give us five minutes, Gwalchmai, then come for him."

The court poet nodded and vanished silently.

"Madoc . . . my son," said Brenda gently. Sniffing loudly, Madoc pulled himself to his feet. He stepped back, but still held his mother's hands in his.

"You are a fair, fine boy, Madoc." Her voice was choked with emotion. "So much like Riryd."

19

Madoc nodded eagerly. "Almost as much as I yearned to meet you, I ached to know that he was my full brother."

The distant blast of a horn brought them back to reality. "Owain Fawr . . . he will be here soon." Brenda's eyes darted to the window. It faced the wrong way to see the road, but it was obvious that the cavalcade was near.

"My father—he knows nothing of me?" asked Madoc impulsively.

His mother shook her head sadly. "He has seventeen sons that he acknowledges—no one has bothered to count the daughters. Several more sons—you included—he banished at birth. He already has too much dissent and competition from his elder sons to want to add to it."

There was a discreet, but urgent tapping on the door and Gwalchmai put his head around the rough boards. "The lad must come, my lady. The royal party is almost at the gates."

Brenda gave a last squeeze to Madoc's shoulders and pushed him towards the bard. "As soon as there is an opportunity, you will come to me again, my son."

Madoc stooped quickly and kissed his mother's hand. As he walked across to the door, Brenda spoke to Gwalchmai. "Where will you hide him? He must be safe; his father is not yet ready to know of his existence."

As Madoc slipped out into the passage under Gwalchmai's arm, the bard reassured his mother. "There are a score of young lads about the castle, one more will not be noticed. If anyone asks, he is Merfyn, a young bard-pupil of mine. I will lodge him with the servants; he will be quite safe."

They hurried out into the courtyard and jostled into the throng that waited there for the arrival of their Prince. Iago, the *Penteulu** of Dolwyddelan, was stalking about, yelling orders to the castle guard who lined the parapet walk of the massive wooden stockade.

"Can I stay and watch my father arrive?" Madoc asked Gwalchmai, as they struggled through the pushing crowd.

The bard flashed startled eyes across at the lad, who was as tall as himself. "Ssh, boy!" he muttered. "Keep your voice down and your thoughts to yourself. There are those here who would delight in carrying tales. I have not suffered that cursed journey by boat just to have it wasted by seeing you hanged."

* Head of the Household.

20

"But may we stay—just for a few moments?" persisted Madoc.

Gwalchmai nodded. "Keep in the background, then. Afterwards, we must go outside to the servants' huts to get you a place to stay."

Moments later, a ragged cheer came from beyond the gate and the leather-jerkined guards on the parapet raised their spears in salute. There was a stir and a shuffling around the gate and then Iago came striding in, leading the royal party. Madoc sensed the natural dignity of the occasion as the Prince of Gwynedd returned to his family—for such was the unity of the Welsh clan, that even the lowliest kitchen-maid felt bound to Prince Owain by chains of affection and loyalty.

And here he was, Owain, the Lion of North Wales, son of the great Gruffudd ap Cynan. Between them, the father and son had held the North against the hated Normans, slowly pushing out further and further, turning Wales into a power that held its head level with many other kingdoms in Europe.

Striding behind Iago, he towered over most of the men nearby. The half Viking blood of his father had come out in full in Owain's generation, giving him a blond massiveness that contrasted strangely with the small darkness of the Welshmen around him.

Madoc, himself fair and taller than average, bent his knees instinctively, partly in awe and partly afraid that his height and colouring might give him away as yet another bastard of the Prince.

But every eye was on Owain Fawr and his eyes were on the stair-case to the keep, where Lady Cristin waited with a cluster of children and hand-maidens. With a roar of welcome, Owain waved his hand to her. The blond giant hurried across the little courtyard, bounded up the stairs and embraced his wife robustly. With a wave to the grinning throng below, he turned and ushered Cristin into the hall of the keep, the great studded door shutting with a bang.

As the rest of the cavalcade straggled into the courtyard, Madoc looked at Gwalchmai who was smiling at him with a curious expression.

"And what did you think of your royal relation?" he murmured.

Madoc shook his head. "He is a great man, both in his size, his dress and his bearing. But he seems more of a stranger than, say,

21

any new sea-captain that drops anchor in the Liffey." He shook his head sadly again. "I don't feel that with Brenda. At once, there was a bond between us."

Gwalchmai shrugged. "To be expected, boy. Your mother bore you and for three weeks, mothered you. You have never clapped eyes on your father before—nor he on you, thank God."

"Do you think my father might ever be made to acknowledge me, Gwalchmai?" he asked sadly, as they left the stockade.

Gwalchmai's grey beard wagged as he rubbed his chin thoughtfully. "Before he can acknowledge you, my son, he must learn of your existence. It is nineteen years since he learned he had yet another brat from Brenda. In those days, all new sons were potential rivals, but now the problem seems to have crystallised down to the jealousies between Iorwerth, Dafydd, Rhodri and Hywel." He stopped on the steps and looked pensively across at the bare moors stretching towards Eryri. "It depends now on whether he sees you as yet another possible contender for the throne of Gwynedd or if he accepts that the four elder boys must fight it out between themselves."

With that rather gloomy opinion, he started down the ramp again, with Madoc walking sadly at his side.

Once across the bridge, they turned left, where stretching along both sides of the rough track were a scattered collection of huts, stables and smithies. Gwalchmai made for one of the largest, around which a group of barefoot children were playing.

The hut was divided into a number of cubicles around a central common area. There was a wide balcony just above head level, also made into little rooms by wattle or cloth screens. Smoke rose from a large cooking fire in the centre, filtering both through a hole in the roof and wafting indiscriminately through the walls and thatch.

"This is a primitive place compared with the Prince's main court at Aberffraw," growled Gwalchmai. He looked around and then strode across to a cubicle against the far wall, where a figure lay on a heap of rushes, softly strumming a small harp.

"Ho, Llywarch . . . get up and meet a friend of mine."

The man looked up and Madoc saw that the face was extraordinarily long, a caricature with a wide upper lip and a long, pointed chin. A pair of humorous brown eyes twinkled in these odd features as he scrambled to his feet.

"This is Merfyn, a young friend of mine from Llŷn. He also has some ability with the harp and a voice that does justice to his playing."

Llywarch was only about thirty years old, but already wore the multi-coloured robe and the pigtailed hair of a professional bard. This was Llywarch ap Llewelyn, one of Prince Owain's official bards. Whereas Gwalchmai was Owain's *Pencerdd* or "Head of Song," Llywarch was only the *Bard teulu*, the resident family songster of Dolwyddelan itself.

"Another of the brotherhood, eh! Welcome, Merfyn, to this pigsty which we call home." He swept his hand about him in a grand gesture, taking in the women baking and washing, the infants squealing and the chickens pecking on the earthen floor.

"Pigsty!" guffawed Gwalchmai. "Is that why they are beginning to call you Llywarch Pryddyd y Moch . . . Poet of the Pigs?"

Madoc sensed that there was no great affection between these two. This was usually the case between bards. It was a highly competitive profession and there were constant jealousies between them for the favour of their royal masters. It was even more so between the younger ones and the older, as the latter constantly feared that the new man would jostle them out of their patronage.

"Merfyn will be here for a few days, until he moves on with me to either Dolbadarn or Aberffraw . . . I promised to show him the great houses of our Lord Owain—and let him hear the real bards at work."

Llywarch nodded and beamed at Madoc. "And he'll be wanting a place to lay his head and fill his belly, no doubt? I'll see to it, never fear. We songsters must keep together, eh?"

Gwalchmai thanked the younger bard and took his leave of Madoc. "I'll call for you in the morning. I'll arrange something then, it cannot be before that." Madoc knew he was referring to another secret visit to his mother.

Llywarch put an arm around Madoc's shoulders and led him to a bench at a table just inside the doorway of the hut.

"Let's talk, Merfyn. Tell me about yourself."

As people came and went past them, Madoc had to keep his wits about him to fabricate a tale of how he came from a sea-faring family at Aberdaron, a little village on the Llyn peninsula some forty miles away. He stuck as closely as he could to the tale that Gwalchmai had thought up for him. The Bard of the Pigs listened politely, then suddenly slapped his thigh. "What an ill-mannered lout you must think me. You've journeyed from Llyn today and not eaten for many hours, I'll wager. Let's get something to keep us alive . . . I could do with it myself."

Madoc was to learn that Llywarch had a thirst and an appetite that was unmatched in the whole of Gwynedd. He called to a girl who had just come from the direction of the castle.

"Annesta! Come and meet a fine young man . . . but before you do, get us a pitcher of beer and some bread, there's a good girl."

Annesta was slim and dark, with a pair of deep set eyes that now turned on Madoc with an interest that matched his own. She smiled quickly, then hurried into the hut.

"Didn't I see her on the steps of the keep when my . . . when Prince Owain came in just now?" he asked Llywarch.

The long face nodded back at him. "No doubt—she would have been standing behind *Yr Arglwyddes** Cristin, as she is one of her maids."

For a moment, all thoughts of his father, his mother and even Wales vanished from Madoc's mind as he recalled Annesta's face and figure into his mind's eye. Llywarch grinned at him crookedly. "She is not spoken for by any man yet, Merfyn . . . and she sleeps in this very hut."

Before they could elaborate on the matter, Annesta herself came out of the doorway, carrying a pitcher of beer, a loaf and some cheese, which she put on the table before Llywarch.

"There you are, bard—my part of the bargain done. Now tell me who your friend is."

Llywarch, though a rising figure in the hierarchy of the household of Owain Gwynedd, never held airs to himself and even a lowly maidservant could talk to him as equal. It was soon clear that Annesta was a girl of independent spirit and carried herself with a natural dignity.

Llywarch introduced Madoc as Merfyn of Aberdaron and the girl slipped on to the bench next to him as they ate. Madoc felt strangely attracted to Annesta. He had had girl friends in plenty in Clochran and in an age when girls became marriageable at twelve and boys at fourteen, he was no stranger to robust love-

* The Lady.

24

making. But after a few moments of listening to her soft voice and looking at her deep, thoughtful eyes, he felt a strangeness inside him that made him glad that he had come to Dolwyddelan.

Half an hour later, the girl had to return to her duties with the Lady Cristin. Llywarch went with her to the keep, to find out from the *Penteulu* what form of entertainment was to be held in the hall that evening. Madoc was left to his own devices. He went up to the little cubicle on the balcony that Llywarch had pointed out and went sound asleep until the sun was almost on the horizon.

He dined that night in the large room under his mother's lodging in the West Tower of the castle, where most of the senior servants and men-at-arms had their meals. The Hall at Dol-wyddelan was too small to hold any more than the Prince, his family, his guests and the chief officers of his court. It was nothing but a large square room occupying the whole of the floor above the basement. In the thickness of one wall was a steep stair running up to the large bedchamber above, where Cristin and Owain slept. All the rest of the household and court had to find what space they could either in the West Tower or in the motley collection of huts outside. When the Prince was in residence, the whole settlement was stuffed with people as tightly as fleas on a hedgehog.

After the meal was over in the hall, Gwalchmai sent word to Madoc, telling him to come up to the main chamber to hear the entertainment. Clustering at the doorway with other castle inhabitants, he saw and heard both the Chief of Song, Gwalchmai himself and the Household Bard, Llywarch, give their traditional recitals to the Prince and his retainers. A very proficient performer himself, Madoc could well appreciate the superb talents of the two bards, both in poetry, song and mastery of the small harp.

As the mead and beer flowed, Gwalchmai sang first of the glory of God and the exploits of Prince Owain of Gwynedd. Then it was the turn of Llywarch, who sang as custom demanded, of ancient heroes and exploits of others nearer their own time. In a century that was filled with almost continual warfare against the invading Normans, there was no lack of tales of bravery, often exaggerated, but full of fire and rhythm.

Eventually the sight-seers on the stairs wandered off, leaving

25

the revellers in the hall to drink and talk the night away.

In spite of his afternoon slumber, Madoc was still tired after the three-day journey from Ireland and he made straight for his straw-filled blanket on the balcony. He knew that he was very fortunate, compared to many in that over-filled castle. Some of these others were lying below on the floor, huddled in their cloaks around the smouldering fire.

His own thick travelling cloak was quite adequate in that spring night and he was almost fast asleep, when he heard a soft rustling in the straw and felt a slight breeze on his face as the hessian was lifted.

Instinctively, his hand slipped down to his knife, but he had taken off the belt before going to bed. But no noctural robber or assassin had entered. A soft tress and long hair brushed lightly over his face as a head was lowered to whisper to him.

"Are you still awake? I felt like talking to you."

He sat bolt upright, his heart hammering suddenly within his chest.

"Annesta?" He shook the remnant of sleep from him in an instant.

The girl, wearing a dark cloak, slid down and sat alongside him on the mattress. Madoc was only too glad to have her company.

They spoke for some time, about all manner of things, keeping their voices low, not for secrecy but to avoid disturbing others in that crowded building. Their talk went on against a background of foot-steps, low conversation, the occasional giggle from other beds.

Privacy was virtually unknown, except to the favoured few and they were oblivious of the nearby snores of sleepers and the whimper of babes, separated from them by no more than wattle screens.

As their talk went on, Madoc's hand went across the bed and took one of hers. Her fingers responded and they edged nearer.

For almost an hour they talked of the castle, the personalities that lived there and of the gossip of Gwynedd.

He found the girl a mine of useful information, as well as being a most intelligent and thoughtful person, without any malice towards those amongst whom she lived. He began teasing her mildly as he felt their relationship becoming closer and their mild flirtation grew into kisses.

But Madoc, through his pleasure, felt that there was still something else that Annesta was trying to bring up in their playful talk. Eventually she broke away from a kiss and pulled her head back far enough to look into the dim blur of his face in the gloom.

"What's your real name, Merfyn? And why are you here in Dolwyddelan?" She asked this with a directness that he was to learn was characteristic of her nature.

The words brought him down to earth from the delights of dalliance, to a slightly suspicious defensiveness. For a moment, he wondered whether the girl had been sent to spy on him, but that idea seemed ridiculous, and he felt that either Gwalchmai or even his own mother might have let fall some incautious remark to the servants "Who am I?" He tried to sound puzzled. "I'm Merfyn, you know that. From Aberdaron."

She reached out her hand again and dug her sharp nails into his wrist.

"Don't tell me that, for I've lived in Llyn myself, since we moved from Dinas Dinlle when I was four years old. I lived in Abersoch, not ten miles from Aberdaron. And I've never heard of a young bard called Merfyn from there." Madoc groaned. Of all the places in Wales, Gwalchmai had to pick upon the one that would sink his story within a few hours.

"But I am!" he muttered feebly.

Annesta jabbed him again. "Even if I were not from Llyn, I could tell by your voice. You're a Welshman all right, but you're from Ireland. I've heard too many sailors in Abersoch, not to recognise the accent." She slid her arms around him and squeezed tighter. "Who are you, fair man?"

Madoc had no heart to lie to this unusual girl. "It's true I have lived long in Ireland, though I was born in this very castle. But I have been in Aberdaron many a time," he added defiantly, for it was true. He often sailed with both Irish and Norse vessels and Aberdaron was one of the main ports of call.

"Then what's your real name—and why are you here?" the dark-haired girl persisted.

Madoc hesitated. "It might be a danger for me if it became common knowledge," he countered.

Annesta kissed his lips. "I'll not bring you into danger."

He believed her and with a feeling of relief at being able to

27

share his secret, he whispered somewhat dramatically into her ear, "I am Madoc and I am of the House of Gwynedd."

Annesta hugged him in a gesture of delight at being allowed into the secret. "You mean . . . you are a bastard of Lord Owain?"

"My mother is Brenda. This is the first time I have seen her since my birth. Gwalchmai brought me secretly from Dublin, where I live with the Welsh at Clochran."

"Then you must be one of those that the older serving women talk about round the fire . . . several sons of our Prince were banished they say. Maybe even killed, some of them."

"I was taken to Ireland. I know not how it was done, I hope to learn something more when I see my mother again tomorrow."

Annesta sat quietly, thinking this over. "Do you think your father would still have emnity against you, after all this time?"

Madoc grunted. "It is a risk I do not care to take until I see which way the wind blows. So if you care for me, Annesta, keep a tight guard on your tongue, especially amongst the other maids."

Fervently, she swore that the secret would be safe, and added, "I must go soon. I sleep in the passage outside the main bed-chamber. Though there are two other girls with me, there may be some disturbance and if Lady Cristin finds me missing, there will be trouble."

"Is she a hard mistress?" asked Madoc curiously.

"No, *Yr Arglwyddes* is a lovely lady. Strict, as befits a princess, but fair-minded even to the lowest scullion."

"And Lord Owain . . . he loves her?" Madoc found it hard to understand how a man who openly had many concubines, could marry a second time, even if it was partly in defiance of Rome.

"He seems greatly attached to her" said Annesta. "They say that since Cristin has been his wife, he has shunned almost all his other women . . . with the exception of Brenda, of course."

"He looks much older than I had expected" mused Madoc, perhaps connecting in his mind his father's waning passions with his advancing age. Annesta wriggled out of his encircling arms and gave him one last kiss in the darkness.

"I must go . . . I will see you again tomorrow. I'll see that you get some good food, too. So, lie back and get some sweet sleep . . . my Madoc" she whispered.

"My name is Merfyn . . . and don't you forget it," he hissed

28

back. "I'll count the minutes until we're here together again tomorrow night."

But fate had other things in store for them.

THREE

JUNE 1160

It was late evening on the next day before Madoc again saw his mother. Gwalchmai came across to his lodging an hour before the evening meal and told him that Brenda had arranged to avoid dining in the hall that evening, so that they might have an undisturbed hour together.

"It seems strange, Gwalchmai, that both my mother and the Lady Cristin share the same table."

The Chief Bard chuckled at the lad's innocence. "I have seen three of Owain's concubines chattering to his wife at the table before now, with every sign of friendship. Both Cristin and his former queen, the Lady Gwladys—Christ rest her soul—held it quite natural that such a virile warrior as Owain Fawr could not manage with merely one woman. Though my Lord Owain gets old now, as I do. He has not the same appetite that he had in days gone by."

Madoc waited until the sounds of dishes and revelry were in full spate in the keep before he went warily up the stairs of the Western tower.

He tapped on the door and went in at his mother's ready command. Again they embraced, then Madoc threw himself across the heavy covers of the bed whilst Brenda sat in the only chair, near the window. Some tallow dips gave a flickering light but bright moonlight from the open shutters helped them to see each other.

"This is little like the castle I expected, lady," he said somewhat ruefully. "It is smaller than Clochran and has less outbuildings. I thought the Prince of Gwynedd would have a great palace. We hear that he has dealings with France and other kingdoms on the continent. There would be little room for their envoys in this eagle's nest."

Brenda smiled in the gloom. "This is but his mountain retreat, Madoc. Aberffraw is much greater and if he listened to Llywarch, it would be the only court of North Wales. But Dolwyddelan has been the saviour of our princes before now, when the Normans march in and prey upon us. From here, we can slip away into *Eryri* within a few hours . . . . and we have had to do it, before now, bag and baggage."

"You live here always, mother?"

"No, my son. I go with the court to Anglesey now and then. But I prefer it here, all my children were born here, including you."

Madoc sighed at all the lost knowledge he had to catch up on. "I do not even know who my brothers and sisters are, except for Riryd of Clochran."

Brenda smiled gently at him again. "You have many, Madoc. I have never lain with any other man but Owain Gwynedd and we have begot six children. Besides you, there is Riryd, Cynan and Rhun, as well as the two girls, Gwenllian and Goeral. So you will never lack for kindred !"

Madoc digested this for a moment, then asked, "What happened at my birth, lady? Why was I banished, and not others?"

Brenda reached out and laid a hand on his. "It was chance, a particular moment when fortunes were pressing hard on Owain. He had had three sons born that year by different women and both you and Riryd were sent away. Owain cared not where or how as long as you both vanished from sight."

"Even now, mother, nineteen years later?"

Brenda made a helpless little movement of her shoulders. "Gwalchmai, who has always been a good friend to me, is to sound out the matter gently with Lord Owain. He is a man that can never be moved by force, but can be led by diplomacy, at which our *pencerdd* is a master. But it will take time."

Madoc plied his mother with questions about his family. He learned that his brother Riryd, seven years his senior, would eventually inherit the lands at Clochran in Ireland, as this was a grant from their grandfather, Hywel, Lord of Carno in Central Wales, to the eldest son of his daughter Brenda. Of his other full brothers, all were dispersed and both the girls had recently been married at the usual wedding age of about thirteen.

"Enough about us and our endless relatives," said Brenda at length. "Tell me about you. It's not every day I have a long-lost boy come back to me. Tell me how you fare and what you do."

31

Madoc squeezed her hand affectionately. "You knew where I was all these years, did you not?" he asked.

"Yes, messages came to me from Clochran. The place is a hive of exiled Welshmen—Ireland was ever a haven for those driven from Gwynedd by family quarrels and the reprisals of the French. I have heard from Riryd often, though I told him not to tell you of your true origins until it was safe for the news to be abroad."

"What did he tell you of me, my best, big brother?" asked Madoc gaily.

"That you were a sweet songster and an even better sailor. Madoc of the Ships, they said you were called over there."

"I love the sea, lady. All the time I can get, I spend at the shipyards and wharfs of Dublin. Already, I can plan and build a boat as well as any Norseman. It must be the blood I had from my father."

Brenda laughed, her handsome face catching the candlelight. "It was certainly not my blood, son. The family of Carno would not trust themselves in a coracle on a rain puddle. It must be your grandfather and his own mother, the Viking girl Ragenhildr, daughter of King Sitric of the Silken Beard."

Madoc nodded eagerly. "Yes, Riryd told me of them. Our blue eyes and fair hair must come straight from the Norselands. One day, I will follow my ancestors across the Great Seas. There are wonderful tales to be heard around the fires in Dublin, of strange lands covered with ice and fairer lands beyond."

His mother became quiet all of a sudden. "Perhaps you would do well to do just that, Madoc," she said sadly. "I fear to think what will happen when your father dies. I hope that I shall be gone myself before then, not to see the feuding and bloodshed that will follow his passing."

He caught the seriousness of her voice and was sad himself. "What will happen, mother? Who will take the throne of Gwynedd?"

Brenda moved restlessly in her chair. "Owain has twenty-eight children as far as people have bothered to count. Of his eighteen sons, only four are to be serious contenders for his power. Hywel, son of Pyfog, the Irishwoman, is one, but it is Dafydd and Rhodri, sons of Cristin, who will stop at nothing."

"What of Iorwerth . . . he is the eldest?" asked Madoc.

"He has this deformity of his face—a birthmark that twists his features so that he is known behind his back as Iorwerth Drwyndwyn—the Crooked-nosed. There is talk of dispossessing him as one who is not fitting to be ruler of North Wales with such a deformity. And it is Dafydd and Rhodri who are in the fore-front of such whispers."

"But my father is a strong robust man . . . he will live for ever."

Brenda shook her head slowly. "He is well over fifty now. That is a good age for a man to survive so many battles and plagues. Already his elder sons are beginning to watch him covertly to see him weaken. I only hope God will take me first, I could not bear to see my man wither or be cut down."

Madoc swung himself off the bed and knelt at his mother's feet. "Neither of you will be taken this many a long year. I will somehow make my peace with my father and come and live in Gwynedd with you. Though I shall make it clear that I will be no contender in this battle for the princedom. All I want is to sail the seas when the whim takes me and to make music on the hillsides when I feel like solitude."

Brenda smoothed his head as he crouched near her. "You are a poet as well as a sailor. And *that* is the blood of Carno, you may be sure."

She seemed quickly restored to cheerfulness and putting her arms about his shoulders, pressed his head lovingly against her breast.

At that moment, the door flew open with a crash and the room suddenly was filled with huge, menacing figures holding blazing torches aloft.

Before the paralysed Brenda and her son could move, they found the great figure of Owain Fawr, Prince of Gwynedd, looming over them.

"So, my Brenda, after all these years, you have palled of my company and taken a younger lover?" His voice was like the edge of a sword drawn across rock, as he pointed contemptuously to the petrified Madoc. "Take this thing and lock him up, until I find the time to dismember him!"

As Madoc opened his mouth to speak, a huge, horny hand was clapped across it and he was dragged on his heels towards the door.

Madoc came groggily back to consciousness to find himself in total darkness. His first act was to be violently sick, a terrible dizziness gripping his brain. Fighting down the nausea, he gradually recovered his senses and found that his main trouble was a severe headache, apparently due to a tender area about his left ear, where a large lump and blood-matted hair told of some recent injury. Gradually memory returned as far as the point where he had been grabbed by Prince Owain's men-at-arms in his mother's chamber.

Madoc groaned, not with pain but with the misery of the memory. The very thing that they had tried to avoid had happened within minutes of his meeting with Brenda of Carno. Now he was discovered, his mother was disgraced and if his father's reputation was true, he had little hope of mercy.

Then his fuddled mind cleared enough to pick out a memory that was at odds with his fears. He remembered his father yelling something about having discovered Brenda with a lover, not a clandestine son. Still, he thought dismally, being hung or beheaded for alleged adultery was no less unpleasant than being executed for being an unwanted bastard.

He gingerly tested his limbs to see if he was injured elsewhere, but all his functions seemed intact, apart from numbness and stiffness after lying crumpled on a hard earthen floor.

There was not a glimmer of light, but he could hear occasional scraping noises and once, some hollow footsteps from above his head. He scrambled to his feet and after fighting down a fresh wave of sickness that the movement aroused, he stumbled around to try to discover his whereabouts. There were boxes, barrels and sacks scattered in the darkness and a mixture of smells ranging from herbs and malt to stale excreta and damp wood. Rats scuttled in the gloom and he knew now that he must be in the basement of the keep.

It must be the middle of the night, as the castle was so quiet. He paced around, until returning nausea and hacked shins from stumbling over obstructions forced him to lie on the ground again. Tiredness, misery and a hovering fear of the unknown drove him into an uneasy sleep. When he woke, there were noises above, the dragging of benches, the stamp of feet and the buzz of voices, broken by shouts and laughter. Soon, smells of cooking wafted through the other odours in the cellar and reminded

34

Madoc that he had not eaten for a long time. His nausea had gone and his head only throbbed slightly now. A consuming thirst came over him, but there was nothing with which to slake it. He felt around and found some small kegs in which liquid sloshed when he shook them, but there was no means of drawing the bung, and in frustration, he dropped them back to the floor. The darkness was now broken by odd slivers of light creeping in through cracks in the floor-boards ten feet above him. As the dawn passed into full morning light, he could dimly see the stacked provisions around him and even the shape of the trap-door near one of the corners.

The noise of the morning meal faded and the hall above became quiet, apart from occasional footsteps and the sound of a broom used on the floor. The day wore on and nothing happened. Madoc did not know whether to be glad or sorry. His tongue was sticking to the roof of his mouth with thirst and his stomach rumbled with hunger, but at least he had not yet been dragged out to be hanged.

What was to happen to him, he wondered miserably. And what would his mother suffer for this escapade? She must surely have told Prince Owain last night, that Madoc was no lover, but a long-lost son . . . would not the old man's heart be softened, at least enough to allow Madoc to slink away back to Ireland.

As he sat on the damp earth of that gloomy cellar, he wondered how they had been discovered so soon. Only one person, apart from Gwalchmai, knew his real identity. And that person was Annesta. He could not see why she should betray him—and in any event, the Prince had burst in shouting about a lover, not a son.

It was all too confusing and Madoc gave up trying to unravel the tragic puzzle.

One thing did remain clear to him, however. This girl Annesta was to be something special in his life. It was not just the romantic episode of the other night that forced this conclusion on him—in an age where lads and lasses matured so early and married in their early 'teens, he was now a relatively old man at nineteen and had had many girl-friends among those at Clochran. But Annesta's face, as calm and self-possessed as his own nature, was branded into his mind with an intensity that survived even

35

the fears and miseries of his present plight.

Hours went by and no one took the slightest notice of him. The tiny rays of light slipping between the oaken planks shifted their position as the sun travelled across the sky and his almost intuitive sense of navigation told him that it was well past noon when the first sign of activity occurred.

He was sitting dejectedly against a sack of corn, rubbing his dry lips, when he heard a slight noise overhead and sensed a change in the light. Looking up quickly, he saw the trap-door opening slightly and a face appearing in the opening.

Quickly, he scrambled up a pile of boxes that he had dragged together earlier, directly under the opening.

"Madoc . . . are you there? I can't see."

It was a girl's voice and as he clambered up towards the ceiling, he could see it was Annesta.

"Annesta . . . what's happening?"

She made a cautious hushing noise at him, peering back over her shoulder. Then she slid a green woollen cloak through the half-open trap.

"Quickly, put that on. It will help disguise you."

He asked no more questions, but flung the cloak around him and climbed onto the topmost box of the precariously balanced pile.

"I waited for hours until there was no one in the hall, but someone may come at any time, so hurry." She disappeared to haul back the heavy trap-door until it was almost upright. "Can you get out . . . I've no rope," she hissed.

Madoc, thankful for his tallness, reached up and gripped the edge of the hole with both hands and with a violent effort swung himself up until he could get his belly onto the floor boards. Then with a twist, he rolled his legs up and lay breathing heavily on the floor of the hall.

"Quickly," urged Annesta. He jumped up and took the heavy trap-door from her, lowering it quietly back into place.

Already the girl was on her way towards the main door, Madoc following close behind. As she reached the little vestibule and peered out on to the top of the wide stairs leading down into the courtyard, she suddenly stopped.

"There's a man coming . . . quickly, and pray that he's not going upstairs."

36

Dragging Madoc by the hand, she slipped past the door into the dark and narrow passageway that led to the stairs. As they cowered around the corner, a serving man banged noisily through the door.

"He's coming this way," hissed Annesta into his ear. In a flash Madoc seized the girl and fixed his mouth passionately on hers, squeezing her closely to his breast.

Surprised and in no mood for loving at that frightening moment, Annesta wriggled.

"Hey, you two, keep that stuff for your bed," bawled the man, as he passed them. He slapped Madoc playfully on the back as he made his way towards the staircase.

As soon as he had gone, they fled to the door. With difficulty, they restrained themselves from running down the steps, then walked together across the courtyard.

As they walked, Madoc found time for a few hurried questions. "What now? The guard on the outer gate. He must know that there was a prisoner in the basement. And he won't recognise me as one of the locals."

Annesta nodded. "Come with me to the servants' room in the West Tower."

They turned towards the building where last night's drama had occurred. It reminded him of Brenda. "What about my mother? What's happened to her?"

Annesta led the way through the double doors at ground level. "She's well enough. Gwalchmai told me that she was going to tell the Prince this morning that you were his son and risk what might happen, but the Lord Owain was called away urgently to Deganwy. There's some talk of the Normans attacking from Chester, so he had no time to waste on you."

For once, Madoc thanked God for King Henry and his French invaders, but he was brought back to reality by having a great bundle of dirty washing thrust at him by the dark-haired girl who was risking so much for him.

"Carry this in front of you—try to keep it before your face as we pass the guard. Come on."

Annesta also had a great armful of grimy clothes and marching ahead of him, she boldly approached the gate.

With the Prince away and no enemies within fifty miles, the sentinels were not taking their duties too seriously. Three of the guards were squatting on the parapet, playing *Tawlbwrdd** and the gate-keeper was sitting on the cat-walk above the gate, whittling a toy sword for his little son.

"I'll tell *Yr Arglwydd* Owain when he returns that his guard is an idle lout," she threatened as she passed underneath, giving him a wink. The man, who had a revealing view of her bosom from his perch as she passed underneath, had no eyes to spare for the fellow who was helping her to carry dirty washing, and a second later they were walking down the steps to the outer settlement. "You'd better not go into the same dwelling," she muttered as they crossed the bridge. "Someone may remember you. Come into the wash-house."

They dumped their load of clothing in a smaller hut where a few drabs were grumbling over their laundry duties, then settled unobtrusively against a wall in a dark corner.

"Annesta, I don't know how to start thanking you for this," Madoc said awkwardly.

She kissed him quickly. "It's not thanks I want, my Madoc, only to know that you get safely away.

"I'll just slip away over the moors. I'll be all right."

She looked at him sternly. "Are you sure that you'll manage. Have you any money for food?"

He felt at his waist. His pouch was still there, with a few coins in it. "Yes, don't worry. I'll make my way to Aberdaron or one of the other harbours on the coast. I know many of the ship-masters that ply on these seas; they'll give me passage back to Dublin."

Annesta kissed him again. "You'd better go soon. They say that Lord Owain returns tonight. Brenda will soon soothe him down, but it's not worth the gamble to face him until you know how the land lies."

Madoc nodded. "How did you know what had happened?"

"Gwalchmai told me. For some reason, he did not confide in Llywarch."

Madoc grunted. "I wondered about Llywarch, Bard of the Pigs, myself. Yet he seemed friendly enough to me yesterday."

Annesta shrugged. "Gwalchmai said that he would send you a message in Clochran, to let you know how things went here."

He nodded and stood up, then looked down sadly at the oval

* A game similar to chess.

38

face of the girl. "Again, my thanks, Annesta. You may well have saved my life."

She smiled. "Probably it would not have come to that. Go now, before some other trouble befalls you."

"I will see you again, Annesta." He made it a firm statement, not a pious hope.

"I hope so, Madoc. I hope so." For a moment, they looked into each other's eyes.

"I will be back as soon as I get word that all is well," he said earnestly. "And if all is not well—then I'll still be back. So wait for me, Annesta of the black hair."

She stood up, they kissed once more under the curious gaze of a nearby washerwoman, then Madoc pulled his borrowed cloak around him and set out westwards for the coast.

FOUR

MAY 1164

Once more, Madoc ab Owain Gwynedd was on a ship coming back to Wales. A larger ship this time and a shorter journey, from Dublin to the royal palace of Aberffraw in Anglesey.

He stood proudly alongside the shipmaster, a rugged young Norseman called Svein. It was Svein's vessel, but Madoc's pride stemmed from the fact that he had designed the ship and supervised its building. It was the maiden voyage of the *Iduna* and the delighted Dane, pleased beyond measure with the handling of his new vessel on its trials off the mouth of the Liffey, had insisted on taking Madoc across the Celtic Sea to his homeland.

This time it was to be a one-way trip for the son of Owain Gwynedd. Almost four years had passed since he had fled from his father's wrath in the castle of Dolwyddelan. As he stood next to the Northman, both swaddled in tightly belted leather tunics against the fresh south-westerly breeze, he could see again the distant blue mass of Eryri across the corner of the flat island of Môn. Behind the highest peak lay Dolwyddelan.

Svein seemed to guess what was in his friend's mind. His grizzled, hairy face turned seriously to Madoc. the big dog's eyes searching the features of the Welshman.

"How does it feel to be going home for good, Madoc?"

With his eyes still on the hazy mountains, Madoc shrugged. "After a whole lifetime spent in Ireland, where is home, Svein? I feel for Wales in my heart, but really it is a strange land to me. Apart from the time of my birth, I have spent only five days there."

Svein whistled noisily through his teeth. "Five days! And you a son of the Welsh King?"

Madoc smiled wanly. "Prince of Gwynedd . . . the north of Wales, though he and the Lord Rhys in the south at last hold most of Wales in unity, for the time being."

Svein grunted, swaying with the pitch of the ship, his long legs braced against the deck with the same ease as Madoc's.

"Though I've known you these ten years, Madoc of the Ships, I know little of your troubles. It seems strange that so many of you royal Welsh exile yourselves in Ireland."

"Not out of choice, friend. Ever since the damned Normans came to our land, we have had to flee from danger across this narrow sea."

For the first time, Svein seemed curious about Madoc's past. Usually, the talk was exclusively about ships and the sea, adventures across the Unknown Ocean—with merrier interludes of song, drink and girls but the solemnity of this last voyage and the approach of the distant shore-line seemed to generate a new curiosity in the Dane.

"Are you sure your father will receive you this time—without a battle-axe in his hands?"

Madoc grinned. He could never remain solemn for long with the amiable Svein around. The Dane was ten years older than Madoc, but his bluff, cheerful manner always made him seem younger—except when the sudden flash of his temper gave him a frenzied strength that recalled the 'berserk' of his Nordic blood.

"According to the bard, Llywarch, all is forgiven. His message two months ago was that Owain, my royal father, gives me not only leave to attend on him at his court at Aberffraw, but a genuine welcome."

"What happened to make him change his mind?"

Madoc's face saddened. "My mother's death. To think that I saw her for hardly an hour in my whole lifetime—the lifetime that I remember, anyway, for she nursed me for three weeks after I was born. But she died two days after Christmas, of a tumour."

Svein clucked his tongue sympathetically. "But how did that bring about your restitution, boy?"

"On her death bed, Brenda—my mother—confessed all to my father. She was his favourite among those women he never married and Llywarch tells me in his message that she told Prince Owain that I still lived and pleaded for his promise to recognise me as his son."

Svein's eyebrows rose. "Told him that you still lived?"

Madoc nodded. "Like others of Owain's bastards, I was supposed to have been disposed of at birth . . . either killed or fostered

41

out to a family who would never know whose child I was."

"Your mother extracted a dying promise from this Prince, eh?"

Madoc nodded. "So Llywarch, one of the court bards, tells me."

"I thought it was he you suspected over the business of your flight from Wales four years back," objected Svein. "So how can you trust him now? Maybe this is a trap to get you into your father's clutches!" He sounded genuinely worried.

Madoc put his mind at ease. "My brother Riryd, who has been acknowledged by our father for many years, came to Aberffraw last month and brought me the direct word of my father that all is now well. As for Llywarch, well, I have to give him the benefit of the doubt. This last message was genuine enough and I have no real reason to suspect him of the treachery last time."

Svein sniffed. "Be wary, my friend, all the same. If any harm befalls you I'll bring the *Iduna* back with a crew of berserks and revenge you against the whole court of Gwynedd."

Madoc slapped the Dane on the shoulder. "Don't worry, friend, I'll be safe enough. In a few months, I'll come across and see you in Dublin and tell you all my news. You'll see plenty of me on the seas, I'm not going to take to the land like my fellow Welshmen."

"What will you do with yourself? You've been so used to the life at the Liffey shipyards and at Clochran, this will be a strange time for you."

Madoc pointed over the bow at the low line of Anglesey ten miles off. "I'll build more ships, Svein. Aberffraw is on the coast —up a small river, so there'll be opportunity for me to carry on with my new ideas about better vessels. In a year's time, I'll have a ship that can do better than sail abeam the wind. It will run circles around your *Iduna*, good as she is."

Svein made a rude noise of disbelief. He pointed down the length of the *Iduna* which was running dead before the wind at a steady clip. "How can you do better than this, Madoc. She's a marvel—a high-sided *knarr*, yet she cuts through the rough water like a longship in a calm lake."

Madoc warmed to the argument, the topic nearest his heart. "I'll do better, Norseman. I'll make the next one even deeper in the keel. I found from those models I made on the pond at Clochran, that the more ship under the water, the closer to the wind can you sail them. One day, I'll make the perfect vessel, if

42

it takes me a life-time. And then I'll sail her out into the Western Ocean, following Saint Brandon and find those Isles of the Blessed and the Fountain of Eternal Youth."

Svein snorted and they resumed the familiar argument that they had had a score of times, about flat-bottomed boats being easier to beach versus deep keels for sailing ability.

They were interrupted a few minutes later by a leadsman in the bows shouting at them and waving his arm.

Svein muttered an instruction to the sailor hanging on the great steering-oar hanging over the steer-board quarter. Then he walked forward, skirting the deep cargo well amidships to get to the man in the bows. The rest of the crew, with the exception of two tending the running rigging, were lying or squatting in the belly of the ship, letting the sail do all the work until they came into calm water.

The leadsman had found bottom with his line and he and Svein now peered over the bow to study the colour of the water and the way the currents were setting, ready for the tricky approach to Aberffraw. After a rapid exchange, the ship-master hurried back along the deck and yelled instructions to the men in the hold, who scrambled out and began making ready for the entry into the little estuary, upon which lay the royal capital of Gwynedd.

"I'll only stop long enough to re-fill my water barrel, Madoc," said Svein when he came back to the stern. "I'm off then down to the Isle of Lundy to give my beautiful *Iduna* a real chance to show off her paces."

Madoc looked enviously at his friend. "I wish I could come with you, I'd give much to see how she handles on a long run against the set of the wind." He slapped Svein on his shoulder. "But you wait until I've built my perfect ship. I'll race you to Lundy or Brittany—or even Iberia and meet you half-way when I am coming back!"

The palace of Aberffraw was no fortress like Dolwyddelan. Sited on the flat open land of south-west Anglesey, it was indefensible in the military sense. When danger threatened the court of the Prince of Gwynedd just took up its bed and vanished into the gaunt mountains of Snowdonia, which towered over the fair island like the backcloth of a stage. Never meant to withstand a siege, it was not fashioned out of stone. Until the coming of the Normans, all Welsh dwellings were wooden and most of them 'disposable', as the pastoral people left their winter dwellings each summer and went with their flocks to their *hafodau* up in the hills. If an enemy came and burnt the house down, well, there was plenty more wood in the forests and plenty of hands to fashion it. After the French of William the Bastard came, the more powerful Welsh nobles began to hanker after more solid and permanent fortresses, like those of their opponents. By the middle of the twelfth century, a few small castles like Dolbadarn and Dolwyddelan began to re-build in masonry. But though Aberffraw never merited stone until the following century, it became the main dwelling of a succession of Welsh princes, some of whom later became rulers of all Wales.

As Madoc walked up the track from the landing stage, he thought that this was a strange way for the Prince's son to come home. No cortège, not a single servant and not even any baggage, apart from the bag slung over his shoulder. This contained a change of clothes, some parchments about shipbuilding and his precious *crwth*.* His other few possessions in Ireland had been shared out between friends, as he wanted to make a clean break with Clochran and a fresh start back in the country of his birth.

He walked up the dusty path through the scattered huts, almost as bare as when he came into the world twenty-three years before. Each step was taking him further from Svein and his last links with his life in Dublin and nearer the unknown that lay ahead in the stockaded palace of Aberffraw.

He remembered his life at Clochran, the ship-yards along the Liffey, reading and writing lessons from William the monk—then the poignant few hours at Dolwyddelan, when he had seen his mother for such a short and final time. The meeting with the enigmatic Llywarch ap Pryddyd Moch ... and by no means least, that startling time with Annesta, whose face had been with him for the past four years. He wondered whether she was still at Dolwyddelan or had been disgraced—or worse—for her part in helping him to escape.

By now, his ponderings had brought him right to the gate in the palisade, where a drawbridge lay over a moat as a token of defence. A guard stood at the side of the wide open gates, again

* A type of lute.

more as a symbol than a sentinel. Madoc felt that if he walked straight past, the sentry would not even have noticed. In fact, just at that moment, two urchins ran screaming past him and vanished into the palace grounds without the sentry batting an eyelid, but Madoc went across and spoke to him.

"Where can I find Riryd, son of Prince Owain, lately come from Ireland?"

The man looked at him rather stupidly, then muttered something and went to the door of a small hut behind the gate and yelled into the interior. Out came a fat man, also wearing a green tunic and white trousers, which seemed to be the uniform of Prince Owain's household.

"You want Riryd ab Owain. You know him?" he asked, rather loftily.

Madoc grinned at him. "I should do, as he's my brother."

The several chins of the fat Porter wobbled. "Brother! Are you lately from Ireland also, sir?"

"Not ten minutes since, did I leave the ship from Dublin."

The Porter, official guardian of the gates of Aberffraw, grasped Madoc by the forearm, in a token of greeting.

"Then you must be that Madoc ab Owain that we have heard whispers about. Welcome, *bonheddig*,* welcome to your own house."

Madoc felt a wave of relief pass over him. In spite of Riryd's reassurances, he had had no direct word from his father that he would be welcome, but now it seemed that the whole household was expecting him and that he was not to be cast into the nearest subterranean store-room.

The Porter himself escorted him, yelling to the nearest passing servant to carry Madoc's sack of belongings. Madoc walked slowly behind the waddling official as they made their way to the central group of buildings. Curious heads popped out of huts and around corners, as the news spread with the extraordinary haste of rumour. Even the two urchins gaped at him in wonder, as they somehow came to know that this was the lost son of the Prince, come back to life after so many years.

"Prince Owain is in the Great Hall, *arglwydd*, in audience with some more Frankish emissaries." The sniff that the Porter added to his words clearly conveyed his opinion of French envoys.

* Gentleman.

45

The largest building was roofed with a great crown of neat thatch that swept down almost to nose-level. The large wooden doors were wide open and inside, a curtain hung across the entrance. The Porter pushed it aside and stood back for Madoc to enter.

As his eyes got used to the dim light, he saw a group of people clustered half-way up the building. They were dwarfed by the row of great tree-trunks that held up the roof, but as he got nearer, he saw that one of them was a good head taller than the rest. Almost instantly, he recognised the face of the terrible apparition that had burst in on him and his mother back in Dolwyddelan. An unreasoning panic gripped him and he stopped so abruptly that the man who carried his bag walked into his back.

He swallowed uneasily as he saw that great head slowly lift and stare down the hall at him.

The discussion died as they came near and half a dozen heads swivelled around to follow the direction of Owain Gwynedd's gaze.

The Porter banged his staff importantly on the hard earthen floor.

"Lord Owain, I bring the visitor we have been expecting." He turned with portentous drama and indicated Madoc like a conjuror performing a trick. "Your son, *Arglwydd* . . . Madoc ab Owain!"

There was a silence one could cut with a sword. Almost paralysed, Madoc at last forced himself to drop quickly onto one knee in a rapid gesture of respect. As he got up, he saw for the first time that his brother Riryd was on the other side of the little group. Riryd smiled quickly at him, rather nervously, Madoc felt. But his attention was soon riveted again on the face of his father, who had been staring at him with an expression that could not be described. His lined and rather ruddy face was partly hidden by a large moustache of a tawny colour, which matched his abundant and rather wild hair. Heavy, leonine features just escaped being cruel; it was the face of no ordinary man, but one of the leaders of men who form the pace-making minority of mankind, for good or evil.

The tableau was suddenly broken by Owain Gwynedd stepping forward a pace towards Madoc. An arm like the branch of a

46

gnarled tree grabbed Madoc's shoulder in a vice-like grip.

"So we meet again, my long lost infant!" The deep voice bellowed from the throat of the Prince and for a moment, Madoc wondered again whether he would be consigned to the nearest prison cell. But the seamy face of the Prince cracked into a smile full of bad teeth as he shook his son violently by the shoulder.

"I'm a fool for admitting yet another bastard to fight me for my kingdom, but I promised your mother, Jesus rest her."

The mood of the group changed instantaneously. Even the Frenchmen, conspicuous in their more flamboyant clothes, grinned and shuffled in the sudden relaxation of the atmosphere.

"I'll have to leave greeting you properly, Madoc of the Ships," grunted his father. "These popinjays from Paris are demanding all my wits at the moment." As he spoke in Welsh, it was obvious that the envoys knew nothing of the native language. "The devil's taken hold of all our tongues today. These idiots know nothing but their Frankish mouthings and Cynan, who is usually our interpreter, is sick with a bloody flux."

He turned away and began speaking to the Frenchmen in a painfully halting brand of Latin, delivered slowly and loudly, as if that would improve its quality. He was trying to ask them in what state of health was their master, Louis VII of France and whether he was likely to be disposed to receive ambassadors from Wales.

To Madoc, who was an accomplished linguist, the whole exchange was painful to the ears. When one of the Frenchmen made a horrible mutilation of the meaning of his reply, Madoc involuntarily came to his aid in rapid and fluent French. It happened almost without thought, an automatic reaction to help another man out of acute embarrassment.

The envoy smiled at him gratefully and replied in his own tongue.

Madoc was suddenly conscious of all the others staring at him, almost open-mouthed.

His father turned hard blue eyes upon him. "So, it's not only Madoc the Minstrel and Madoc of the Ships . . . Madoc of the Many Tongues, eh?"

Madoc was not sure whether the Prince's voice held amusement or censure. He reddened. "I have been many a time to Brittany, sire. I spent a whole summer there and though their own tongue is our Celtic, there are many Franks who speak as these gentlemen do."

Riryd spoke up, half defensive, half-proud of his favourite brother. "Prince and father, our brother has a gift of languages, aided by his travelling in the Norse ships. He has Irish and Norse, as well as a good command of French. His Latin and even English are passable, also."

Owain Gwynedd's bushy eyebrows rose up his forehead. "I have a long-lost prodigy, it seems! Perhaps it were better that I had banished one of the other louts that plague me, rather than this seeming angel."

This time, Madoc felt that his words held no sarcasm, but a thoughtful admiration. He bowed his head to his father. "My services, such as they are, are yours, sire, until Cynan recovers."

For the next hour, he smoothed out the course of the discussion between the two French envoys and his father. It soon became apparent that his father was engaged in sounding out the possibility of gaining French aid against the English king, Henry II.

Louis VII of France had no love for Henry, partly because of the offence arising out of Henry having married Louis' divorced wife, Eleanor of Aquitaine. Even more than this slight, was the loss of half France to Henry, by his acquisition of her dowry lands of Aquitaine, Gascony and Poitou.

The dispute between Henry and the new Archbishop of Canterbury, Thomas à Becket, was beginning to boil over and Louis had openly offered the cleric sanctuary.

Madoc soon gathered that Owain would like an alliance with France; Wales was now becoming an influential nation in Western Europe, since Owain had formed such strong links with the Lord Rhys in the south. It was premier in matters of literature and had a model legal system, so that in spite of its relatively small size, it was a worthwhile member of any alliance and a valuable ally against Norman England.

However, Madoc gathered that matters were still in a very early and delicate state. Prince Owain was still supposed to be adhering to the peace settlement of 1157, when he and Henry had fought themselves to a standstill. There had been an uneasy peace for the last seven years and Owain wanted to tread carefully with his negotiations with France, so that he did not bring down another English army on him before the help of Louis VII was signed and sealed.

So far, all the initiative had come from Owain and as far as Madoc could make out, the French king was not yet aware of what the Welsh ruler had in mind.

"We must send envoys of our own," declared Owain, after an hour of skirting round the subject. "This court of Paris has never seen a Welshman yet. We have to convince them that we are real live people, with brains and a culture, as well as strong muscles."

At this point, serving men brought in a long trestle table and began laying it for a meal. Owain had retired to a large chair near the fire, which smouldered under its peat blocks in the centre of the hall. As it was a mild May day, it was banked down until the chill of the evening, but the royal chair, which passed for a throne, stood ready in the place of honour. All the rest stood in a half-circle around him, except the Chief Judge of the Court of Gwynedd, whose corpulence and feeble legs, as well as his precedence, allowed him to have a small chair on the Prince's right hand.

Women began bringing food and drink and benches were brought to place around the table.

They all sat down and for the moment, the affairs of state were put aside. Madoc talked eagerly with his brother Riryd.

"The French? It all stems from the Prince's actions, not theirs. These are the first emissaries we have seen here; they are but a scouting party. I doubt if Louis himself knows they are here; it is more like to be the initiative of his Chancellor, Hugh de Soissons, as far as I could gather from Cynan's interpreting, before he went off with his sickness of the gut."

Riryd's neighbour on the other side engaged him in talk at that moment and Madoc was left to his food and his thoughts. All seemed to be going well on this second return. By the fortunate chance of his gift with tongues, he may well have made a good first impression on his royal father.

Owain was deep in talk with his Chief Justice and another younger man, whom Madoc suspected was one of his own half-brothers. The Frenchmen were talking earnestly among themselves—there was no one else for them to speak to, except Madoc, unless they wanted to labour away in halting Latin again. Madoc looked around the large hall, at the scurrying serving women and the servants carrying in more wine.

Suddenly his attention was riveted by a slim shape standing just inside the back door that led to the kitchens. He immediately recognised her. Annesta! She seemed to be searching the hall and without a second's hesitation, Madoc slid from his bench and hurried across to her.

She saw him coming and her face lit up as she ran forward. "Madoc . . . they said you were here."

Behind the shelter of one of the great roof pillars, Madoc pulled her into his arms and kissed her, oblivious of the curious looks of passing servants.

"Annesta . . . I thought you would still be in Dolwyddelan. I was going to seek you there as soon as I had the chance."

She pulled back, still holding his hands and looked at him with a glowing smile. "And I thought you would have forgotten all about the little maidservant you flirted with four years ago."

Madoc grimaced at her. "Don't talk like that . . . you saved my life, in all probability. Helping me out of that dungeon put me in your debt for life."

She pretended to pout. "So I'm only a debt to be honoured, Madoc ab Owain?" Then she laughed and he pulled her gaily into his arms again and hugged her. "It's so good to see you. Are you still serving the Lady Cristin?" She nodded against his chest. With the dark-haired girl close against him, he felt both excited and at peace at the same time. He knew, quite clearly, that this was the woman for him and that sooner or later, he must marry her.

"I'm here for good now, Annesta . . . you'll not get rid of me easily again."

"And I'm here until high summer, when they go back to Dolwyddelan. Are you never going back to Ireland, then?"

Madoc shrugged and gently disengaged himself. "Much depends on what the Prince wishes. During the last hour, I seem to have become his chief interpreter. I have the feeling that he will find more work for my tongue."

There was movement in the group near the fire and Madoc squeezed Annesta's hand quickly. "I must get back there . . . I have been here little more than an hour, yet it seems a day. I'll see you as soon as I can."

Within minutes, he found that his guess about his father finding

50

more work for him was already true. Owain Gwynedd, standing in front of his big chair, beckoned to him. As Madoc went near and bobbed his head respectfully, he noticed the podgy judge smiling benignly at him and a young man with flashily fashionable clothes scowling at him.

"You haven't so much as said a word to your brother, Madoc," boomed the Prince of Gwynedd, waving his gnarled hand at the young man. "This is Dafydd, the brat that most desires my power when I've gone."

Dafydd, some two years older than Madoc, forced a mechanical smile as he made some deprecating noises towards his father's wit. Madoc felt that here was a natural enemy that needed watching twenty-four hours in every day. It was obvious that the ambitious older son saw Madoc as a new challenge to his hopes of becoming chief heir to the lands of Gwynedd. As such, to say that he was not welcome, was a gross understatement. However, etiquette demanded that they made some formal greetings, especially in front of the Frenchmen, who were ambassadors not only of France, but of the new craze of courtly chivalry and manners that had been so enthusiastically taken up by Eleanor, England's new queen.

They murmured and nodded at each other, then Madoc looked back expectantly at Owain his father, who as always dominated any gathering at which he was present.

"I have found you a job already, my son . . . though you be hardly off the sea, I must send you journeying straight away." His eyes flicked towards the Frenchmen and Madoc immediately knew what the task was to be.

Owain Gwynedd stood looking as if he was carved out of the very granite of Snowdonia. "I want you to go back to the French lands with these men, to sound out how things lie in Paris. You have heard what I propose . . . an alliance with Louis their king, against Henry Plantagenet. We must move soon and until we know how the Franks view the matter, I do not wish to provoke the Normans."

Madoc nodded. He regretted having to leave Annesta so soon after having found her again, but his father's wishes and his father's benevolence were all-important. "When shall we leave, sire?"

Owain grinned under his big moustache. "That's what I like,

51

Dafydd." He turned to his petulant-looking son and slapped him roughly on the back. "Madoc doesn't ask questions or argue, like you. He just says 'when do we leave'."

Madoc sadly sensed that this hearty criticism, however jovial, only served to deepen Dafydd's enmity against him.

"You leave tomorrow, lad. They call you Madoc of the Ships, and you'll have your fill of them this month. On the way to Paris I want you to call at *Ynys Wair*, the island the Norsemen call Lund or Ely. Do you know it?"

Madoc nodded. "I have been there a number of times, sire. There is a brisk trade between Lund and the Norse settlements in Dublin. It is also a shelter from storms on the passage to Brittany."

The Prince's smile grew broader and he jabbed a fist into Dafydd's side. "This Madoc becomes a greater paragon of virtues with every question I set to him, eh?"

If Dafydd's look could have killed, Madoc would have lain dead at his feet.

"Is the visit to Lund of the same nature as to France, *arglwydd*?" asked Madoc.

Owain wagged his great head. "Jordan de Marisco, who rules the island, has no love for King Henry and some time ago offered his help should it be needed. I wish to confirm the treaty with him, to strengthen all the power at my command against this coming battle with Plantagenet."

The meeting broke up soon afterwards, with a promise from Owain Gwynedd that final details would be settled after the evening's feasting.

Aberffraw was more of a scattered encampment than a palace. Around the great hall was a collection of thatched wooden buildings. The largest, adjacent to the hall, was the dwelling of Owain and Cristin and a number of the other larger erections housed the other members of the immediate family and the more important officers, like the Chancellor, the Chief Judge and the *Penteulu*, the Chief of the Royal Household. Less imposing buildings tailed off from the central group towards the boundary palisade, with kitchens, servants' quarters, barracks, stables and the huts of the more lowly families. Chickens, goats, dogs and urchins wandered about freely. The whole atmosphere was one of peaceful and leisurely routine, that seemed at odds with the preparations for war that were being so actively planned.

The fat Porter took him into one of the medium-sized buildings and found him a bed in a small room on the upper level, reached by a wooden stairway outside. There were three wooden bunks in the room. Each had a woollen sack stuffed with hay and a rolled blanket at the foot.

"There is no one else in the other beds this night, Prince Madoc," commented the old man and gave a knowing wink. Again Madoc marvelled at the efficiency of the local grape-vine —he half expected the Porter to offer to take a message to Annesta, but he waddled off, still wearing a smirk on his face.

Madoc threw himself onto the mattress and stared at the straw-weaving under the thatch above him. His home-coming had been nothing like he expected, but had gone off far better than he could have hoped. Finding Annesta so quickly was the high spot, as far as he was concerned. During the years he had been back in Ireland, he had always had Annesta in the forefront of his mind. He had thought that she might have been married off by now, being a good many years past the betrothal age for girls. But when he heard that he was coming back to Wales, he had made special enquiries through Riryd and found that Annesta was still un-married. As he had told her, he was intent on seeking her out in Dolwyddelan and to find her right under his nose in Aberffraw was indeed a bonus.

He turned his mind to the weightier matters that had so rapidly been placed on his shoulders. The business with the French envoys had been equally fortunate, in that it had so rapidly cemented his acceptance by Owain Gwynedd. But for leaving Annesta so soon, the prospect of sea voyaging to the Isle of Lund and then to France was something to be relished. Madoc's feet felt more at home on a swelling, creaking deck than on the solid turf of land.

All in all, it had been a memorable day—and one that was not yet over, he thought with a warm glow of anticipation. But there was one black cloud in his otherwise rosy sky. It was obvious that Dafydd, his half-brother, was to be an implacable enemy. Riryd had already told him of the present intrigues that were boiling up amongst the sons of Owain. Madoc, though loth to condemn such a close relation, felt that there was evil in his sullen-faced brother and that some of it was going to be directed at himself, if he was not careful.

His reverie was interrupted by the sound of feet on the stairway. A moment later, the moonlight from the bare doorway was dimmed by the silhouette of Riryd, his full brother and greatest friend.

"Are you staying here too, brother?" asked Madoc, as Riryd stretched himself out on the bunk opposite.

Riryd turned his head and grinned at him. "Never fear, Madoc. I'm lodged nearer the aristocracy. I'll not play gooseberry this night."

Madoc flushed in spite of himself. "Does every man, woman and child in this place know my private business?" he muttered.

"Aye and every dog and goat," cackled his brother mercilessly. "The other maidservants have been talking of nothing else since you walked through the gate today."

Madoc changed the subject. "What think you of this business that I am pressed into the moment my face is shown to our father?"

Riryd became serious. "You are very fortunate, brother. This sets you in good stead with Prince Owain. Carry out this mission well and you will have no fear of him ever again. Rough and cruel he may be, but he is a man of his word. What he promised to our mother Brenda on her death-bed, that will he carry out. And if you show him you are a man of action as well as words, he will value you for yourself, as well as for the pledge."

Madoc pondered for a moment. "I want to keep well out of this game between the many sons, Riryd. I am afraid that if I gain too much favour with Lord Owain, that I will fall foul of these others. I liked the looks of brother Dafydd not one little bit."

Riryd swung his legs back to the floor and bent earnestly toward Madoc. He was smaller than his younger brother, but had the same blond looks and fine blue eyes, though there was a thinness of his face that gave him something of an impish look. "Madoc, I fear for what will happen when our father leaves this life. I have told you before, when we were in Clochran, of the feuds and intrigues that go on here, but I see on this visit that it is becoming much worse. As our father gets older and nearer death, so does the rivalry increase."

Madoc was silent. There seemed nothing to say.

"I hope to be well out of it when the time comes," went on

Riryd, "and unless you have any aspirations for the throne of Gwynedd, I suggest you try to do the same. Be in Brittany or Ireland when Owain's time comes, otherwise you may wake up one morning and find your throat cut!"

Madoc stared at him. "Could it be as bad as that?"

Riryd nodded. "The main contenders are Iorwerth Drwyndwyn . . . the one with the deformed nose whom you have never seen. There is now talk among the other brothers of getting Owain to disinherit Iorwerth on the grounds that such a disfigurement cannot be consistent with the Princedom."

"They will never manage to do that," said Madoc, aghast.

"They are well on the way to doing it. They have many of the court officers agreeing with them, too. Dafydd, Hywel, Cynan and Rhodri, though they hate each other, are all willing to reduce the odds by one. That means one less for each of them to fight against when the time arrives."

Madoc shook his head sadly. "You are right, Riryd. It will be well to be a long way from here. I would like to build a ship . . . the best ship in the world . . . and sail her away over the western horizon to seek the Isles of the Blessed and the Fountain of Eternal Youth."

Riryd stood up and grinned. "And what about your Annesta then, brother?"

Madoc looked up at him. "I'll take her with me, of course . . . and never come back to this land of eternal strife."

FIVE

JUNE 1164

No one would have recognised the figure on the rather sad pony as being that of a young Welsh prince, fresh from the winds around western Britain. Madoc was swathed in the drab habit and cowl of a Cistercian monk. The long ride from the ship at Saint Valéry had bowed his back with discomfort and fatigue.

Yet as his party trudged up to the gates of Paris, the novelty of the moment made him straighten up a little to see all that was to be seen of this fabled city, centre of continental learning and the new arts of romantic chivalry. He was a little disappointed to see yet another grey-walled town, albeit much larger than any other. Some of the flanking towers had pinnacled roofs that looked slightly exotic, but there was still the usual cluster of tattered huts with their ragged inhabitants clustered against the outside walls.

His companions were the two emissaries from the court of France that had been visiting his father, together with a priest— a real Cistercian—and four retainers from Aberffraw to see them safe from footpads. Madoc was still not clear just why the French courtiers had insisted that he swaddle himself in cleric's robes and use the title of Brother Moses for this venture, but they knew best the curious ways of Louis le Jaune's court and he bowed to their advice. He had a letter in his pouch that he had written under his father's direction on the morning that they had left Anglesey, three weeks earlier, but he also had Owain's instructions to amplify this by word of mouth, if he got the chance to plead the case before Louis.

The little cortège plodded through the narrow streets inside the west gate of the city and eventually came to some larger dwellings that were within sight of the towers of the palace and cathedral. The lodgings, Madoc discovered later, were reserved for visitors to the court and the university.

The two Frenchmen introduced the Welsh party to the concierge, then vanished in the direction of the royal court with promises to send for him on the following day. The four guards were taken off to some more modest accommodation and the concierge showed 'Brother Moses' and his colleague Brother Padraig to a small room which held nothing but three truckle beds and a large pitcher of water. "We eat in the hall at dusk," muttered the Parisian as he left and when the door curtain had dropped behind him, Madoc knew that he was in for several hours of utter boredom. This was because his companion, a lean, aesthetic Irish priest, was as near speechless as made no difference. Why he had been sent by Owain's Chief Judge, Madoc could not fathom—unless it be that the court welcomed any opportunity to get rid of the morose, introverted cleric.

Padraig went to the bed and knelt against it, prepared for at least an hour of silent prayer, so Madoc took himself to the unglazed window opening and leaned on the sill to look at Paris. All he could see was a confused pattern of roofs, walls and a few spires—a conglomeration of tiles, thatch and stone. Below him was a narrow lane with the usual collection of town sights and sounds—tradesmen, passers-by, children and strident house-wives. Apart from the language and some difference in dress, there was nothing that was excitingly new.

With nothing to hold his attention, his mind turned to the task his father had set him. He had already completed part of it, in visiting the island in the Severn Sea which most people were now calling Lundy. One of Owain Gwynedd's ships had taken him there from Aberffraw and though the vessel could not compare with Svein's *Iduna*, it was sound enough to reach Lundy in three days, even across the prevailing wind.

His visit to Jordan de Marisco, the flamboyant ruler, had been moderately successful. De Marisco hated King Henry of England and was keen to join in any military alliance, but certain threats of annihilation had been sent to Lundy by the English court, should he take up arms against Henry.

Jordan wanted definite assurances of support from the Welsh Princes before he openly declared his defiance. Madoc did his best to reassure him and promised to return at a later date with further proposals from Owain.

The ship took them on after a few days, going from Lundy around the treacherous tip of Cornwall into the Western Channel. Here a fair wind took them up and across to the French coast and into the port of Saint Valéry at the mouth of the Somme, as Harfleur on the Seine was firmly in English hands.

Now his task was to open up a line of communication with the court of France.

How to get the ear of the French king was another matter. The two courtiers who had returned with him from Wales were more than a little vague as to when an audience would be granted, murmuring about having to wait upon the grace of Hugh de Soissons. It seemed that this nobleman was a major figure in the court of Paris, overshadowing the weak king in matters of diplomacy.

And vague the hopes turned out to be. Madoc waited for three days before anyone so much as came near the lodgings. He had no one to turn to for advice, as the semi-mute Brother Padraig was as much use as a deaf dog in matters of this kind.

Eventually a young, effeminate page came with a verbal message from Charles, one of the envoys to Wales, apologising for the delay and hoping that something could be arranged within a few more days.

"Tell Monsieur Charles that I very much trust it will," snapped Madoc to the disinterested messenger. "I am the accredited ambassador of Prince Owain ap Gwynedd, ruler of North Wales, not some villager seeking a petty favour."

The foppish youth shrugged at Madoc's foreign accent and minced away, leaving the Welshman fuming at the door of the chamber.

"Take little hope from a promise of that sort, friend," came a deep voice. Madoc turned and saw a tall middle-aged man in the garb of a priest, leaning against a nearby wall. He had a large bundle wrapped in a cloth and a few manuscripts tied with a leather thong. "The curator told me to find my bed in here," he said, walking to the door of the bed-chamber and peering in. "That will be it there, no doubt."

He threw his bundle on the vacant couch and nodded at Padraig, who was in his usual posture, kneeling on the floor with his hands clasped in front of him.

"You'll get little sense from him," said Madoc sitting on his own bed. "He talks only to God, except when he wants food."

The big man, with blue sailor's eyes like Madoc, grinned. "Three clerics together, eh. They've put us in here to form a holy choir, no doubt. I'm Guiot . . . Guiot de Provins they call me, as I'm from Arles in the old Roman province."

Guiot turned out to be a scholar of all manner of things connected with science and discovery, some very near Madoc's heart. As not a word came from the court for another week, the company of Guiot was manna from heaven for the Welshman.

One of Guiot's interests was navigation. In fact, he was in Paris partly to research a book he was writing on all manner of natural phenomena. It was to be called "Le Bible Guiot" and the author and Madoc spent many hours talking of ships, the legendary voyages of explorers and new exciting ideas that were filtering into Europe from the new routes to the East, often via the returning Crusaders.

Guiot was intrigued to hear the tale of the Irish Saint Brandon, who vanished into the Western Ocean centuries before, looking for the "Isles of the Blessed." Even the dumb-struck Padraig came briefly to life on this topic, as being an Irish monk, the tales of St Brandon were a matter of national pride.

"The Holy Saint Brandon—there was a book written on his life back in eleven-twenty-one by one of our brothers for Queen Aelis of Louvain," he murmured, as if a low voice was nearer silence than a more profane stridency. "Born in Trallee, was the good man, in the year of the Lord four-eighty-four."

Madoc and Guiot stared in amazement at Padraig. This was the longest speech they had ever heard from him. And yet more was to come. "Brendan he was also called—Brendan son of Finnloga. Eight years he sailed the great seas, before coming home in the care of Holy God to become abbot of the Benedictines at the abbey of Clonfert in Galway."

Guiot was intrigued, seeing potential material for his book emerging. "And what did the good Brandon discover in the west, brother?"

Padraig's eyes rolled and he cranked up his voice to a loud whisper. "The Isle of St. Brendan, of course—the island that moved, as if it were the back of a whale."

Guiot made a derisive noise of disappointment. "That old tale —half the Arab sailors have the same story."

Padraig became almost voluble in his indignation at this slur on his countryman. "The holy man would tell no lies—he set forth in a curragh, a small boat of osiers covered with tanned

59

hides and carefully greased, provisioned for seven years."

Guiot grinned. "He must have had a small appetite, then. And what of this Island?"

"The abode of the Saints in the western sea—he found it to the west and south-west sailing from Ireland—it was full of singing birds and the trees were full of fruit, but when he lit a fire upon it, St. Brendan's Isle of the Blessed shuddered and moved." Having delivered this marathon speech, Padraig subsided into silent prayer again.

Guiot and Madoc whiled away the time by exchanging more stories of sea ventures.

Madoc found a fascination growing within him about what lay to the west of the coastal fringes of Britain and France. Superstitious sailors crossed themselves and told of the precipice out in the mists where the edge of the world lay in wait for any blasphemous ship-master who dared to go beyond the bounds that God ordained. But he knew that for hundreds of years, Vikings had sailed their boats far beyond the settlements in Iceland and Greenland, without being annihilated by divine vengeance.

Guiot used to go to the university for some part of every day, to pore through the manuscripts in the library and to talk with other sages. Madoc gathered it was more of a debating society than a school. One day Guiot brought home another priest, an Englishman, who seemed to be a pupil of Guiot's. He also intended writing yet another book sometime in the future. This was Alexander Neckham, a monk of St. Albans, near London, who shared their interest in novel methods of navigation and new-found scientific trickeries. He was much less knowledgeable than Guiot de Provins, but good company, especially by contrast with Padraig, who had sunk back into his stupor after his brief revitalisation on the subject of Saint Brendan.

The visit to the court of Louis turned out to be an anti-climax. When Madoc was eventually summoned there, he did no more than kiss the hand of the King, who seemed to know nothing of Madoc's identity or purpose.

The only satisfaction he got was a brief interview with Hugh de Soissons, to whom he delivered his father's letter. This seemed to impress the French nobleman, but he was still not very forthcoming. "We must think on this and meet again when matters with Henry Plantagenet are settled," he told Madoc, this being almost the sum total of the result of the Welsh emissary's visit. But he was promised a letter to take back to Owain Gwynedd and was requested to wait in his lodgings until it was delivered.

"Spend your time with Brother Padraig in praying for a rapid answer," chaffed Guiot de Provins.

They laughed, then Madoc said, "I'd rather have more details of these navigation methods you spoke of to Brother Neckham. One day I'm going to build the best ship in the world and sail her to unknown parts—this magic stone you speak of would be a boon when sun and stars are shrouded in fog."

Guiot reached for his pouch that lay on the window-sill. "I'll do better than tell you about it, I'll give you some of this remarkable substance." He unwrapped a cloth and took out a little leather bag. Shaking it over the table, he displayed three pieces of ragged, brown stone each about the size and shape of a little finger. "These are the magic-makers—they come from the land of the infidels beyond Byzantium, but more and more are appearing in the Mediterrannean as Crusaders and Arabian travellers bring them from the eastern lands. Here, take one, I can get more when I return to Provins." He held out one of the slivers to Madoc, who took it gingerly and turned it over reverently in his fingers.

"It is too precious to just give away like that," he said.

Guiot brushed away his feeble protests. "Take it, friend. You are a man who can make true use of it. Do not drop it or allow it to get heated, as I have discovered that this makes its properties weaker or even vanish."

Madoc gazed down at the ordinary-looking piece of rock with awe. "Lodestone . . . for this alone, my visit to Paris has been worthwhile a hundred times over. How can I thank you?"

Guiot grunted. "By remembering how to use it. You heard Alexander Neckham and I talking of how the Arabian ship-masters manage it . They take a needle and lay it in a split of straw, like a baby in a cradle, then float it on a bowl of water. . . . Understand?"

Madoc nodded, hanging on to every word of the scientist-poet. "Then the lodestone is approached closely to the needle and whirled around twenty times, so that the needle spins in the bowl. Then the lodestone is taken to a distance and the floating needle watched until it comes to rest—when it will always be north and south."

Guiot fixed him with a beady eye. "But which is north and which is south, eh? Do you remember how to tell?"

Madoc nodded eagerly. Anything connected with ships was branded into his mind, never to be lost. "You mark one end of the lodestone and always use that to approach the needle . . . then point it to the sharper end of the spike, so that that end follows the stone around. Do this when north and south are known from landmarks or sun or stars, so that when all is hidden, the needle will behave in a like fashion."

Guiot nodded. "But more easily said than done, boy. I have heard recently—just before I came from the southern coast— that some ship-masters use a new method. They actually stroke the needle in one direction only with a known point of the lodestone. This both sets the north-seeking end and also makes the needle more powerful for searching out the lode-star, which must be the heavenly body that attracts the needle."

Madoc stared down at the grubby piece of rock, fascinated. "All this I will try—on the journey home."

Guiot had a word of caution. "I would not say too much abroad of this device. Some folk think it is witchcraft and others would cut your throat for possession of the stone. Use it discreetly and keep the knowledge amongst fellow ship-masters for the time being."

Madoc wrapped up his precious lode-rock in a piece of linen and hid it inside his shirt.

"If this really can set the bows of our vessels in the right direction at night and in mists, then this surely must be the ultimate marvel in nature and in human ingenuity," he said fervently to Guiot as they parted next morning.

The older man shook his head slowly. "There is no ultimate for the mind of man, Madoc. Some of us are fated to advance knowledge and so it will be until doomsday. We can never stand still—either we go on and on or we slip back into savagery. Somehow, I think that one day, you will be reckoned amongst those men who have done some deed that will mark their names on the book of history."

SIX

MAY 1169

"It's like the Liffey river all over again," said Madoc gaily, bouncing his little daughter into the air in time to the ringing sound of a heavy hammer aboard the ship.

They stood on the bank of a little creek, the Afon Gele, a few yards from the sea-coast of North Wales. A little group was watching the final stages of the completion of the vessel that had been Madoc's dream-ship for more years than he could now remember.

There was Madoc, his brother Riryd, his half-brother Einion and, of course, his wife Annesta and their four-year-old daughter Gwenllian.

Riryd was now Lord of Clochran, as Merfyn had died and as Brenda, his cousin, had also passed away, the land came to Riryd, the eldest of her sons.

Einion was the son of Prince Owain and one of his minor mistresses who had died when Einion was a child. He was no contender at all in the power struggle and had been allowed to live in court all his life, being fostered by one of the Chief Falconers to Owain.

Einion was barely twenty and a cheerful, happy-go-lucky youth, liked by everyone who knew him. He was stocky and dark, quite different from Riryd and Madoc, thanks to a different mother. He became deeply attached to Madoc, having an admiration almost amounting to hero-worship for his elder brother.

They were all in holiday mood, come to admire the new ship and enjoy their bread and meat, sitting in the spring sunshine away from the intrigues and bustle of the court.

To bless the ship properly, they had brought a priest, the same Padraig who had mutely accompanied Madoc on his first visit to the court of France and who had in the succeeding years, found that his voice improved with advancing age.

Madoc let Gwenllian scuttle to her mother and then sank down on the grass, supporting himself on his hands so that he could watch the last touches of the shipwrights on the *Gwennan Gorn* which lay in the little river waiting for the tide to float her down to the sea.

Riryd, and Einion sat alongside him, their eyes also glued to the little vessel rocking on the incoming swell. As soon as the last rigging was finished and there was enough water under the keel, they were going to take the vessel back along the coast a few miles to Aber Cerrig Gwynion—another little creek named after some 'white rocks'.

"What's so special about your precious ship, brother?" asked Einion, who had not set eyes on it until today.

Annesta gave a mock groan. "Don't say such a thing, Einion. You'll set him talking from now till dusk, explaining every splinter of wood and every piece of thonging on board."

Madoc grinned, delighted with life today and quite impervious to wifely sarcasm.

"The *Gwennan Gorn*, the best ship in the world," he exclaimed. "Not a wooden dowel in any of her planks, but all stag horn to secure the best oak that the forests of Nant Gwynant could provide."

"Stag horn! Why such expense, brother?" asked Einion. "I know the Norsemen use such horn for fairleads and rowlocks, but you must have used hundreds to pin her planking to the frames."

Madoc nodded, delighted to have the chance to lecture on his favourite topic. "When our father offered to meet the cost of any ship I cared to build—as a reward for my services as his envoy— I felt it improper to stint on any gift that came from such a notable prince."

Riryd poked him hard in the ribs. "Conceit ill becomes you, brother! We know you have been a good ambassador and gained our father's favour . . . much to the disgust of certain persons." There was a general guffaw at this, not unmarked by bitterness. "But spare us the innuendoes about why our rashly generous father met the shipwrights' bill for this." He waved at the *Gwennan Gorn*.

Madoc's blue eyes swung back to the vessel with pride. "The best ship in the world," he repeated.

Einion groaned. "It looks like any other Viking *knarr* to me."

"It *is* a Norse boat," Madoc retorted. "They've had five hundred years to perfect them in the storms of the Western Ocean. But I've added some things that more southerly sailormen have found useful, like the longer main-yard set lower on the mast . . . and above all, these strong stag-horns to hold the planks. . . . I'll not risk another fright like that in the channel of Ynys Ennlli*
last year, when we were in Svein's *Iduna*."

Annesta shuddered. "I was nearly a widow and little Gwenllian half an orphan. I don't know why you risk your lives, you men, just to prove that a certain ship is stronger than another."

"This one wasn't," observed Riryd shrewdly.

"I came nearer to drowning then than ever before," agreed Madoc. "The ship was a good one, but those races and whirlpools shook her near to pieces. When we limped into Aberdaron, we had to leave the *Iduna* on the beach for the villagers to use as fire-wood."

Riryd gave Madoc an elder brother's smile. "Are you going to pit this one against the channel of Bardsey, then?"

Madoc ran a hand through his fair hair. "I might. But we'll try her on some milder water first, come the next week or two."

Annesta looked sharply at him. "Indeed? Where will this be, then? I'm always the last to know where you're off to."

Madoc looked with placid devotion at her. He loved even her solitary fault, the beginnings of a sharp tongue. "Brittany, my wife . . . where they speak our Welsh tongue, thank God."

"Next week?"

"Prince Owain has become embroiled with some of the Breton barons who are revolting against Conan, their King. He has messages and men to exchange with them."

Einion grunted "Be careful then, brother ambassador. I hear that this Conan is getting deeper in league with our Henry of England, who wishes to get his feet under the Breton table."

Padraig the monk nodded vigorously, a trick which he found helped him to get his tongue moving. "Henry wishes to marry that odious son of his, Geoffrey, to Conan's daughter Constance. . . . So be careful that the king's men do not use your precious ship for target practice."

Madoc held up his hand placatingly. "Thank you all, but our father has warned me already. Never fear, Annesta," he said

* Bardsey Island off the tip of the Llyn Peninsula.

hastily, as he saw her opening her mouth, "we will slip into the harbour of Saint Pol de Leone, miles from the King's city of Rennes. We'll not even beach the vessel, just slip men over the side and pick up others. A quiet maiden voyage for the *Gwennan Gorn.*"

There was a shout from the direction of the creek. A huge blond figure was advancing across the grass to them, waving his arms.

"Svein . . . is it finished!" Madoc jumped up and ran towards him.

The big Viking grabbed him by the arms and lifted him clear from the ground.

"Did you not hear the hammering stop, Madoc. They've driven the last wedge alongside the mast after tautening the rigging . . . she's finished, man. Finished!"

Every one rose and ran gaily down the green banks to the water's edge, joined by a dozen men, who were the shipwrights of the Afon Gele.

Madoc stood with his feet in the advancing tide.

"The *Gwennan Gorn* . . . the ship that will take us far, far out into the Western Ocean," he said quietly, almost to himself.

Riryd heard him. "Beyond the Isles of Africa!" he shouted more exuberantly, caught up by the emotion of the moment.

Einion went one better, though he was new to the *Gwennan Gorn.* "To the Island of Eternal Youth . . . wherever that is," he added as an afterthought.

The tide was flowing rapidly, rippling up quickly into the creek and the waterways of the big marsh that stretched away eastwards from the Gele towards the big river, the Clwyd, a few miles away. The flat-bottomed vessel was already beginning to rock gently with the advancing ripples.

Svein, his arm around Madoc's shoulders, began to wade out to the vessel, pulling his friend with him. "Another hour and we'll be afloat and ready to go," he roared in his bull-like voice. "These good men who masted her will tow us down to the surf, I'm sure."

The shipwrights grinned their assent and two of them offered to crew the *Gwennan Gorn* on its short trip back to Aber Cerrig Gwynion. "We'll charge your royal father no more," the leader said cheerfully. "He's already sent gold and goods to cover most of the cost of masting her and has promised the balance by the month's end."

Madoc tugged around in Svein's giant grip. "Let's put Annesta and Gwenllian aboard. No need for us all to get wet legs."

Soon they were all aboard, the five men and the shipwrights making ready to move the new vessel off. Padraig said the appropriate prayers for blessing her, then Annesta, Einion and Gwenllian went on a tour of inspection.

"I never knew a thing about sea-going until I married you, Madoc," said Annesta severely. "Now you insist that I become an expert."

Madoc smiled forbearingly at her. "This ship will do great things, my love. It will weather any storm, like a good Norse ship should. Look at that high prow and stern."

It was Einion who showed the most interest in learning about the vessel. He had no great knowledge of the sea, like his two brothers Madoc and Riryd. "That is higher than usual, then?" he asked.

Svein answered for Madoc. "The Norse ships that sail the deep oceans have high sides and high ends, land-man—but never quite so high as this one."

"That is to ride the heavy seas and to prevent waves running behind from breaking into the waist of the vessel," added Riryd.

The deck was planked only over the bow and stern thirds of the ship. Narrow gangways joined these platforms at the sides, so much of the interior of the vessel was a gaping hole, from the centre of which the stubby mast rose.

"Where are you going to live on these great expeditions of yours?" objected Annesta, looking around the bare boards of the quarter deck. "You will die of exposure within a day of setting out."

Svein grinned and squeezed her round the waist. He was the only man who dared take liberties with her. "Don't worry, wife of Madoc . . . he will be snug enough under here." He took her to the edge of the central hold and pointed down. "Under there —the rearmost parts of the hull—when it's furnished with straw pallets and blankets, it will be as luxurious as Prince Owain's chamber in Aberffraw . . . and not much more damp, either!"

Einion stood looking at the lines of the boat, now rocking more vigorously, with scraping sounds underneath as she began lifting

67

off the bottom.

"She's nothing like those long-ships that used to terrorise these parts years ago," he commented. "They were slim and flat. This is like a sow compared to a greyhound, alongside one of those dragon-boats."

Svein pushed him playfully, almost knocking him into the six-feet deep hold.

"Call our lovely ship a sow, would you, you rogue! But you are right, the *langskips* would be useless in a long ocean voyage. They're too vulnerable to heavy seas and they offer no shelter for the crew. They were only for quick war expeditions, with crazy tough men like me, obsessed with fighting, looting and raping."

Madoc nodded his agreement. "This is a *haf-skip*, the Norse word for ocean ship, only I've exaggerated the lines even more. Deep in the body, so the water can't flow in over a low waist and shorter and heavier to be more stable."

Einion looked forward to the rising bow. "How long is it . . . how many men will you carry?"

"About forty feet. The crew need only be about ten, as far as the sailing is concerned, but if we need to use the long oars in calm waters when the wind fails, then a few more strong arms would be wanted. But for cargo or passengers, there's room for two to three dozen people in the hold there, as well as a few sheep and cattle, with their fodder."

Einion clambered down the short ladder into the hold and stood on the rough planking that covered the bottom. Moving to the curved inner side of the hull, he ran his hands down the overlapping planks and the sturdy frames that looked like the ribs of a huge beast.

The others watched him from above. "Every plank of best oak from the Gwynant valley," offered one of the shipbuilders. "Pinned with sawn stag horn, as Lord Madoc directed. Stronger than any other vessel in the world."

"And with the best mast in the world," added another Gele man. "Our spars and rigging are the best in Wales. They may build good hulls on the banks of the Conwy, but they send them to the Gele for masting."

This was true and was why Madoc had taken the trouble to have had the hull rowed around from Deganwy to this creek, after the main building had been completed on the Conwy. The men at this little boat-yard community on the Gele were undisputed masters of the delicate job of lowering a twenty-foot tree trunk into place, without dropping its foot through the bottom of the vessel. They also had the art of making a good sail and rigging, which not only would affect the performance of the *Gwennan Gorn*, but might make all the difference between life and death in really bad weather.

Annesta settled herself and the child comfortably while they waited for the tide to flow in far enough for the men on the shore to start pulling the vessel down to the sea.

In an hour, to the cheers of farewell from the Gele shipwrights and their families, the *Gwennan Gorn* slid through the low surf, pulled along by four of the men using long oars poked through little windows in the sides. "Even the oar sockets have stoppers to keep the sea out when sailing," Riryd proudly pointed out to Einion.

"Right, let's let the wind do the work now," shouted Madoc, as the breakers were left behind. He took the big steering oar that hung over the steer-board side of the stern, whilst Svein and Riryd hoisted the single yard that carried the oblong sail of wadmal fabric, strongly reinforced at the edges and in strips by bands of leather. "Do you like our new machine, Einion?" he called, pointing to the innovation that the Norseman and Riryd were using.

"What's it called?" asked Einion, staring at the three-foot length of tree trunk that rested in sockets on the stern deck. Four spokes stuck out from each end and the rope that hoisted the sail was wrapped around the drum formed by the cylindrical log.

"A windlass—used by modern Norsemen these days. The sail-spar can be hauled up by two men, instead of needing four struggling and slipping on a wet deck, as before."

Einion shook his head in wonder, thinking that progress these days was getting too rapid for his liking. As Svein and Riryd heaved at the spokes, the sail rattled up and began bellying in the breeze. The wind was coming off the land, but thankfully from the east, so the *Gwennan Gorn* soon pulled away from the coast and went along at a steady pace, the water gurgling and slapping under her bluff bows, music to the ears of Madoc and those others aboard with salt water in their veins.

"It rolls and pitches a lot," complained Annesta, looking rather white about the cheeks already.

Svein, Riryd and Madoc laughed aloud. "This is like sailing an acorn cup on a dish of water, girl," yelled Svein, as he jammed the spokes of the windlass with a piece of wood. "Wait until you're off Brittany in a sudden storm . . . you'll not know which way is up nor which is down then."

"No, thank you very much," snapped the young woman, now looking decidedly pale. "I don't mind this for myself, but I'm thinking of poor Gwenllian."

The little girl looked perfectly happy, gripping the edge of the bulwarks and laughing delightedly as the breeze and a few drops of spray tangled her dark hair.

It was over all too quickly and before long they came around and headed back towards the land. The ship heeled slightly, having no cargo or ballast and Annesta's protests became more vociferous, though her voice had become weaker as the pallor of her face took on a greenish tinge.

Her discomfort was to be short, however, as soon the *Gwennan Gorn* reached her destination. This was another little tidal creek, the Afon Ganol, a mile or two from the great mass of the Orme Head. Here a little stone quayside gave shelter and loading facilities for small vessels that squeezed through the surf at high tide and beached themselves in the creek under the gaze of Llandrillo church. The *Gwennan Gorn* was rowed into this haven, called Aber Cerrig Gwynion and Annesta's ordeal was over. Svein dropped the bow anchor, a great stone perforated with a hole through which the walrus-hide cable was attached and the little vessel was home.

70

SEVEN

JUNE 1169

A month after the completion of the *Gwennan Gorn,* she was safely anchored in the creek near the palace of Aberffraw. The court was again in full residence in Anglesey—it was the only one of the royal residences large enough to accommodate all the family, officers, servants and assorted hangers-on that made up the full court of Owain Gwynedd. And this June, everyone seemed to be at Aberffraw, excepting the eldest son, Iorwerth . . . Iorwerth Drwyndwyn, he of the Flat Nose, who was ostracised and virtually banished, skulking in a manor on the shores of the Menai Straits.

The main contenders for the princedom of North Wales were all there—Owain's sons Dafydd, Rhodri, Cynan and Hywel. The first two were the pace-makers of the court, the finest dressed, and the loudest-mouthed.

Though Owain Gwynedd was far ahead of any of them in both personality and presence, Madoc could see the clear and ominous signs of the familiar scramble for power in the not too distant future.

"It's like those monkeys we saw in Spain, Riryd," he said sadly to his brother one evening. "Remember, they were in a great pit at the court of some prince near Cadiz. The young males fought amongst themselves, then when the old leader grew tired, they crept up behind him and bit him."

Riryd nodded. "It seems that monkeys and men are pretty near relations, Madoc."

"Our brothers have fine clothes and no tails, but there is little difference otherwise. I tell you, it sickens me. I hate to think to the future, when our father goes to his rest. Whilst these popinjays are squabbling, Henry of England will march in and hang them all."

They were sitting in the great hall at the evening meal, looking around at the familiar scene, no women were present, only being admitted to the hall on festive days. The strict observance of the

71

old Welsh court protocols of Hywel Dda had begun to fade, after more than a century of contamination by Norman influences, but the Prince and his immediate following still sat at the upper end of the hall above the great fire. Owain Gwynedd had the place of honour on the right-hand side, with his bards, judges and chief officers around him. The three elder legitimate sons were nearby, but during the years that Madoc had been serving his father, his reliability and popularity with the old man had gradually earned him a place above the fire and now he sat with Riryd at the bottom of the benches that lined the wall of the upper hall. The traditional wattle screens between upper and lower hall had vanished in the name of progress, but a low step demarcated the large nave of the hall, where all the lesser men sat in serried ranks of benches behind their food-filled trestle tables. The floor was now of roughly slabbed stone instead of beaten earth, but the great roof trees that supported the massive thatch were much the same design that had persisted since the Romans left Britain.

On the surface, there was a comfortable air of permanency and security, but to those in the know—like the two brothers and the sharp-eyed bards—there was an ominous tension that grew month by month.

Servants were clearing the tables of platters and scraps, to make room for the serious business of drinking. There was beer, mead and even French wine for the select group around Prince Owain. The contact that Madoc had substantially helped to form across the sea had resulted not only in treaties, but in trade. Ships the size of the *Gwennan Gorn*, as well as more flimsy hide-covered curraghs, shipped Welsh wool and Anglesey corn across the channel in exchange for the more exotic produce of France.

It was time for song and verse, as well as for drink. The court Silentiary yelled and banged his staff for quiet and Owain Gwynedd rose to order Llywarch, now one of the court bards, to entertain them. The wily long-faced singer looked no older than when he had first met him, thought Madoc.

As the Prince spoke, Madoc looked with foreboding at his lined and tired face. Owain was now in his late sixties, an advanced age indeed for a warrior in those times. Though he had been as strong as an ox—and almost as large—for most of those seven decades, he seemed to have shrunk and bent during

72

the past year. Several old wounds, each of which would have been fatal in a lesser man, had at last begun to weaken him and the rapid onset of old age seemed to have withered him pitifully. His voice and eye were as sound as ever, but by the way he leaned on the table and the way his clothes hung on his shrunken body, Madoc could almost see the finger of death upon him.

Riryd had the same feelings. "Our royal father looks ill tonight," he murmured to his brother.

Madoc nodded. "Annesta told me that he had blood in his phlegm last night. She hears everything from her old friends in the Queen's bedchamber." His eyes swivelled to the opposite table. "Someone else has noticed it too, damn them."

Riryd followed his gaze and saw Dafydd and Hywel staring up at their father and talking behind their hands.

"Discussing the share-out already, I'll wager," muttered Madoc angrily.

Suddenly Dafydd looked across at them and must have intercepted Madoc's expression. He scowled and nudged his brother. Hywel also stared across the hall and his face began to show undisguised hatred and contempt.

The two of them never tried to hide their open jealousy of Madoc. It was made worse by the fact that Owain knew it only too well and goaded them with it by openly favouring Madoc, especially since he had proved such a successful ambassador and courier.

Several times there had been heated exchanges in the court, with Dafydd commenting loudly on Madoc's bastardy and previous banishment.

Since Owain had publicly rewarded Madoc with the cost of building the *Gwennan Gorn*, Dafydd's seething hate had been a permanent feature of court life. Though Owain, in his strength, had pretended to make a joke of it, Madoc sensed that he sent Madoc away on voyages and errands merely to cool off an embarrassing situation.

The very next day, the *Gwennan Gorn* was to leave on her first long trip to Spain. This was really quite unnecessary from the diplomatic point of view, as any shipmaster could have delivered the letters that Owain was sending to the ruler of Leon and Castille. Madoc strongly suspected that the open breach between the legitimate and bastard brothers had prompted Owain to invent this bogus errand for the *Gwennan Gorn* and her pilot, but he was glad of the opportunity both to escape from the evil atmosphere and to put his new vessel to sterner tests. After calling at Spain, he was going to take his ship much further south to the Fortunate Isles off the coast of Africa.

But tonight was yet to be lived through. At the end of the songs and poems from the bards, the hall dissolved into drinking groups and isolated centres of singing and tale-telling. The orderly ranks of benches were broken up and those who did not wander off to go wenching or back to their families, remained far into the night to revel or talk or play games of *tawlbwrdd* and dice.

Madoc did not want to remain too long, as he would rather spend the time with Annesta, talking and watching the sleeping Gwenllian. However, he stayed for a while in a group consisting of Riryd, Einion, Svein and a few others who had an interest in ships and voyaging.

Einion was proudly declaring his brother's naval prowess—since the *Gwennan Gorn* was launched, he had developed a passion for the sea and had been with Madoc on every proving trip that the new ship had made. He was going with Madoc on the voyage to Spain and his enthusiasm was unbounded.

"We're not coming straight back," he was telling those outside the *Gwennan Gorn* family. "Madoc of the Ships here is going to sail her down to the Fortunate Islands,* far beyond Spain, off the hot coast of Africa."

A few of the other ship-men had heard of the Fortunate Islands, which lay in the great ocean off the Pillars of Hercules, but none had ever been there, as this was beyond the ultimate limits of navigators from Britain.

"They are at the very edge of the world," said one confidently. "Nothing lies beyond them, save the mists of the rim of the world . . . then the great void."

Madoc had little time for those who described the bounds of the world from the safety of their chairs.

"How do you know, if you've never been there, Iestyn?" he asked. "There are other islands in the Western Ocean. . . . Brandon the Blessed found them . . . many of them, hundreds of years ago."

* The Canary Islands.

74

Iestyn scoffed at this. "Legends, Madoc . . . hundreds of years ago! The babblings of a mad Irish priest, like that Padraig of yours."

Madoc nodded. "Very well, let's forget Brandon for the moment. There are islands not far from the Fortunate Isles—which even you will not deny exist. They lie to the north and further out into the ocean."

Iestyn was shaken by the quiet confidence in Madoc's voice. "How do you know?" he asked dubiously.

"When I was in Paris, I spent much time with a philosopher from the shores of the Mediterranean . . . Guiot by name. He had great knowledge of the seas in that part of the world and had many friends amongst Arabian ship-men who used Massilia and often sailed the coast of Africa and out beyond the Pillars of Hercules."

"So . . . what did this oracle tell you?" asked Iestyn.

"That not only were there these Fortunate Islands, but others about three days sailing northward from the Fortunate Isles. They had no inhabitants, though there were some animals . . . the most noticeable being the profusion of hawks."*

Madoc was so definite that the others lost their cynical attitude.

"What else did this man tell you?" asked Iestyn.

Madoc exchanged a quick glance with Einion. Einion shook his head slightly, telling Madoc not to say any more about the secret navigating device that Guiot de Provins had given him.

Madoc covered up. "That there are seven or more islands, some very small. A few rise to a great height, sheer out of the sea there, which cannot be plumbed with a line even close inshore. These must be the tips of underwater mountains—Guiot thinks they may be the remnants of the fabled continent of Atlantis that the Greeks described."

"Can you land at these distant isles?" asked one of them, a practical man.

"They are very steep, but there are a few bays and coves that are accessible. There is fresh water and an abundance of fruit."

Iestyn looked thoughtful. "The Irish talk much of the Isles of the Blessed and the Isle of the Fountain of Youth, far out in the Great Ocean . . . are these supposed to be they?"

Einion answered for Madoc. "No, those are the Gwerddonau

* The modern Azores.

75

Llion—the Isles of Llion—that Brandon sought. It is said that they have wondrous fruit and trees full of birds and the seas around them have strange fish of enormous size . . . though as no one has ever returned from there, I fail to see how such tales ever came about," he added practically.

"These are the blasphemous tales that you have been filling my father's head with," cut in a new voice from the edge of the group.

Madoc looked up at the newcomer. It was Dafydd, accompanied by several of his burly, extravagantly costumed acolytes.

"I was merely retelling old legends, brother," said Madoc mildly.

"Brother! You are no brother of mine, Madoc the Bastard," snarled Dafydd, his face flushed with drink and his voice slightly slurred by both hatred and French wine.

Riryd started forward in anger, but Madoc restrained him with a hand on his arm. "Those are hard words, Dafydd ab Owain Gwynedd," he said evenly, striving always to avoid confrontation.

"They are true words, you interloper, you snake in the grass!" Dafydd was nearly shouting now. "Son of one of my weak father's whores, expelled in disgrace . . . then you come worming your way back into his favours, hoping to carve out some inheritance for yourself when he dies."

Madoc's face began to redden. He had one of the slowest tempers in Wales, but to hear his mother being insulted like that began to tax even his iron self-control. "I think you are not well —or over tired, brother," he said with icy quietness.

"I am very well, well enough to recognise deceit and fawning treachery when I see it," raved Dafydd. He staggered a little and one of his creatures took him by the arms to support him. His fair hair was a legacy from his father, just as Madoc's, but a big frame and handsome face was spoiled by a petulant mouth and weak chin.

Riryd took a step forward. "Dafydd, you are drunk," he said bluntly. He was older and more pugnacious than his brother and had the independence that came from a settled domain across the Irish Sea. He cared for nothing for Dafydd or his jealousies and made the fact quite obvious. "You are an insulting knave, brother . . . and brother you are, to me, to Madoc and to twenty others and more, whether you like it or not. So take yourself off, you and your rabble here. Brood elsewhere on your envy and jealousy."

Dafydd lurched around and faced him with seething hatred. He opened his mouth to spit insults, but Riryd took another step nearer and glared right into Dafydd's face.

The fair dandy stared back, then his eyes dropped. He turned and swayed into his companions. "Let us leave this band of bastards . . . but you, Madoc of the Ships"—he turned and gave his half-brother a look of crazed, drunken malice—"you will regret ever coming back to this court. I will see to that." He made his way unsteadily across to the high tables.

"There goes an evil man—and a dangerous one, Madoc," muttered Riryd.

"I hate this bickering and ill-feeling between us," said Madoc sadly. "I think he is right, I will regret coming back here. I could have stayed at your court of Clochran and built my ships there on the Liffey."

"And never met Annesta and never been father to Gwenllian?" asked Einion.

"That is true," sighed Madoc, "but I am very happy to be leaving Aberffraw tomorrow, to get away from Dafydd and his vile tongue."

"He is sorely afraid that you will be granted some of the princedom when Owain dies . . . he is already plotting against Hywel's chances and I would not trust his intentions with brother Rhodri, for all they seem so friendly."

As they left the hall, Riryd put his arm around Madoc's shoulders. "Tread carefully, Madoc. I know that you are not interested in power in Gwynedd, but until Dafydd and Rhodri get that message through their jealous heads, you might well be in some danger."

Madoc smiled in the darkness. "I know, Riryd, and thanks for your caring for me. But in a few hours, just after dawn, Einion and I will be down the river and safely away from all this turmoil."

"Let's hope that Dafydd's blood will have cooled by the time you return," murmured the Lord of Clochran, as they parted to go to their separate huts in the compound.

As Madoc walked through the starlit night, he thought of

77

leaving Annesta and the child, of the delights of sailing the *Gwennan Gorn* through the bluer seas to the south and the excitement of re-discovering islands that were still mysterious to all but a few intrepid ship-masters. He was taking Einion, this time, a brother of whom he had become as fond as he was of the old and reliable Riryd. Only the thought of two or three months' separation from his family marred the anticipation of next morning's departure.

On an impulse, he turned off the path to his lodging and walked towards the gate that led to the river. He wanted to look at his vessel once again, as she lay at anchor in the creek.

Passing through the quiet compound, he took his fill of land sounds and smells, which he would not get in any quantity until he returned in the summer. He listened to the noises from the various huts as he passed, the snores, the talk, the occasional shouts, the child's cries and the giggles. He smelled the wood smoke as it drifted from the eaves and through the holes in the thatch, the cruder smells of humanity, and as he neared the gate, the smell of wet mud from the marshes and river.

There was a night porter on duty at the gate leaning drowsily against the lodge-hut. As Madoc passed the last dwelling on the path to the gate, he heard a sudden rustle and a menacing swish of feet in damp grass.

He turned swiftly, but not fast enough. A dark figure, arm upraised, materialised before him and he felt—momentarily—a frightful pain in his head.

Lights flashed in his eyes, all the colours of the rainbow. The world swirled around him as he crumpled to the ground.

Three figures stood on the grassy bank above the beach, gazing out to sea. Far to the south-west, the sun glinted on the sail of the *Gwennan Gorn* as she vanished over the horizon.

"He'll be back by midsummer's day, Annesta," said Riryd comfortingly, as he gently led her back towards the palace.

"Safer there than in this hot-bed of passions," muttered Llywarch. "I pray that these intrigues and jealousies have died down before Madoc returns."

"Thank God he was able to go at all," said Riryd feelingly, as they trod slowly up the river path. "That blow on the head would have laid a lesser man in his bed for a week."

Annesta coloured and her voice quaked with anger. "It was Dafydd . . . I know it was Dafydd!"

"You can't say that without proof, girl," pleaded Llywarch earnestly. "It could have been any common thief . . . or some mistaken identity in the gloom."

"Ha . . . some mistake!" snapped Madoc's wife heatedly. "Not half an hour before, that Dafydd and his foul friends had been baiting and threatening Madoc in the hall itself. A strange coincidence that so soon afterwards he is laid low by some assassin. But for Einion happening to have followed him, no doubt my man would have been beaten to death or found floating in the river next day."

The three of them walked silently on as the *Gwennan Gorn* disappeared over the edge of the world behind them.

The bard gave a deep sigh. "I don't see what's to happen to Gwynedd when Owain goes to his rest—and he looks older and weaker every day. These sons of his will tear the land apart like dogs snarling over a bone."

"They can do what they like—Madoc and I want no part of it. We have agreed to leave Aberffraw when he returns and set up our dwelling elsewhere. Maybe down on the Llyn peninsula—or even back across the sea in Ireland. Perhaps you'll have us in Clochran, brother Riryd?"

The elder brother nodded gravely. "You are ever welcome, sister. But I think that while Owain has need of Madoc, he will stay. He feels that having had so many years without a father, he must make the most of the time whilst Owain lives."

"There lies the danger," murmured Llywarch. "It is this very trust that the Prince puts in Madoc that brings the fear and hate of his other brothers upon him."

Riryd looked at the "Poet of the Pigs" as some of his more unkind critics called him. "Can you not use your influence with Owain to tactfully show him the danger to Madoc?"

Llywarch shrugged. "I have my position to think of," he said evasively. "I do not have Owain's ear as well as I would wish." His face darkened. "There is that damned Gwilym Ryfel, who calls himself a bard, also trying to ingratiate himself with the Prince . . . and of course, that senile old fool Gwalchmai, who still flaunts himself as the grand old man of the Court, sage and adviser to Kings . . . and I can run circles around him when it comes to devising an elegy or an ode."

Riryd and Annesta made faces at each other behind Llywelyn ap Llywarch's back. The jealousies and professional rivalries between the court bards was almost as bad as the in-fighting of the king's sons.

"Madoc is safe now, out on the sea that he loves so much," said Riryd.

"Until he returns," added Annesta, sadly. "I hope that I can persuade him to leave this place straight away. Anywhere would be preferable after that attack last night. Brittany, Ireland, the south of Wales, anywhere."

She turned round and looked back at the sea. There was now nothing visible of the dot on the horizon.

"Farewell, husband," she breathed, pulling Gwenllian close against her skirts. "Find your Isles of the Blessed, then come home to me, safely."

It was ninety-four days before the *Gwennan Gorn* climbed back up that same horizon and saw the blue peaks of Snowdonia lowering over Anglesey. In that time, Madoc's vessel had done everything that he had expected of it and more. The few summer storms had been ridden through with no damage. The stag-horned hull had hardly leaked a bucketful of water in each day. Svein, who had given the ship its basic Norse design, had grinned almost continually between each landfall, so pleased was he with her performance. The oars had hardly been used, so favourable were the currents and the winds.

"She sails at a quarter angle to the breezes," he exulted one day. "Impossible in theory for a wind to blow one way and the vessel to move straight across it, but our *Gwennan Gorn* does it!"

Madoc was equally—if more sedately—delighted. "One day, my Norse friend, some genius will get a vessel to sail nearer the wind than a square angle . . . but it'll not be in our time!"

"By magic, maybe . . . but magic we already have in that little bowl." He nodded at a wooden broth bowl which now lay empty on the planks of the stern deck. It was the one in which Madoc floated his enchanted lodestone needle, when the sun was hidden and no land was in sight.

"With that and the birds and the waves we could sail round the edge of the world if we so wished," he yelled.

80

He had cause for celebration as the voyage had achieved all that Madoc had hoped. After their duty visit to Spain, they had sailed down the coast and sold all of their small cargo of woollen cloth and a few unhappy sheep to the inhabitants of the small ports. In return they had collected a little gold and silver and some curious goods brought round from the Mediterranean . . . fine earthenware from Italy, strange spices from somewhere further east and some flasks of wine. But these were but fringe activities—this was no trading trip, but a voyage of discovery. Twenty days out from Aberffraw, Madoc turned the ship's prow away from the Iberian coast and travelled on a slow but strong current southwards, so that every day at noon, the shadows of the sun grew shorter.

On the twenty-ninth day they sighted the Fortunate Islands, warm and basking in the heat blown off the great deserts of Africa, said to lie not far to the east.

The islands had high mountains, especially one of them, which was shrouded in cloud most of the time. The people were a primitive race, dressed in goat-skins, calling themselves Guanches. One Arab dhow was anchored off the islands and there was obviously regular trade with the Berbers of the mainland. The natives had few possessions to barter, but Madoc and his crew exchanged some woollen cloth for some rough pottery, decorated with finger-nail marks and some quite attractive necklaces of bone, shell and carved wood.

The *Gwennan Gorn* stayed only a few days, moving from island to island, taking on fresh water in her casks and some fresh fruit and a few goats as an addition to their stores.

Then the tiny vessel hauled up her stone anchor and headed north and west from the Fortunate Isles, out into the almost unknown sea. They had tried asking the aborigines if they knew of other islands beyond their own, by sign-language and attempts at drawing maps in the sand, but they got no response.

Madoc's only guide was the conversations several years earlier with Guiot of Provins and a few vague guesses of Breton and Irish ship-masters, who had heard of men who had heard of the Isles of Hawks.

This time the wind was not so kind to them, as they had to set themselves across the breezes that came from Africa. The current also was against them, but the *Gwennan Gorn* made slow but steady progress northwest. Every noon, the shadow of the mast crept longer across the deck, but they had no means of telling how far they had progressed in the direction of the setting sun.

For twenty days, they ranged out into the Great Ocean—for two of these days and nights, a storm drove them south, losing them much of their previous progress.

There were a few mutterings amongst the crew, not rebellious or fearful, but rather grumbling about wasting time searching for islands which might not even exist.

The situation was saved by Svein, whose sea-sense verged on the uncanny. Suddenly one morning, he raised his head and slowly scanned the horizon to the steer-board side. "There is land somewhere, Madoc," he announced in a matter-of-fact way.

The Welshman was content to believe him, though he could not sense anything different. He had experience of the Norseman's near-magical powers on other occasions.

Later that day, even Madoc was persuading himself that the edge of the world, now visible over the prow, looked a slightly different colour compared with other directions. Svein was hanging over the side, and an hour later he gave a grunt of satisfaction. "Seaweed, Madoc," was all he said. Next morning they awoke to find a large bird, resembling a fulmar, circling overhead, before it flew away with easy wingbeats to the north. Madoc ordered the steersman to go on the other tack and the *Gwennan* did its best to follow the bird, though until evening the wind was not very co-operative.

On the third morning, there were several other birds, guillemots and a herring gull.

At the next dawn, high mountain peaks were spread across the horizon and by evening they were anchored in the lee of great cliffs of volcanic rock.

This time there were no aboriginal natives to deal with—the islands seemed deserted and almost barren, apart from birds and small vermin. There was fresh water and berries in abundance. The crew launched one of their coracles* which were kept lashed upside down on the fore-deck and in the next few days they made many trips to the beaches that crouched between the high precipices.

* A tiny, bowl-shaped boat made of hides stretched over a wicker frame.

The conical mountain peaks were often wreathed in cloud, but the climate was mild. There was no sign of any human visitation, apart from some trees felled with an axe, looking as if this had been done many years earlier.

"The Arabians told the truth, then," murmured Einion, as they gazed for the last time at the islands.

Madoc nodded. "Guiot was right in many things—about the Fortunate Isles, these Isles of Hawks—and many hawks and buzzards there are. And also about the lodestone, though so far we have had little need of it in this clear weather, with good sightings of the sun and stars."

Svein looked at the misted peaks as they clawed away towards the east. "These are not the Isles of the Blest or the Fountain of Eternal Youth that you Celts keep bleating about, then?" he asked with good-natured sarcasm.

"You Norsemen have your sacred places, your Valhalla and your Asgard. Let us have our fabled islands in return, Svein the Doubter."

The Viking grinned. "You can keep these barren rocks, Welshman—if you can find them again, without my help."

Madoc became serious at this. "We must take the exact point of the shadow of noon sun for this day of the year . . . then follow it exactly to the east until we meet the mainland. That way we will be able to find these isles again, as long as we come at the same month of the year. We sail southward from Brittany until the shadow is the same length and then turn westward."

Svein nodded. "I have heard that my fellow ship-masters in Norway now use a device for doing just that. One that can even be adjusted for different seasons of the year. When we return, I will ask amongst the *knarr*-masters that come into the Liffey, whether they have such a device or know how to make one."

Madoc thought about this during the long haul back across the current and the wind, trying to keep the mast-head shadow on a marked point on the deck each noontide. It was ridiculous to be bound to a certain month of the year to make each similar journey. The sailing season was from May to September, but the sun's shadow varied greatly during that time and he would be overjoyed to hear of Svein's Viking sun-board which could compensate for this defect.

It took another twenty-seven days to reach the Iberian coastline and after sailing north for a day, the crew of *Gwennan Gorn* recognised that they were approaching the mouth of the Tagus, land which had recently been won for the new Kingdom of Portugal.

From then on, all was plain—if laborious—sailing, until they reached the south-westerly winds beyond the tip of Spain, which sent them up the now almost familiar coastline to Brittany and then across to Cornwall and the Severn Sea.

Now they were within sight of the Isle of Môn* and the palace of Gwynedd.

Madoc stood with his brother Einion and Svein on the stern deck and looked at the low line of Anglesey ahead.

"We have seen many marvellous things and many strange places, friends. But what stead will they be to us if we plunge back again into hatred and treachery in my father's palace." A cold wind suddenly seemed to ripple down Madoc's spine. "Just as you sensed the Isles of Hawks, Svein, so do I sense great trouble ahead."

Silently the three stood watching as the little ship laboured its way home, their pleasure at the safe return being muted by a sense of foreboding.

* Anglesey.

EIGHT

EASTER 1170

During the autumn of 1169 and on into the winter, Owain ap Gruffudd, Prince of Gwynedd, grew steadily more infirm. Though his mind was still keen and his strong will remained as sharp, he seemed to shrink and wither away. By the New Year, he needed either a stick or the arm of one of his family to help his steps. He ceased going to Dolwyddelan, finding it too hard to mount a horse and to deal with the steep slopes of that craggy place.

Yet his political and diplomatic intrigues were as active as they had ever been. He continued his jousting with both the See of Canterbury and the Pope, over his marriage to Cristin, mother of Dafydd and Rhodri, who were still incensed by their illegitimacy in the eyes of the official Church. Though Becket had been exiled to France by Henry of England, he had excommunicated Owain Gwynedd six years earlier, for his unlawful marriage to his second-cousin, which was outside the bonds of sanguinity recognised by Rome. With typical contempt for English ordinances Owain ignored the terrible prospect of an eternity in hell and continued to receive communion from the hugely-pleased Welsh bishops. He also continued to keep out any bishops nominated by Canterbury to his domains, which now covered all Wales except the south, which was held by his ally, the Lord Rhys.

He also maintained his links with France and the court of Louis, both tactfully avoiding the subject of Thomas à Becket, who was fretting away in the Monastery of Pontigny.

The campaign against Henry Plantagenet had not materialised, mainly because Henry had kept well clear of conflict with the Welsh. He had enough to do in his French possessions, where he was gradually eroding Louis's territory north of Paris.

In the spring of 1170, Owain again sent Madoc to France to keep up the contacts with Louis. Though it was early in the season for sea-faring, the *Gwennan Gorn* had proved herself so well, that the short crossing could be risked.

Svein had gone back to Dublin after the 'Long Voyage' to the Fortunate Isles, promising to return again in the spring for another adventure.

Einion had become Madoc's sea-faring companion now. He had proved himself well on the Long Voyage, showing himself to be a natural sailor and a reliable navigator. Madoc grew as fond of him as he was of Riryd.

On the return trip from France good winds had sped them quickly northwards from Lundy, and they were several days in advance of their expected arrival at Aberffraw.

The *Gwennan Gorn* was off the tip of West Wales, a mile from the cruel coast near the cathedral of St. David, when Madoc, who had been staring at the surf smashing against the rocks of Ramsey Island, suddenly called to Einion above the whistle of the wind and the creak of rigging and planks. "Brother, let us give our magic ship the supreme test . . . take her through the maelstrom of Ynys Enlli."

For once Einion's bluff features failed to respond with a grin. He stared back at his brother. "That devil's mill-race? Would you wreck our vessel and drown us all, just on a whim?"

Madoc, beat his fist into his palm. "It will be the final trial, Einion! If she can weather that boiling water in this wind, it will be an omen that she is indestructible."

For half a day they argued back and forth, but the battle was lost from the beginning for Einion, for secretly he wanted to prove that the *Gwennan Gorn* could survive in that hellish channel where so many vessels had been pounded to pieces, including Svein's *Iduna*. The channel was the narrow sound between Ynys Enlli, the sacred island where the saints were buried, that the Norsemen called Bardsey. Between there and the mainland of the Llyn peninsula, was the most fearsome stretch of water south of the Caledonian coasts.

As the tide ebbed from the Irish Sea, it raced down the north coast of Llyn and was funnelled into the mile-wide gap between the lonely island and the headland of Braich-y-Pwyll. Here under-water crags and rocky bars caused the sea to boil and writhe into whirlpools and cataracts of white water that could spin a small vessel round like a top and either shake her planking apart or overwhelm her steering and smash her against the steep grey cliffs. Anyone cast into the water was sucked down, never to be seen again in one piece. The wreckage of shattered ships was smashed into matchwood and the mangled remains vomited up on distant beaches.

The twenty men who were the crew of the *Gwennan Gorn* had all had experience of the hell-race of Bardsey. Though most of them had passed through in carefully chosen circumstances—when the tide was slack on the turn and when there was no swell or wind to speak of—they all had a healthy respect for it even in those calmest of moments. None of them would have dreamed of attempting the passage as Madoc intended, in this stiff wind, deliberately picking the middle of the ebb tide.

Einion, came to see this as the ultimate test of the ship—more than that, a portent of future infallibility, for if they survived it, what worse could the unknown world offer?

The crew were soon infected with the same feelings. It was daring the devil, twisting the tail of fate, to win immunity for the future. As the little ship ploughed across the great bay which lay between Dyfed and Llyn, they began to feel a reckless fatalism which grew as the rounded hump of Ynys Enlli rose higher over the horizon.

"We shall go around the island to seaward, then come down through the sound with the tide," decided Madoc. They were only a few dozen miles from Anglesey by now and it was only their perversity that made them attempt this horrific doubling-back on their course to prove that Svein's design, Madoc's modifications and the stag-horn pegs could defeat the buffeting of Bardsey's treacherous waters.

They drew into position north of the island, far enough off-shore to remain clear of the tide rip that was beginning to build up.

"Every loose thing must be lashed down, every box and barrel," yelled Einion from the stern deck, where he stood next to the steersman, ready to throw his weight on the great oar that was lashed to a pole projecting from the ship's side.

Thankfully, they had no live sheep or other animals aboard and the crew had only themselves to look out for.

"Bring her to the shore," commanded Madoc, who had placed himself right in the high blunt prow. He hung on to the great post that formed the stem, so that he could see the water directly ahead of the vessel.

Gwilym, the steersman, twisted the shaft of oar and slowly the *Gwennan Gorn* came around towards the east, then the south. As Madoc had expected, the wind had changed with the time of day and now blew strongly down the coast with the tide, coming off the mountains. Yet the swell was hurling itself northward against the tide and the wind, due to the prevailing westerlies coming from the Great Ocean. Where the three elements met in conflict, the channel between the gaunt cliffs was alive with leaping wavelets and turbulent, churning waters.

The ship turned right around and by the time it was two miles north of the narrowest part of the sound, the tide was racing its fastest, just as Madoc had calculated. They now had the worst possible conditions, short of waiting for a winter gale which would have wrecked any ship in the world, including their own.

But this was bad enough and every fathom nearer the narrows made it worse.

"Here we go!" screamed Einion, scared and exhilarated. Every man aboard felt the tide grip the hull and she seemed to lurch forward as if grasped by a giant hand. Most of the crew were either clinging on to the bulwarks or braced in the hold, ready to bale with the leather buckets. Only those tailing on to the running rigging had to stand free on the deck.

Madoc was not trying to avoid the worst areas, but rather to deliberately seek them out. He had little difficulty in finding trouble. As the straits narrowed, the surface of the sea turned into a maelstrom of white-caps and writhing currents. Right before him he saw a huge patch where water was bubbling upwards, as if from some subterranean spring, leaping in great streams from the bottom and spreading out in fluid snakes that flattened even the cresting waves in the vicinity.

"To the lee-side . . . lee-side," he yelled, motioning with his hand so that the bow was made to point directly at this cauldron of boiling coldness.

Gwilym, now being juddered about by the vibrations of his oar, turned the ship's head to the left and with a jerk, the forty feet of cockleshell was simultaneously twisted, heeled and battered. There was a wail from one of the crew, as the lurch threw him off balance into the hold, then the ship lurched through a quarter of a circle until the opposite rail was touching the water.

"To steer-board, for Jesus' sake," screamed Madoc, suddenly aware that they were in trouble enough, without actively looking for more.

The *Gwennan*'s head suddenly dipped and she took a sea full over the prow, soaking Madoc and almost sweeping him aft to join the injured man in the hold. Then she spun around and lay broach-to while parallel lines of white waves battered her sides like ranks of soldiers charging in battle. The hull shuddered and the empty sail flapped as the wind hit it on the wrong side.

Einion, leaping onto the steering oar to help Gwilym, yelled at the men on the sheet roopes to pull the yard around to catch the wind and get them under way again, rather than be wallowing helpless across the current. Then a sudden blast of spray on his neck made him look aft and nearly faint with fright and despair.

A sudden blackness and rough water was sweeping down on them from the north, in the shape of a squall from Snowdonia.

Half a moment later it hit them.

The vessel, already jumping about like a cow in a fit, was hit abeam by the wind, just when the sail had been dragged around into the worst possible position.

With a crack like thunder, the mast snapped off half way up and the sail fell over the side, held only by the lower yard and the sheet ropes. One man was knocked clean overboard by the mast, his last scream drowned by the wind.

Out of control, the *Gwennan Gorn* spun around madly, rotating in great circles and being jolted from one whirlpool to another.

The white horses of the tide-rip splashed one after the other onto the deck and into the hold. The rolling and the pitching threw all the crew into a bruised heap, some of them falling over the rim of the deck into the flooded hold.

"Bale . . . for God's sake, bale," yelled Madoc, crawling hand over hand along the bulwarks, drenched, cold and shivering.

There was nothing else to do but bale. Gwilym's steering oar had been torn from his grasp and it and the post to which it was secured had vanished into the hell over the side.

With no sail, no mast and no steering, they were moving at the speed of a galloping horse.

"Bale . . . bale!" sobbed Einion, crawling to the edge of the hold and grabbing a leather bucket that a man—up to his waist

89

in water—shakily handed up to him.

"We are losing fast," shouted Rhys, a black-bearded senior crewman. With every roll of the ship, Rhys was alternately up to his ankles, then up to his chest in water as he heroically scooped bucket after bucket of water from the hold and handed it up to men above. But with every roll, more water poured over the side of the ship and cascaded into the central well.

"We're done for," yelled Gwilym. "We must swim for it."

Madoc grabbed him by the neck and shook him like a dog, an action so unlike him that it emphasised the extraordinary situation. "Fool—can you swim in that?" howled the ship-master. "And only four of us can swim at all."

But Einion interrupted with fresh worries. "The cliffs, we are getting under the cliffs!"

The current, which so far had taken them rapidly into the neck of the channel, now seemed to curve away towards the mainland. There, not four hundred yards away, was a wall of sea-swept rock climbing from the spray to the grey sky above. At its foot, the water made the rest of the channel look like the palace fishpond on a calm day. From the pitching deck, the surface looked like the teeth of a great saw, with jagged serrations jumping up and down, the tops being blown white by the wind that still howled down the coastline.

"We are lost!" screamed one of the men, holding a bucket at the side. He dropped the bucket and scrambled on to the wooden rail. Einion managed to catch his leg, but the bare foot slipped in his grasp and the next second the man had leapt into the water.

"Stay with the ship, you fools," screamed Madoc. "Another minute and we'll be through."

It was now a gamble between the speed at which the ship was being pulled through the sound and the speed at which it was sliding towards the rocks. They hit the saw-toothed water and the vessel began shaking, as if a giant hammer was hitting the keel.

As the ship shook unmercifully, the cliff seemed to race towards them.

Madoc was thrown to the deck and found himself grasping someone. It was Einion. Together they looked up at the grey rocks almost overhead.

Einion, even when staring death in the face, could not resist

90

a jest. "We are to end on *Trwyn-y-Gwyddel*, the Irishman's Nose, brother. It's appropriate for you, being raised there. At least, it's better than dying on a Englishman's nose."

Just as they were about to strike and all aboard had passed into their own personal state of terror or resignation, the freak currents that had brought them there, just as suddenly took them away. The sea, rebounding from the cliffs, roared round the Irishman's Nose in a cascading semicircle. This was the narrowest part of the channel and the most shallow. The bar of rock under water that had forced the rip-tide to rise from the bottom, dropped away and the increased depth could accommodate the volume in relative peace, as a deep mill-stream runs silently.

In a matter of seconds, the *Gwennan Gorn* was back on an even keel, and slowed down almost to walking pace.

Unbelieving, the men stared up from wherever they lay or crouched.

Gradually, the reality of salvation dawned on them. Ragged cheers, mixed with sobs and half-drowned coughing echoed across the suddenly quiet water. Once round the corner, they were drifting on a swell with not a white horse anywhere near them.

"We live . . . we came through!" Madoc's voice held more surprise than joy at first.

They all rose shakily to their feet and looked around them. Behind, a line of terrible broken water marked the sudden end of the maelstrom.

"The bane of our life, Madoc. *Gwennan*'s bane," said Einion shakily.

Madoc looked aback, still shivering with emotion and cold. "Let it be known as that for eternity, then . . . *Ffrydiau Caswenann*, the Currents of *Gwennan*'s Bane. But we did it, Einion, we did it."

"Unless we sink in the next hour," came a deep voice from somewhere near their feet. In the hold, the bearded Rhys was barely able to keep his black chin above water. By now the level was not far below the edge of the deck. Over the side of the ship, the freeboard was reduced to less than half that it was an hour before.

"Bale or perish," yelled Einion, jumping in alongside Rhys and grabbing a floating bucket. They were able to reduce the flood to something approaching safety level in about an hour, though the vessel was still unfit to tackle any more rough water.

"The oars, Rhys . . . can you unlash them?" The *Gwennan Gorn* was drifting uncomfortably near to the cliffs again and though there was none of the watery Hades like that further up the coast, the breakers were large enough to pound her to pieces should she drift ashore.

"Around to Aberdaron—we'll beach her there," ordered Madoc.

There was a small inlet just past Trwyn-y-Gwyddel, called Porth Felen, but they had drifted too far to get into it. The cliffs that they were so uncomfortably close to now were the Great Wall of Parwyd, but around the corner was the placid bay with the village of Aberdaron.

The long oars were taken from the lashings along the sides of the hold, after Rhys and two other men had groped for them under the remaining water. The little doors opened for them and they were pushed out over the side.

The haul around to Aberdaron was long and laborious, as the waterlogged vessel was heavy and unmanœuvrable, but danger was past and Madoc saw with pride that the water level inside did not rise at all, even with no further baling.

"Not a single leak . . . not a single sprung plank in all that buffeting, Einion," he enthused. "Stag horn and Welsh oak . . . an unbeatable combination. Now we can sail across the world and be confident of survival."

Einion paused from wringing the water out of his sodden tunic. "You mean row across the world, brother." He pointed to the tattered remnants of the sail and rigging and the shattered stump of the mast.

NINE

APRIL 1170

It took Madoc and his crew another week to get the *Gwennan Gorn* back to the coast of North Wales. At Aberdaron they rigged up a temporary mast and a day or two later, limped back along the coast, keeping well to seaward of the treacherous, but now defeated Sound of Bardsey.

Madoc left the vessel at Aberffraw, but Einion and his crew took the *Gwennan Gorn* on to the Gele river, where the experts who had masted her could carry out the best possible repairs.

Madoc waded ashore through the shallow surf of Aberffraw beach. He was torn between a desire to go on with them to Abergele to make sure that a good job was made of stepping a new mast or the joy of seeing Annesta and Gwenllian again.

In reality he had no choice, as he was obliged to report to his father on the results of the visit to Paris.

The Porter, who knew and loved him well, gave him a cheerful greeting and walked with him across the compound towards his own hut, where the family waited for him.

"What's been happening while I was away, Idwal?" he asked the gatekeeper.

Idwal's round face became serious. "The Lord Owain . . . he fails a little each day, though he still holds court and tries to keep these louts of his in order." This was dangerous talk, but the Porter knew that his tongue was safe with Madoc. "They have been setting upon Hywel's reputation lately, that Dafydd and Rhodri. He is not here to defend himself and they are out to destroy his character, as they have already done with Iorwerth." Idwal looked furtively around and lowered his voice. "Madoc ab Owain, though it is no place for me to advise a man of royal blood, I would be careful where you walk in the dark."

Madoc laid a hand on the officer's shoulder. "Thank you, good man. I shall watch for myself well enough."

Idwal turned a concerned face towards Madoc. "Watch out

for your family as well, Prince. It would be better for you to take them far away, for all we love your gentle ways here." With this cryptic remark, he walked back to his gatehouse, leaving Madoc standing thoughtfully outside his thatched home.

The homecoming was as happy as Madoc could have expected, with quiet contentment from Annesta—who was pregnant again —and sheer exuberance from little Gwenllian.

The quarters in Aberffraw were cramped, as even a royal son had to make do with a dwelling that an ordinary farmer would have used in the countryside.

"We must leave here soon, my love, and find a permanent home," said Madoc, after their morning meal the next day.

"You have been saying that for four years, husband," answered Annesta with a touch of the impatience that was in her nature. "Now that the Prince never leaves Aberffraw, we are as cramped here as bees huddled in a hive."

"Ireland . . . we must go back to Clochran," decided Madoc. "Riryd says that he will be glad to have us on his lands. With the profit I have made from trading in the *Gwennan Gorn* over the past years, we could build a new winter dwelling within sight of the river. In the summer, we could come back to Wales for a few months."

"When you are not gadding about the world, Madoc," retorted his wife, this time with a smile. She was secretly proud of her husband's reputation as "Madoc of the Ships."

For a few days, all was quiet, as the premier sons were away. Dafydd was skirmishing away to the east, where he was pushing back some Normans from the banks of the Clwyd. King Henry seemed indifferent to the fate of the Welsh border. The power of Gwynedd was such that local barons and knights were impotent to defy the sudden attacks of the Welsh as they descended out of the rain and mists of the hills.

In the absence of Dafydd and Rhodri, the palace was peaceful. Madoc had long sessions with his father, explaining what had happened in France. This time, Hugh de Soissons had again confirmed the French alliance with Wales, but appeared cautious in making any plans to move against England. They had a military problem already in containing Henry's pressure in Normandy and would not contemplate any more outright action for the moment.

Owain seemed to take this philosophically and indeed seemed almost indifferent to expanding his outside influence. His mind seemed occupied completely with worrying about the succession and Madoc feared that he knew that his days were limited. "I'll not see the Christ Mass of this year, son," he muttered one night. "All these years I have worked to bring North Wales together—and even join it politically with the south. But I fear that in a few short months, my labours will be unravelled by my kinsfolk. Even Cristin prefers her own blood amongst them. She encourages every move of her two sons against the others, which is natural, but thank God I will not be here to see the ruin that must follow."

He never said a word about any bequests for Madoc after his death, though he was generous to him with his purse during life. When he heard of the conquest of Bardsey Sound by the *Gwennan Gorn*, he cheered up, the old glint coming back into his eye as Madoc recounted the story of their ordeal and triumph. He insisted on paying for the repairs to the vessel, saying that it was vital to restore her to exactly the same degree of safety and seaworthiness as before.

Word came from Einion some days later that the builders on the Gele were fully occupied with other ships, it being the start of the new season, but that the *Gwennan Gorn* would be re-masted at Aber Cerrig Gwynion, the little creek with a quay-wall between the Conwy and Abergele.

The peaceful time lasted about ten days. Then early one evening, a long cortège clattered into Aberffraw, headed by Dafydd. A few hours later, while they were all at meat in the hall, Rhodri arrived with his retainers and the palace, already overcrowded, now became unbearably packed.

Madoc kept out of the way that night, but the next evening brought the beginning of trouble.

Owain Gwynedd seemed to have rallied a little and cast aside the usual weariness and apathy that had lately engulfed him. There was a long session of the bards, with Llywarch y Pryddyd Moch and the elder Gwalchmai regaling the packed hall with song and poetry, then an impromptu contest between lesser singers, poets and story-tellers.

An hour before midnight the smoky hall was almost bursting at the seams with roistering men.

Madoc studiously avoided his half-brothers and sat with Einion, as Riryd had returned to Ireland. Dafydd threw a sneer of contempt at them across the upper hall from time to time.

But later in the night, when the formal songs and stories were finished, Prince Owain, rose from his chair and began walking around amongst his court, goblet of mead in one hand and a stout stick in the other. He was dutifully attended by his Chancellor, Chief Judge, the bards Gwalchmai and Llywarch and other officers of the hierarchy. He chatted and joked with many of his family—for scores could claim blood relations with him. Dafydd and Rhodri stuck close by him, for though their anxiety to see his funeral was great, they were attentive to the last degree during his life, for fear of incurring his great displeasure and somehow standing at a disadvantage when the great share-out came.

Owain passed from group to group, in high spirits that pleased everyone except his senior sons. Then he came across to Einion and Madoc, who had been sitting with three of their immediate friends, talking ships and adventure, as usual.

They rose to their feet and greeted Owain warmly. Madoc's father slapped him on the shoulder.

"Son, you have given us something new to talk of . . . the exploit in the channel of Ynys Enlli was after my own heart. I was something of a sailor myself in my youth. How could I be otherwise with the Viking Sitric Silken-beard for a grandfather."

He had drunk a good deal and was in an expansive, paternal mood. He put his arm round Madoc's shoulders and squeezed him hard. "To think that I missed a son like this for so many years. Thank God Brenda of Carno had the good sense to put that to rights—even though it was on her death bed, God rest her."

Madoc caught sight of Dafydd's face and saw the sheer unadulterated hate in his half-brother's eyes.

"You must give me a voyage in your wonderful magic ship, Madoc," went on Owain in his deep rumble, which seemed to have strengthened with the mead. "Not through the Currents of Gwennan's Bane, for I could not stand that at my age . . . but a short trip around Mona, before I die . . . eh!"

Madoc looked fondly at this emaciated giant, his heart full. "You'll not die yet awhile, Lord Owain," he said feelingly, "Gwynedd needs you too much . . . especially when Louis of France moves with us and forces this Henry Plantagenet to

96

recognise our frontiers for a century to come."

Dafydd cut in sharply, "You are the great architect of the French liaison, I suppose," he sneered. "Madoc the Great Sailor, Madoc the Great Diplomat . . . Madoc the aspiring bard . . . what else do you aspire to, *brother*?"

The tone was insulting and Owain turned sharply on him, swaying a little. "Hold your tongue, you over-dressed popinjay," he roared. "If you had half the courage and devotion of this Madoc, I'd not look ahead to my death with such consternation!"

Dafydd seemed on the verge of hysterical raging, but the more phlegmatic Rhodri laid a hand on his arm and pulled at him. "Easy, brother . . . settle your differences in a less public place, eh?"

The meaning of this muttered advice managed to penetrate Dafydd's hate-ridden mind and with an effort he backed away. He was about to throw a parting threat at Madoc, but again Rhodri pulled at him and the two sons thrust their way through the curious onlookers and left the hall.

Owain shrugged. "There must be some good in every man," he said enigmatically and moved on down the hall with his entourage to talk to others of his household. Madoc and Einion stood uneasily, watching the last of Dafydd's henchmen leaving by the small wicket door opposite.

"You are heaping much trouble for yourself," murmured a voice.

They turned to see Llywarch, the bard, who was trailing behind Owain.

"The heaping is none of our doing, Llywarch. I say not a word, and yet those ambitious brothers seem intent on shaming me, especially Dafydd," answered Madoc sadly.

Llywarch sighed. "Take a warning and look over your shoulder this night when you walk in the dark."

He hurried on after Owain and the others, afraid of losing his place in his own constant battle for prominence amongst the bards.

"I trust that Poet of the Pigs about as far as I can throw my horse," muttered Einion, scowling after the retreating figure in the gaudy robes.

"So far, we have no grounds for suspecting his honesty," objected Madoc, always ready to see the best in any man.

Einion shook his head knowingly. "He tries to run with both the hunter and the hunted. Several times I have seen him capering and grinning with Dafydd and Rhodri. He probably tells them how evil you are, at the same time as he warns you of them. I trust him not one little bit."

Madoc thought back to the episode in the castle of Dolwyddelan many years before, when his father had burst in to his mother's chamber. He had wondered about Llywarch's part in the affair, but no proof had ever been found.

"My thirst and my spirits are quenched, Einion," he said sadly, picking his woollen cloak from the bench. "I feel tired and out of sorts. Let's go to bed."

"A walk first, then. I've too much ale and *meddyglyn** inside me to lie on my bed for a while yet."

They walked down to the river in the moonlight, not without a few glances over their shoulders. Neither remarked on it, but both were well aware of what had happened to Madoc the night before they left on the Long Voyage. But all was quiet and they spent almost an hour strolling down towards the great beach that lay off the mouth of the river.

"The *Gwennan Gorn* will be ready for sea by now," reported Einion, who had returned from the boat-fitters at Aber Cerrig Gwynion only the day before.

"What of our crew . . . are they ready too?"

Einion nodded, his chin wagging into the collar of his cloak. "They will all be there by tonight. I told them that I would ride back tomorrow and bring the vessel round to Aberffraw as soon as the present contrary wind had died down."

Madoc stared gloomily at the palace walls. "I think I will take Annesta and Gwenllian to Ireland for a time. Riryd is there now and I feel that with the unpleasantness here, it will be better for us to have a month or two at Clochran, while Dafydd's blood turns less sour. Our father has no need of me for any diplomatic voyages at the moment, so I'll take leave of Wales for a time. Maybe it would be a good idea if you joined us."

Einion shook his head. "I'll voyage with you to Dublin, but then I'll return in some other vessel or bring the *Gwennan Gorn* home, if you wish it."

"Why the sudden devotion to Aberffraw?" asked Madoc

* A type of mead.

98

curiously.

Einion grinned sheepishly in the gloom. "I have a certain interest that might develop into something good," he murmured.

Madoc laughed. "You bachelors . . . it seems a long time since I went tumbling young girls behind barns. But make the most of it, brother, one of them will get you up before the priest one day and then it's goodbye to the sweet and easy life."

Einion made a derisive noise at his brother. "You revel in being tied to your Annesta . . . don't you?" he added rather wistfully.

"I am happy enough, Einion. Her tongue is a little sharp now and then, but she is good and faithful and has given me the prettiest daughter in Wales." He thought for a moment as they walked. "No, you can have your tumbling in the hay—I'll settle for my wife, even if she does accuse me of loving another woman better than she."

"Another woman . . . you must be jesting! Annesta has nothing to be jealous of in you." Einion sounded indignant.

Madoc laughed. "The 'she' is no other woman, brother—it's the *Gwennan Gorn*. Annesta says I talk of her as if she lives and breathes."

Einion's indignation increased. "Lives and breathes! Of course she does! And recently she's been sick and injured, but if those physicians at Aber Cerrig Gwynion know their job, she should be fully restored to health by today!"

Amused by their symbolism and the ever-welcome talk of their beloved ship, the brothers walked through the gate into the palace compound.

Immediately they sensed something wrong.

There was something wrong with the air, with the noise and with the colour of the night.

Then Madoc sniffed. "Something's on fire . . . and there are people shouting."

They stopped and looked around. Over to the left, the grey night was visibly changing to an angry red, away behind some of the stables and thatched dwellings.

Slowly a swelling of voices was heard in the distance and then running feet.

"Fire! Come on, run," yelled Madoc. They hammered away across the grass towards the glow, which was increasing by every second that passed. "It's near our own hut," he panted. "God

99

grant that the wind keeps it away from us . . . the thatch is like tinder in this weather."

They raced across the compound in a gloom that steadily lightened with the rise of the fire. As they dashed between other huts and buildings, actual flames and showers of sparks began to crackle up into the sky. Yelling voices, other running figures and the neighing of terrified horses began to make the night a bedlam.

They rounded the last hut and came out right in front of the fire. Aghast, Madoc stopped so abruptly that Einion cannoned into his back.

"God . . . Oh God! It *is* our dwelling!" he wailed, then began running straight towards the inferno like a man demented.

The hut, made of wood with a thatched roof that came right down to face level, was burning like a great candle, the red and yellow flames rising straight up with a low roaring noise. So far the stout walls had not burnt, the whole conflagration being confined to the roof.

"Madoc . . . careful!" yelled Einion, as his brother raced without hesitation straight towards the doorway.

There was a small crowd outside the doorway and a few were making futile efforts with leathern buckets of water. Just as Madoc ran wildly into the doorway, two men met him coming out, one of them with a white bundle in his arms. Madoc slithered to a stop, unconscious of the red sparks falling on him.

The two men pushed him aside and staggered out into the open, coughing and spluttering, tears streaming from their smoke-filled eyes.

"It's the little girl . . ." gasped one of the men. Einion caught up with them just as Madoc was scrabbling at the bundle in their arms.

"Gwenllian . . . Gwenllian," he sobbed.

"She's all right, Madoc." The man staggered further away from the hut and gave the bundle, which now began coughing and wailing, to a woman onlooker. "Take her, wife, look after her."

Madoc seemed numbed. Then with a great shout of anguish, he turned and dashed back into the hut, which was by this time roaring like a demented soul with the current of burning flame that shot upward from the circular walls of wood.

100

Einion dashed after him. "Madoc . . . for God's sake, you'll fry in there!"

Within the doorway was nothing but a sheet of flame. Both brothers were pulled up short, their hair singeing from the heat. Einion grabbed Madoc and pulled at him, but he was shaken off violently.

"Annesta. . . . Annesta!" screamed the elder brother, trying vainly to go forward into the inferno, arm over his face. The front of his cloak began to curl and the wool melted, then began to smoulder before he allowed Einion, himself half-roasted, to pull him back away from the flames.

There was a sudden crashing and hammering from the other side of the hut. Madoc raced around the building, his clothes still burning as he tore them off and dropped them on the ground.

At the back of the dwelling, four men, including the *Penteulu*, the Chief of the Household, were smashing with axes at the wall of the hut where it was pierced by the single window opening. Flames were licking out of the top of the window, but the bottom of the wall was intact. As Madoc and Einion arrived, the wall collapsed under their desperate onslaught and two men dived into the hole, closely followed by Madoc.

Almost immediately, the first pair crawled out backwards, singed and breathless. They were dragging a body, dressed in a white night robe, which they pulled clear of the hut and laid on the grass. Madoc came clambering back on all fours, like an animal. He fell sobbing across the still body on the scorched grass.

"Annesta. . . . Annesta!" The cries were torn from him as if they were part of his flesh.

Einion pulled at Madoc, trying to see if the woman was living, but the *Penteulu* laid a hand on his shoulder. "It is useless, look at her head."

Madoc still lay with his head on his wife's breast, as his brother slowly rose and looked down to where the Chief of the Household was pointing.

"God was merciful, Einion. She has no burning save some of her clothes. Her head has taken a great blow, she must have died quickly."

As Einion looked at the bloody hair and the crushed skull, one of the men who had recovered the body managed to get some of

101

his voice back. "One of the main roof beams had struck her to the ground. Its end must have burnt through and it fell from its support, striking her down. The fire had not quite reached her, as she lay near the window. I think she must have been trying to climb out when she was hit."

Madoc slowly lifted his face from his wife's body and looked numbly at his brother. "Einion, she is dead," he said tonelessly.

Einion dropped down again and put his arm around Madoc's shoulders. "Yes, brother. But she died cleanly and quickly. And your daughter is safe and well. She will need you now. Annesta is beyond our need, Madoc—she is with Christ."

As Madoc pulled himself painfully from the floor, his eyes fixed on the peaceful, if smoke-stained face of his wife, a crowd of people hurried around the hut from the front. Foremost among them was Prince Owain, leaning heavily on his stick, but moving faster than usual. Llywarch, the Chief Judge, the Chancellor and a number of courtiers and guests accompanied him.

"Madoc's wife . . . she is dead, sire," called the *Penteulu* as they approached.

"The child . . . what of the child?" snapped Owain, his face hollowed with concern.

"She was saved, *arglwydd*. She is with the wife of Llowarch ap Bran, Lord of Menai. They are caring for her."

Owain came forward and stood before Madoc who still stood silently, looking down at Annesta. The court chaplain dropped to his knees by the body and began arranging the hands, murmuring prayers as he did so.

Owain looked gravely at his son. "Sorrow has come to you, Madoc. There is nothing I can say that will heal the pain you feel. You are a strong man and you will survive it. Death comes to us all, sooner to some than to others. Annesta still lives in your daughter. The flesh continues from one generation to another." He put out a hand and rested it briefly at the side of Madoc's neck in a gesture of total compassion.

Then he turned and spoke in a harder tone to his Chief of the Household, who was responsible for the safety of the palace. "How did this thing come about?"

The *Penteulu* threw up his hands. "It happened in the winking of an eye. I myself passed here not a quarter of an hour ago and all was well then. It must have been some fault with the cooking

102

fire, some fallen kindling."

Madoc spoke, his voice taut with the effort of holding his emotions in check. "That could not be . . . my wife was ever cautious with the fire. It would have been banked down for the night, as it was so late. And by no means could the thatch have caught so ferociously from a small fire on the hearth."

One of the palace servants had been muttering to the *Penteulu* while Madoc was speaking. The *Penteulu* came forward to the Prince, holding something in his hand.

"Meurig Gam thinks this may be something to think on, lord." He held out a piece of stick, as long as a man's forearm, around the end of which was wrapped the charred remnants of a linen cloth.

Prince Owain took it, whilst everyone stared in silence. Owain turned it in his hand, then held it to his nose. "There is oil upon this," he announced.

A murmur rippled round the crowd, now several score strong.

"An incendiary device . . . a fire stick," rapped out Einion.

Madoc's apathy and sorrow vanished in the splitting of a second. "Murder . . . it is murder!" he yelled. He glared wildly around the circle surrounding him and his eye fell on Dafydd, lurking well in the background.

Every drop of Viking blood in his body congealed into the makings of a *berserk*. A film redder than the fire dropped before his eyes as he screamed at the top of his voice, "Dafydd . . . Dafydd, the murderer! This is your doing."

As the words left his mouth, he leapt, eyes staring like a madman. Both Einion and the burly *Penteulu* tried to block his path, but he swept them aside like chaff before the winnow and charged straight at the cringing figure of Dafydd, who though no physical coward, was momentarily terrified by this crazed blond figure, red eyes glaring in a soot-blackened face, who was tearing at him like an enraged bull.

The crowd automatically parted and in an instant the normally placid, gentle Madoc was on him, tearing at his throat. They fell to the ground and with incoherent yells, Madoc was squeezing Dafydd's throat with one hand and punching him frenziedly with the other.

Owain Gwynedd himself was the first to regain his presence of mind. "Stop them . . . pull them apart for the sake of Christ, or

103

he'll kill him."

The authority in the voice galvanised the onlookers into action. Several leapt upon the fanatical, thrashing body that was tearing at Dafydd and dragged him upright. Still flailing his arms and almost foaming at the mouth, Madoc was babbling incoherently, eyes staring like someone in a fit.

"See to him . . . get him away," roared Owain, pointing his stick as the tattered form of Dafydd tried to crawl away on his hands and knees.

Several of his retainers helped him to stagger to his feet. His right eye was closed, blood streamed from his nose and around his neck were bruises and scratches where Madoc's fingers had narrowly missed throttling him.

Owain groaned. "Oh God, what have I done to have my declining years so plagued!" he muttered.

TEN

APRIL 1170

Dawn was not long past when solemn men left their dwellings inside the palace of Aberffraw and made their way to the great hall, past the blackened shell of the burnt hut, a wisp of smoke still rising from its centre.

They converged on the central building, where Owain Gwynedd already sat with his chief officers and the two score men of his personal fighting retinue.

When they were all assembled, he stood up and looked sadly down at the faces of his people. Then he sought out one particular face, "Madoc . . . come near."

Madoc walked up to stand in front of his father, his feet moving as if they were made of lead. A few paces behind came Einion, unasked but as faithful to his elder brother in adversity as he was in triumph. Madoc wore his best clothes and his face was clean and shaven, the smoke of the previous night gone, though his eyebrows and some of his hair still showed singeing from the fire.

"Dafydd . . . come here."

Owain spoke straight in front of him, though the other son was standing a few paces to one side. Sullenly, Dafydd moved across and stood at his father's side, glowering at Madoc, who made no sign of recognition.

"Madoc, last night you attacked your brother Dafydd and would have killed him had we not stopped you."

Madoc remained silent, but his eyes rose until they rested on Dafydd's face. There was no fury or malice in them, just a blankness that reflected the emptiness and weariness of his soul.

The Prince turned to Dafydd.

"Dafydd, your brother attacked you because he believed that you were responsible for the fire that burned his dwelling and killed his wife Annesta. What say you to that?"

Dafydd was torn between sneers and indignation. "Why should I soil my hands with petty arson . . . what need have I to meddle in the affairs of a half-brother, who is no consequence in this land, apart from being a messenger and a ship-master?"

Owain glared at him. "I asked you for an answer, not for a speech. Tell me again, did you fire or cause to have fired the hut which Annesta occupied? And in which Madoc should have been but that he went walking in the night?"

Dafydd's face went red with sudden rage. "I did not, sire! I am Dafydd, Lord of Teigeingl and Rhuddlan, not some poacher to be accused of petty crimes. I have better things to do than to soil my fingers and waste my time with . . . with landless peasants such as he."

He swung away and walked a few steps, before turning and giving his father a cursory salute. "You will excuse me, Lord Prince, but I have business with my brother Rhodri and the hour gets late."

Jerking a finger at his minions he threw his cloak over his shoulder and walked out.

Llywarch, the bard, started to go after him, then thought better of it after seeing the expression on the face of Owain Gwynedd.

The Prince recovered control of himself with difficulty after this high-handed insult from his arrogant son. He turned back to Madoc, who had stood with a bowed head all through the tirade from Dafydd.

"Madoc, the officers have made all possible inquiries through the night. There is nothing . . . I repeat, nothing at all . . . to link anyone with a deliberate act of of fire-raising. True, there was that brand found near the hut, but it was a brand such as is used daily for carrying fire from one hearth to another and may have been there for some time."

He waited for Madoc to answer, but the blond head did not rise an inch.

Owain sighed. "I have no alternative, both for your own safety when Dafydd returns and for the attack you made upon him with clear intention of murder, but to send you from the court for the time being."

Madoc lifted his head at last. "Sire, you need not send me. I was going to leave as soon as I had your leave."

Owain nodded. "It is well. I wish you to go to your brother Riryd, Lord of Clochran in Ireland, a place you know so well. You have done much good work for me lately; you could do with some ease, especially now that you have sorrow to defeat."

Madoc nodded wearily. "I shall have to take my wife to her home for burial," he muttered. "Her mother now lives in Dinas Dinlle, a village near Aberseiont."*

Owain laid a hand on his shoulder. "Do that, Madoc, then take ship from Aberseiont straight to Dublin. I want you away from here as soon as possible. Take Llywarch, bard of the court with you, I want news from him that you left these shores safely."

"I can take the *Gwennan Gorn*, Lord Owain," answered Madoc, but his father shook his head emphatically.

"You go by the quickest and straightest route. I want you out of Wales by today."

So was Madoc's banishment announced. It was partly for Madoc's safety, as the Prince knew full well that Dafydd was behind the campaign of violence. But he wished to stifle any vendetta, not favour a new claimant. The easiest thing was to separate the contestants and also to confirm the rule that the strongest and most legitimate must continue the royal line. He feared for what would happen in Gwynedd when his own heart stopped beating, but at least he could try to reduce the number of combatants in the future struggle.

Madoc, innocent Madoc, had to be sacrificed, at least until things had cooled down.

But Madoc had other ideas. As soon as the congress in the great hall was over, he whispered some instructions to Einion, who found his horse and the four men who always rode with him. They slid away into the morning light, leaving Madoc to say farewell to little Gwenllian. She was being left in the guardianship of Llowarch, Lord of Menai, and his amiable wife.

Then came the sadness of lashing on to a pack horse the long wicker basket that contained the white-shrouded body of Annesta. With two priests, four men at arms and Llywarch, Poet of the Pigs, the sad cavalcade left the palace of Aberffraw.

They went south to the ferry over the Menai Straits and by afternoon were standing at a hastily dug grave outside the little wattle church where Annesta had been christened twenty-four years earlier. Her father was dead and her mother, who Madoc had met twice before, took the sudden tragic death with the fortitude of one who knows long life as the exception, rather

* Caernarfon.

107

than the rule.

The priests had their say and the grave was filled in, as Madoc stood by and thought again of the days and nights when his woman had loved him, comforted him and sometimes fought with him.

Llywarch, whose cunning was matched by his perception and intelligence, said all the right things for such an occasion.

As they walked away from the church, Madoc felt a total revulsion with all things connected with this place, this land and these people. He thought he had loved this land, yet it was not only this land that offended him. Ireland was no answer. Owain had banished him there and he now felt that he could no more face life in Ireland than he could in Gwynedd.

They reached their horses and swung into the saddles. "The priests and the other men are returning to the ferry," said Llywarch. "We ride alone now, to Aberseiont, as your father has charged me to see you safely aboard a vessel for Dublin."

Madoc had other ideas, but he trotted alongside the bard until the right moment presented itself. The village where Annesta had been born and had been buried was Dinas Dinlle, on the sea coast where the old Roman road ended. From there, the ruinous track of a Roman causeway led northward the few miles to Aberseiont, which wise men said was the Roman fortress of Segontium and where the Roman Emperor *Macsen Wledig** came after his dream to claim his bride, Elen of the Mighty Host. Madoc planned a way to give Llywarch the slip. With the burial of Annesta, his mind had cleared of the confusing sorrows and hates of the past day. He was resigned, bitter but no longer bemused.

After a mile or so, he began fidgeting with his reins, deliberately making his beast stumble and jerk. Llywarch looked at him enquiringly. "She feels lame. Stop a while," he told the bard.

They both slid off their mounts and Madoc pretended to examine one of his horse's hooves.

"Look at this . . . stuck in the hoof! Here, give me your horse."

As soon as he had Llywarch's horse and the bard was peering to study a non-existent flint in the hoof, Madoc gave the other stallion a stinging blow on the flank with the flat of his sword. The horse whinnied with pain and bolted wildly up the long grassy slope towards the inland hills to their right.

* Magnus Maximus.

"What in God's name are you doing?" yelled Llywarch, jerking upright as if he had been stabbed.

But there was no one to answer him, for Madoc had swung into the saddle of his own horse and galloped away up the same slope.

Ignoring the pleas and then curses of Llywarch, he went at full tilt for a mile, when he reined briefly to look behind him. He could just see the tiny dot that was the bard, hopelessly struggling up the long slope in his impracticable robe, yelling at his horse, who by now had stopped, but was looking with suspicion from a distance.

Madoc turned and galloped on, the hills getting nearer with every hoofbeat. Before Llywarch could persuade the horse to come to him again, he would be far beyond pursuit and by sunset he would be in the valleys that would take him through the mountains to the Conwy River. By morning he would be at Aber Cerrig Gwynion and the *Gwennan Gorn,* with Llywarch none the wiser as to where he had vanished.

A month later, another royal inquest was held in the great hall at Aberffraw, but this time it was Llywarch Pryddyd y Moch who was standing on the hot spot before the Prince of Gwynedd.

Dafydd, Rhodri and Hywel, the poet prince were there. The chief complainant this time was Madoc's full brother, Riryd, Lord of Clochran.

The hall was full of other men, curious and indignant at the accusations and denials being bandied about.

"Then where is he?" cried Riryd, flushed and angry. "Our royal father gave orders that my brother Madoc should travel to my lands in Ireland that very day, to escape the plots and dangers that were set against him and which had already evilly killed his wife and made his child motherless!"

"And so he did . . . who are you to put your accusations against us?" shouted Dafydd.

"How would you know . . . you were not even here," retorted Riryd. "You left in high dudgeon, before Madoc set off to bury his murdered wife."

Owain Gwynedd held up a hand. "Wait, Riryd. No one has said that Madoc's wife was murdered. Dafydd was not involved in that . . . nor was he near when Madoc disappeared. We have ample witnesses to that."

Riryd was contemptuous of such proof. "Dafydd can command as many witnesses as folk who live in this part of Gwynedd. That means little."

Llywarch, fearful for his life as a scapegoat in this affair, earnestly broke into the argument. "Sire, I told the truth. Madoc tricked me, sent my horse bolting and rode off into the hills."

"A likely tale, Llywarch ap Llywelyn. Try telling it to your pigs," snapped Riryd sarcastically.

Llywarch could see his neck in a rope noose or his chest spitted on a sword unless he convinced someone. "He did, Lord Riryd . . . he vanished like a shadow into Eryri. I swear it. Test me on the hot iron if you doubt me."

Riryd snorted. "I doubt it well enough. Your tongue is well used to making up legends and fairy tales, but it has never excelled more than it does now. You were put up to some trick, Llywarch, confess it."

"I was not! I swear it. I'll take the hot iron on it!"

"You were alone with Madoc, you confess that already. You took him unawares and slew him in some secret place."

"No, no, I did not. I swear it."

"At the behest of some other party . . . for whom we do not have to look far." Riryd, the protector of Madoc in his younger years, was in a towering rage. He was a big, commanding man, like his father and living in independence in Ireland felt little deference to other courts and princes.

But Llywarch denied it again, almost weeping in his earnestness. "He ran away, lord, leaving me on foot. How can I convince you?"

"Then where is he now? Both I and our Lord Prince have have made enquiries in Aberseiont, Aberdaron, Deganwy, Conwy . . . not a sign of him!"

Owain Gwynedd broke in. "But his ship . . . the *Gwennan Gorn*. Where is that?"

Riryd shrugged. "It is in some small creek along the coast, being repaired after its sore damage."

"But Einion . . . his closest brother and friend. He also has vanished from the face of the earth. Maybe the ship has sailed, with Einion and Madoc upon it."

Riryd shook his head. "He was coming to Clochran . . . you

ordered it yourself. Two days it would have taken him . . . and now we are a month away and no *Gwennan Gorn* has been seen in the Liffey or anywhere near it." He swung round again to face Dafydd and Llywarch. "It smells evil to me that Madoc, my brother, should have been attacked, abused, his dwelling burned to the ground, his wife killed . . . and now he vanishes! If that is coincidence, then I shall become a monk. You are the key to this, Llywarch Pryddyd y Moch . . . you were the last to be with him alone."

The bard groaned and looked beseechingly at Owain Gwynedd. "*Ayglwydd*, I swear I am innocent of any harm to Madoc. Find the *Gwennan Gorn* and you find Madoc ap Owain!"

ELEVEN

MAY 1170

At the time when the distraught bard was trying to convince the Lord of Clochran, the ship in question was just taking up her anchor off the Fortunate Isles.

Within four weeks of leaving Wales, the *Gwennan Gorn* had reached the strange islands where the primitive Guanches dwelled.

They had filled their water barrels to the brim as well as some leather and skin containers of the precious liquid. The barter of some woollen cloth, together with a couple of silver coins, had added several goats to their provisions, also as much sweet fruits as they could pack away in the hold and under the two decks.

Now they stood off from the land, in the fairest of weather, with both a steady wind and a slow but definite current setting them in the one direction . . . the south-west.

"God seems to will us to go that way, Madoc," said Einion.

Madoc shrugged resignedly. "We have made our decision, Einion. Whether God wills it or not, I do not know. But it is better to go on to a possible heaven, than back to certain hell."

He was responsible for the decision, though it was democratically put to all the crew. As the prow of the little ship ploughed bravely into the Great Ocean and the last known land in the world fell over the horizon behind them, he thought back— not without some guilt—over the events of the last month, since Annesta had died.

After he had given Llywarch the slip, he had ridden north to the Conwy river, fording it well away from the settlements near its mouth. He reached the little creek of Afon Ganol around noon and rode down to Aber Cerrig Gwynion at its mouth, where the *Gwennan Gorn* was berthed. Here, below the old church of Llandrillo, was a stone pier, pierced with low arches.

There was no other ship there that day when Madoc rode up to see his precious vessel sitting on the mud alongside the quay.

112

The tide was out and some of the crew were sitting on the deck, playing *tawlbwrdd*. The rest were in a small tavern amongst the few cottages on the slope.

When Madoc strode across the stones of the quay, he was level with the after-deck and could see Einion kneeling at the edge of the hold, talking to someone below. He was overjoyed to find that the man in the hold was Svein.

Einion had already told the crew the news of the sad happenings at Aberffraw, but he knew nothing of Madoc's evasion of Llywarch the bard.

Madoc related the whole story, the seamen and his friends clustering around to listen with renewed anger against the brothers who had perpetrated this crime.

"What will you do about it?" muttered Gwilym, the steersman, his face glowering with anger.

Madoc shrugged. "I am banished by my father—gently and for my own good, but none the less banished."

"Why did you give Llywarch the slip like that?" asked Svein, compassion and rage vying with each other in his concern for his friend.

"I was ordered to Ireland by the quickest route . . . as a passenger on some worm-ridden ship from Aberseiont. That was not for me—I wanted the company of my men and the feel of the *Gwennan Gorn* beneath my feet. Having you as well, is a welcome bonus, Svein. How did you come to be here?"

"I was on my way to Abergele to select new spars for the Liffey yards—there are none better. As I passed this creek of Afon Ganold, I spied the unmistakable shape of the *Gwennan Gorn*, so I came ashore here yesterday. I was going on to the Gele tomorrow, but if you are journeying to Ireland, I will sail back with you for company."

Madoc stood up and looked out at the sea. "I have a fancy not to go to Ireland, Svein. I have a yearning to go much farther." He looked at his friend and brother. "Will you come with me again?" All had been with him on the Long Voyage and, except for Svein, through the maelstrom of Bardsey Sound.

"Aye, we'll come," came a chorus, unhesitatingly.

"Where?" asked Einion, after a short pause.

"To the Isles of the Blessed—to look for the Fountain of Eternal Youth!'"

113

There was a silence and each man looked at his neighbour.

"We'll come with you, Madoc," grunted Svein.

"This land is not fit for decent men at the moment," agreed Einion, "I'd as soon be at the bottom of a clean ocean as live in company with those who would murder women and children."

There was a ripple of assent around the circle of crewmen.

Einion stood up. "Go to the tavern, Gwilym, fetch the rest of the men."

Within a few hours, the crew were ready to sail with the high tide. Not a man had objected to the sudden crazy plan to sail out of the known world. Those who had families nearby had taken a hasty farewell. Their wives, were quite used to months of separation at short notice.

Towards evening, the *Gwennan Gorn* was a dot on the horizon, sailing well out to sea to avoid the coastal look-outs on Anglesey. They put in to a small port on the coast of Cornwall, to take on enough provisions to last them across the short seas to Brittany. Madoc had all his personal fortune of a number of gold and silver coins, which was more than enough to purchase their simple needs.

As Madoc had done several times before, they went in a few land-hugging hops down to the coast of Spain, where they revictualled again and then set out on the next leg of their journey, this time repeating the voyage of the previous year into the warmer waters that led to the Fortunate Isles.

Now these in turn were behind them and they set their faces towards the Unknown.

There were thirty-four souls aboard the *Gwennan Gorn*, as she glided before her fair wind across the Western Ocean. In a boat only forty-five feet long, this allowed little space, but the vessel could have carried another dozen if necessary. Before a good wind, half a dozen men were enough to manage the vessel, so the remainder had to find a place to put themselves and find things to occupy them. A great sheet of sewn ox-hides was stretched across the well of the hold, which took up a third of the ship. This had the double purpose of collecting any rain that might fall, to add to the drinking water and also to protect the stores, animals and crew. Lashed on top of the hold were six flimsy coracles, little boats made of leather-covered wicker-work.

114

Svein and Madoc were standing together on the stern deck, on the afternoon of the tenth day out from the Fortunate Isles. The weather was perfect, with high white clouds scudding south-westerly across a blue sky.

"How long will we sail for, Madoc?" asked Svein contem-platively.

Madoc shook his head slowly. "Neither I nor any mortal knows that, good friend, as no one has ever been here before."

"Unless it was this good Saint Brandon you often speak of," retorted the Viking, with a grin splitting his fair beard.

"Not even he, I think. The stories tell how he left the coast of Ireland and sailed West. We are many a hundred leagues from there, though maybe . . . and God trust . . . our paths will come together eventually."

Svein grinned again. "It is a pointless question, asking for how long we will sail this way."

Madoc stared at him. "Why so?"

"We have no choice, that's why!" cackled the big Norseman. "Look over the side, look into the sky . . . both wind and current are whisking us along at the pace of a horse's canter. If we turned around, we would merely carry on in the same direction, at the same speed, only backwards!"

Madoc nodded, unperturbed. "We all know that, Svein. We have been at the mercy of these elements since we left the coast of Spain. But if the need arose, we can force ourselves across the wind and ocean stream to a small degree. That may eventually bring us to a part of the sea where different elements prevail."

Svein poked him in the shoulder with a hand like a ham. "But as we do not know where we are going, why should we want to change direction?"

Madoc had no answer to this, but it was a question that was to come up more than once in the future.

After more than another week, the whole crew—except a couple at the ropes and the steersman—were assembled on the deck for a holy service to celebrate White Sunday, six weeks after the Easter of the year of Christ eleven hundred and seventy.

The priest Padraig, who had developed into a keen and able seaman, gave the sacrament, the making of which came from a large cloth bag which constituted the whole of his luggage. After the service, Madoc stood right at the after end, against the stern-post and made something of a speech. On such a tiny vessel, with the men cheek by jowl with each other, every day and every night, there was never any lack of communication, but this was a formal occasion and the crew seemed to desire their leader to speak to them.

The pure tones of the Welsh language rang out across the empty sea, accompanied by the splash of water under the hull, the creak of the timbers and the plaited leather of the rigging.

"Friends, we are from the land called Cymru, so we are the Cymry, an ancient word meaning 'comrades'. And comrades is our relationship. Not lord and servant, master and slave. We do what we do, because we have agreed on this thing. Not one of you need have left that quay at Aber Cerrig Gwynion, unless he had wished it—and I would not have thought a whit less of any man who had decided that exploring the Great Ocean was not an occupation for him. But every one of you did me the loyalty and honour of accepting."

There was a growl of assent around the ship. Every Welshman loved oratory almost as much as verse and song.

"You accepted freely and now we are sitting in the middle of God-knows-where, for I do not know. Nor does our tame giant from Ireland, Svein Olafsen, know where we are! It is now eight weeks since we left Gwynedd and over three since the Fortunate Isles vanished from view, the last land we have seen. The weather has been good to us and we must be many hundreds of miles from the coasts of the known world. With the rain showers last week we have as much water now as when we left land and with the fish we catch daily, our food is holding well. So far, God has given us his blessing. There is little we can do to alter our course and until some sign of land appears, we may as well take the fastest route, as any other."

He stopped and looked expectantly around the other twenty-five faces, waiting for comments. He was not disappointed.

"Madoc of the Ships, if anyone can lead us to new lands, it is you," said Alun, a wiry man with a bad turn in his eye. "But how do we know there *is* a new land? How can we tell that we are not sailing into eternity, ever onward until we die of hunger and thirst?"

There were a couple of grunts of assent to this, which enabled Madoc to identify the men who might be the first to become

116

troublesome if things became difficult.

"I cannot answer you from my own knowledge, Alun. But I can tell you that other men have found land across this ocean. I have heard as much from scholars in France and here on this very ship, we have men who have better stories than that, both from Ireland and from the North." He jerked his head at the big figure of Svein, and at Padraig, who had abandoned his monk's habit for this voyage.

Padraig raised his hands as if in benediction. "I have bored you all too much in the past with stories of the Blessed Brandon. He spent seven years on these seas. He sailed from western Ireland and must have journeyed further to the north, where the sun stands lower at noon."

Madoc looked at Svein. "What about your Norse tales, friend? We have not heard so much of them as from our Irish patriot here."

Svein ran a hand over his moustache and beard thoughtfully. "Land there is in the west, without a doubt, for the Northmen have had settlements there for a century or two. Iceland is now an ancient kingdom of ours and just before the thousandth year after Christ, Eirik the Red, from Jaeder, discovered and settled in the land he called Gronland, which was many days sailing west of Norway."

He stopped, but Madoc spurred him on. "There were even more discoveries after that, so I heard."

Svein nodded. "The son of this same Eirik, called Leif, sighted other lands far to the west and south of Gronland. Other adventurers took his sailing directions and for some years there were settlements in fair countries where even vines and corn grew. These facts are all recorded in the sagas of Iceland, but I know nothing of what befell them. There is now no talk of these places amongst the ship-masters that call in the Liffey, but it is an undoubted fact that there are great lands far to the west."

Madoc looked round the faces before him and saw interest and reassurance in most of them. But again, it was Alun of the crooked eye that spoke up. "These things may well be true, but you say yourself that all these voyages were far to the north of us. Why then did we come to these southerly levels, where the sun stands almost overhead at midday? Why should there be lands in front of us here?"

Again there were one or two rumbles of agreement.

"I came down to these warmer places to find better weather, Alun," replied Madoc. "Svein has told me that his fellow Vikings have had terrible passages when they try to reach their northern settlements. Some years, indeed, they are unable to reach them, other times they get blown God knows where and spend months limping home. Many other *knarrs* are never heard of again, being sunk by the hellish northern waters. So by coming down here, off the coast of Africa, we have the Fortunate Isles as a jumping-off place, better weather, a longer season for safety and the benefit of these fair winds and ocean river to waft us across to the west."

The meeting dispersed, giving the men much to talk about as they lay on their blankets that evening.

Madoc, Einion and Svein sat that night on the after-deck, on the opposite side to the steersman, looking up at the incredibly bright stars.

"We are not going in exactly the same direction as we were a few days ago," observed Svein critically, staring up at a group of bright stars shaped like a cooking pan with a long handle. Einion, who was not so expert yet in reading the sky, followed his gaze, then scratched his head. "They look the same to me."

"No, there is a change. We are pointing slightly more to the west and not so much to the south. Don't you agree, Madoc?"

Madoc studied the sky intently for a few moments. "I thought that last night, but felt it might be imagination. But tonight, I agree, there is no doubt, Svein. Yet the wind and the current are exactly upon our stern, just as before."

The Viking slapped the deck planks. "Then they too have changed direction and are bearing us with them."

Einion looked ahead to where the phosphorescent sea was dipping and rising with the ship's motion. "What does it mean?"

"It means that we have changed direction," said the ever-practical Svein. "No more, no less. I think the change is like a great circle, swinging around in the ocean."

"May be we will wake up one morning and find we have travelled the full circle and Aberffraw will be under our bows!" jested Einion.

In a way, he was not all that far from the truth.

118

Five days later it was obvious to every seaman on the *Gwennan Gorn* that they were indeed in the grip of different currents and winds. The sun, which had been climbing higher in the sky at every noon, slowed its progress, though some slight change was still to be expected, as it was the last day of May and the summer solstice had not yet arrived. The breeze began to freshen, the sea became friskier and the vessel made even faster progress. The timbers creaked more and the leather-bound sail cracked and flapped with more energy.

The hull was still as sound as a bell and needed only one man baling with his leathern bucket, to keep it dry below the bilge planks.

Eight weeks away from Wales, the three leaders again held a navigation conference on the stern deck, this time with all their available apparatus. A circle of curious crewmen stood around them as they fiddled with the strange instruments.

"It becomes hard to correct the peg of the *skuggafjol* for the season," grumbled Svein, as he tugged at the gnomon of his sunboard. When he had adjusted it as well he could, he floated the wooden contrivance in a large earthenware dish of water, which slopped wildly onto the decking as the *Gwennan Gorn* rolled and pitched.

One of the younger seamen came nearer, obviously fascinated by the instrument. "I have seen you do this before, yellow beard," he said, "but I still fail to understand its mysteries."

Ever ready to teach the ways of the sea, Svein demonstrated. "All it is, is a square board with a small hole in the middle, lad. In the hole is the peg, called the gnomon, which can be slid up or down. Around the peg are circles carved in the wood, like an archer's target. We float it in water, so that it stays nearly level, whatever the motion of the ship."

"But how does it tell you where we are?"

"At midday, the shadow of the peg will reach out and its length can be measured by counting the circles. If we go south, the shadow moves in. If we go north, it reaches out further. So to carry on a steady course, say from Bergen to Iceland, we steer so that the shadow stays on the same circle each noon."

The young man nodded. "But why move the pin?"

Svein snorted, "Come on, any shepherd can tell you that! The shadow will move back and forth according to the seasons, without ever shifting the ship from its moorings. The peg must be lengthened every few days up to mid-summer, then pulled down again as the autumn approaches. Einion here keeps a record of each day on his notched stick."

Madoc produced a sheet of parchment, which he carefully guarded from spray in a sheepskin wallet. "This is better than a notched stick, though not so robust," he said. "Ever since leaving Gwynedd, I have marked our progress here as well as I am able."

He spread out the sheet on the deck and the men craned their necks to see the spidery charcoal lines that represented their voyage into the unknown.

"Every day is written as a small cross," explained Madoc. "With such a constantly fair wind, I have made the distance between each cross the same. We have the direction of each day's sailing from the sun and the stars." He pointed with his finger at the parchment. "Until a few days ago we were sailing south and west, but from now on I will have to bring the line upward, almost straight across to the west."

Svein stared critically at the map. He could not read the notes that Madoc had written in Welsh and Latin alongside some of the marks, but other things were obvious. "That marking you have on the right side of your map . . . that is the known land?"

Madoc nodded. "Here are the promontories of Llyn, of Menevia,* of Cornwall, of Brittany, of Spain, and here is the entrance to the Pillars of Hercules. The Fortunate Isles were as far south of the harbour called Lisbon, as Lisbon is south of Cornwall."

"And we are now twice that distance further south," commented Alun, peering over Einion's shoulder.

"But also twice that distance out into the Great Ocean, if your reckoning is right," grunted Svein.

Madoc folded up the parchment and put it carefully into the wallet. "Yes, but I make no claim to much accuracy. All we can use as a measure of westering is an average day's sailing. We have had such fair winds these past weeks that perhaps we have travelled further than this course suggests."

Gwilym, for once off steering duty, had a question. "Why is it that the nights are closing in both earlier and more abruptly?

* St. David's

120

By the sand glass, yesterday had a good five hours less daylight than we should get at home on this date of the year."

No one had any convincing explanation, though all had noticed the peculiar behaviour of the sun, as it raced faster across the sky.

"We are getting into strange waters, where the very sun itself no longer acts as it does in Christian countries," growled Alun, who was becoming the spokesman of the discontents aboard the *Gwennan Gorn*.

In a few days, at long last, the fine weather began to break up. Great masses of cloud chased the vessel, at first white, then grey. The wind, swinging round even more until it came almost directly from the east, strengthened so much that the *Gwennan Gorn* began racing through the sea, her timbers groaning and creaking with the strain. On the third day, the sea became so restless that every wave sprayed over her stern, making the life of the steersman and those on the stern-deck, wet and miserable.

The sun disappeared altogether.

Madoc was glad of the idea that Svein had suggested when the vessel was being built—that of copying the Norse trick of rolling up part of the sail and tying it with thongs to decrease the effect of the wind upon it. Without this, he would have feared for the safety of his sail. He had one spare tucked away under the deck, but they were too precious to be allowed to blow to ribbons.

As well as becoming wild, the wind began to act capriciously as to direction, changing within the hour almost a quarter of a circle, then back again.

"How do we keep to any sort of course?" asked Einion, clinging to the bulwark alongside Madoc, as the *Gwennan Gorn* charged along, bucking like some mad horse.

"We have to go where the wind takes us for the moment," he yelled back. "When it quietens after dark, we will see what Guiot de Provins' magic will tell us."

It was well after dark before the wind dropped appreciably, as it had done the two previous nights. When the ship was sailing more evenly, the crew began really energetic baling, to get rid of the water that now lapped a foot deep over the bottom boards. While they were doing this, the three navigators crouched on the fore-deck, trying to keep some water in the big pottery vessel that they used to float their sun-board. This time, they had a long iron needle that was used for mending sails. This was housed in a piece of straw taken from the sheep pen, which Einion had slit lengthways with his knife. They carefully floated the straw and needle in the pot, then Madoc carefully unwrapped the piece of lodestone that he had been given in Paris, years before.

One end was marked with paint and this he pointed at the floating needle. "I'll try this method first. It's a new needle, so it has no power in it from past usage," he muttered. Going as close as he could to the straw without letting the steel jump up to the piece of rock, he slowly rotated the lodestone around and around in a circle, the needle faithfully turning after it.

Einion, who never ceased to be fascinated by this magic, gazed in breath-holding wonder at the moving steel. "It's still impossible," he hissed, above the wind and the ship noises.

"The damned water is slopping about so much that I can't do it properly!" complained Madoc. He persevered for forty circles of the needle, then wrapped up the stone and placed it safely in a bag which he left on the deck a number of paces away.

The three of them stared intently at the needle jerking about on the miniature waves in the jar.

"I can't see it pointing any particular way," objected Svein, who was reluctant to believe in this new-fangled method.

Madoc had to admit that the straw seemed to be veering around in a quite haphazard manner. "Perhaps it's the wind," he muttered, shielding the jar with the edge of his cloak. But even then, the needle refused to settle into any definite direction. "Guiot warned me of this and I have proved it before, with other needles . . . I will use the touch of the lodestone this time."

He retrieved his magic rock and this time pinned the needle to the deck with a forefinger and gave it twenty strokes with the painted end of the stone, always drawing it towards the sharp tip of the needle, away from the eye.

Perhaps a sudden lull in the wind helped, for the water in the jar was less turbulent this time. The needle in its little straw boat seemed to prefer pointing to the steer-board side of the *Gwennan Gorn*. "It directs itself always that way . . . look!" said Madoc triumphantly. "When I poke it with my finger, so that it is forced the other way . . . so, it comes back! See that!"

True enough, after half a dozen tries, they agreed that the needle always pointed slightly in front of the line that crossed the vessel from side to side.

"That means we are moving west, with a little north in it, if your devil's toy here always seeks the lode-star," observed Svein. He stood up and his great figure towered over the stem of the vessel, heedless of the spray that soaked him. "I feel a difference," he announced eventually. "Not definitely land, perhaps, but I feel that there is something ahead. I smell it," he muttered defiantly, as if challenging anyone to deny him his sailor's sixth sense.

"Then God grant it is something good, Svein," answered Madoc fervently, "or Alun Crookeye will nag us to the bottom of the ocean."

The wind and the heavy cloud persisted another two days and nights, but the sea remained the same, uncomfortable for the tiny ship, but not dangerous. Twice more they checked with their lodestone that the course was roughly the same. On the fourth morning, before dawn, the clouds began splitting and the twinkling heavens peered through. A great red dawn followed and with the appearance of the sun, the wind dropped. During the day the sea subsided into a long swell with no broken waves at all. There was still a fresh breeze and when they checked their direction, they found that they had shifted their position to about a day's sailing north of their furthest southerly point.

Later in the day, they were sailing steadily on into the void, the current now being dead before the south-easterly wind.

"God knows where we are or where we are going," growled Svein, looking over the side.

"Do you see any signs of change in the waters, with your eagle eyes?" asked Einion, half bantering, half hopeful.

Svein pointed out across the green water, a ship's length from the *Gwennan Gorn*.

They followed with their eyes and Madoc gave a shout.

"Men, look . . . look out there!"

A score of heads turned and a few ran to the bulwarks. "What do you see?" someone called.

"A branch . . . a tree-log floating," yelled Svein.

True enough, they were passing a brownish black tree trunk, wallowing along in the same ocean current as themselves.

"It has a green shoot . . . it has not been in the water more than a week or two," yelled the Norseman, alert to every detail and meaning of the flotsam. "There must be land within a few days' sailing."

There was a ragged cheer from the throat of every man. The feeling had been growing in every mind that perhaps they had left the realms of men for ever. In the long nights, as each man lay curled on his blanket, these thoughts of being condemned for ever to sail the empty sea, perhaps skeletons in a tattered hulk, came upon the crew. Only the calm confidence of their leader, Prince Madoc ab Owain, gave them the will to face another day of staring at the ever-empty ocean. Alun Crook-eye would be the catalyst to set their fears alight, for though he was a good man and so far faithful to his masters, he was the weakest link in the chain aboard the *Gwennan Gorn*.

But now this tiny sign sent their spirits soaring and their fears receded. No longer were they afraid of being in a watery waste that stretched untold leagues back to the familiar coasts of Britain. Where there was a branch, there was a tree, and where there was a tree, there was land . . . land with water and fertility, animals and who knows, maybe even men.

Einion, Madoc and the Viking watched the log until it vanished beyond their stern. "It puts me in mind of the story in the sacred testament," said a voice from further down the ship's side. It was Padraig, the monk, now dressed in a jerkin and short breeches, like the rest of the crew.

"What story, Irish priest?" bellowed Svein, who concealed his liking for this cleric with a patently false ferocity.

"The story of Noah . . . who when in the ark, knew of the subsidence of the flood by the olive branch brought back by his bird."

Madoc and Einion looked at each other and grinned happily. "Then God grant it has the same significance for the *Gwennan Gorn* as it did for Noah's ark," said Madoc. "For we could do with a landfall before many days are out. How are the stores lasting, Einion?"

His brother was the quartermaster, responsible for the supply of food and water. He shrugged non-committally. "We have enough water for at least another two weeks, thanks to the rain caught in the ox-hides. The food situation is not too good. Both sheep have gone, as you know, and I think the men slaughtered the last chicken yesterday. We have enough flour and oatmeal for a week or so. Otherwise, the fish we catch remains our main diet."

"Anything else left?"

"Some dried fish from Gwynedd—it is as hard as the very rocks of that fair land!" replied Einion dryly. "Also some dried meat, which would do well to replace our anchor stone, should it be lost!"

"We need a landfall soon, then, or we shall be eating each other inside a couple of weeks," murmured Madoc. "Svein, keep all your senses at full pitch. We need land, my friend, both for sustenance and for the sake of our souls, lest we go mad with looking at this empty sea."

Einion looked around the full circle of the horizon, as he did a hundred times a day. "Nothing . . . not even a cloud now. What if the world is circular, like a shield or dinner platter. Maybe we have come round in a great arc and are now bearing down on our own lands."

Madoc shook his head. "Impossible . . . the sun tells us that we are far from our climate in Wales. It is so warm here and the nights are almost as long as the days. We cannot be anywhere near Christian lands."

"That tree we passed," said Svein. "It was one of the type that grows in southern Spain and in the Fortunate Isles . . . I could see the feathery remnant of the twig and the rough scales of the bark. Wherever we are, it is a hot, southern climate." He thought for a moment. "Those Norse settlers that went out from Gronland, many years ago. They came back with tales of lush meadows and places where wild vines grow. Maybe we are approaching the same region by another route, far to the south."

Madoc gave a mock groan. "The saints forbid that we be met on the beach by a hairy band of Norsemen, all shouting welcome to our brother Svein!"

They had no wine or beer, but even the stale water from the leather casks tasted better that day.

And tomorrow was to be even better.

125

TWELVE

MAY 1170

As soon as dawn broke, it was obvious that something had changed. When the light streamed over the *Gwennan Gorn* from the eastern sky, the lookout in the bow saw that the water round the ship was different in colour. It did not need the Viking's expert eye to tell that a deeper blue, a vivid ultramarine was lapping the ship's sides. At full light, everyone on board was crowding to the bulwarks and looking at the changed sea. The wind had dropped considerably.

"We are near land," said Svein confidently. "I said that yesterday and though I have not seen a sea this colour before, I am sure it heralds a coastline not far away."

Pressed to explain, he stroked his tawny beard, always an indication of deep thought.

"Off Norway, where the deep fjords come to the foot of the high mountains, there is a colour something like this . . . and I have seen it elsewhere. It seems that at the edge of land, there is often a great trench in the ocean, which gives this dark blueness."

"We seem to be moving less speedily today," observed Einion. "Is that also due to deep water?"

Svein shrugged. Picking up a piece of wood that had been part of the sheep pen, he threw it over the side, well away from the ship. The *Gwennan Gorn* soon left it behind, but noticeably slower than a few days earlier. "The current is less active here. Whether that is due to the deep water beneath us, I do not know. But I do know that things are changing rapidly and soon we shall see other signs."

He went forward to the deck below the stem post and climbed up onto the stout timber that acted as a rail. Gripping the high post right in the eye of the ship, he shaded his eyes with the other hand and looked intently ahead. In a few moments, he came back.

"There is nothing to see . . . no cloud, no land, but I still have

126

the feeling that there is something out there, not far away."

Madoc went about his business, getting the instruments ready for the noon sighting of the sun, which now blazed clearly in a pale blue sky. He too felt that this was to be a different day.

He fervently hoped that some landfall would be made soon, as he had checked the stores himself the previous evening and was not nearly so confident as Einion that they had enough to last for a few more weeks.

Later in the morning, Svein, who had been prowling around like a caged bear, climbed for the fourth time to the crossing of the main spar and the mast. A few minutes later, he let out a great shout and stood erect on the spar, heedless of the twenty foot drop below him.

"What is it, Norseman . . . do you see land?" yelled Madoc.

"No . . . not land. Not yet . . . but there is a change in the water, away there to the port side of the ship." He jabbed a great arm away to the left, the side of the ship that was always brought to port or the quayside, as the steering oar encumbered the other side.

No one could see anything from deck level.

"Shall we steer toward it, Svein?" yelled Madoc to the man up the mast. The Norseman nodded vigorously and shouted back, "Yes, try it. It seems to be a great shallow, stretching away as far as I can see."

Madoc ran to the steersman and helped him twist the great oar so that the bow of the *Gwennan Gorn* slowly came across the horizon. The breeze came on to her opposite quarter, but was still well behind her as she sailed on at almost the same speed.

Madoc joined the men on the fore-deck. As he looked ahead, Einion came up from the hold and Svein slid back down the rigging to join him.

Within half an hour, the change in the deep blue of the water became noticeable. It became a light greenish blue and more turbulent, almost milky in appearance, though the actual water was clear.

"It has suddenly become shallow," muttered Svein. "Cast the line, Alun."

The crooked eyed seaman took up a long line of thin twine, with a heavy stone lashed to the end with leather thongs. He threw it over the side and let the line slide through his fingers,

127

counting the knots spaced at regular intervals.

"No bottom here," he announced.

"It will come . . . let us follow this new avenue."

The line of pale water was only about a mile broad, but carried on north-eastwards as far as they could see. The *Gwennan Gorn* moved slightly back on to her old course to follow it.

As dusk approached, Madoc began to feel a sense of anticlimax and disappointment when nothing further appeared, but as the sun was touching the western rim of the ocean, one of the men on the steer-board side suddenly let out a great yell.

"A bird . . . look, a bird."

Men left their evening meal to jump up and stare wildly about them, craning their necks to scan the evening sky.

Cries of "Where? . . . where?" rang out over the quiet sea.

"There . . . straight up. A great bird."

Sure enough, circling high overhead was a white sea-bird, something like a gull, but with a greater wing span. It soared in wide circles, obviously looking down on the *Gwennan Gorn* as intently as the crew stared back at the first living thing except fish that they had seen since leaving the Fortunate Isles.

It stayed within sight for another few minutes, but as the quick sunset darkened the sky, it began flying with great slow wing-beats towards the west, its silhouette diminishing to a dot against the pink sky.

"That way lies land," said Einion, as Svein felt it too obvious to mention.

"Do we keep on our course or follow it?" mused Madoc.

"The pale water has widened to several miles since the afternoon," replied the Viking. "I think we shall soon be at a landfall whichever path we choose, but we may as well take the sign the bird has given us."

Madoc ordered the steersman to head due west. Four men had to drag the sail around to catch the wind, as it was now almost coming at them from the beam. At this angle of sailing, the *Gwennan Gorn* heeled over slightly with the wind, but after dark, the breeze became so slight that they made little distance.

Madoc lay on the deck in the warm summer night. He could not sleep and let his thoughts range unchallenged through his head.

It seemed a lifetime since he had left Wales, though it was little more than two months. The memory of Annesta was at once both vivid and distant. He found her face difficult to focus in his mind. His thoughts of her were of a tender, but painless nature, as if she were some familiar saint whom he had grown to adore, though never really known. He no longer loathed Dafydd, whom he was firmly convinced had plotted her death, even if his own hand had not itself carried the torch. Madoc knew that he had been intended to fuel that blazing hut himself, Annesta being the innocent victim of circumstances.

Not for the first time, his thoughts wandered to what in God's name he was doing here, out in the unknown, risking his own life and that of thirty other men. If it was escapism from Gwynedd he wanted, he could have had that in France or at the Crusades or even in Ireland.

Yet he found himself over the edge of the world, in places where eternal mists, waterfalls of the ocean and fearsome nothingness were supposed to hold reign.

He recognised that this was something that had been sleeping dormant inside him for many years—perhaps even since he heard tales in Clochran of St. Brandon and the other Gaelic monks who had ventured out centuries ago onto the deep waters.

Certainly since the *Gwennan Gorn* had been built and since the Long Voyage last year, this ultimate adventure had been inevitable. Escapism was the immediate excuse, but he recognised that it went deeper than that—a desire, a need to know the truth about what lay beyond the confines of the minds of cautious men.

Maybe tomorrow he would find out, for all the signs now pointed to land near at hand. It had hardly needed the fine powers of Svein Olafsen to guide them here . . . the wind and the currents had done that for them. Yet much lay ahead and it might be that the mysteries of this strange sea would yet tax the ship as much as the Currents of Gwennan's Bane.

Though sleep came late to Madoc ap Owain Gwynedd, he suddenly found himself awakening with a start, the light of dawn on his face and the stars paling above him.

All the memories of the previous evening poured back over him and he clambered stiffly to his feet. A quick look up at the heavens and at the lightening horizon told Madoc that they were still on a westerly course. With the dawn came the wind and gently the

Gwennan Gorn began heeling as the wind caught the sail, which was braced well forward by the tacking boom—a device which Svein had introduced from the Norsemen, who called it the *beitas*.

It was still too dark to see any distance and Madoc lay down again, though other men were stirring to make their poor breakfasts from what was left of the flour and oat-meal. With the ship heeling in the wind, there would be no fire under the fore-deck to cook anything. When the vessel was riding steadily, a dull fire was made with peat blocks and some kindling, on a thick slab of slate that acted as a hearth, but because of the ever terrifying risk of fire, this could only be done in ideal conditions.

The hour wore on and the sky blazed into reds, greens and then the blue of full daylight. There was a man up the stubby mast, but so far he was silent.

Half the day went by and still nothing was seen. The pale water had been left behind the previous evening but before noon another came into view—perhaps the same one winding its way to the north-west.

"Let's follow it," shouted Madoc to Svein, who was up at his favourite place, the stem post.

The big man waved his assent and again the ship came around slightly, this time with ease, as she was taking the strain off herself by coming back before the wind.

Madoc stood with his brother on the stern-deck and stared ahead with the deflated feeling of anti-climax.

"That damned bird must have had strong wings," muttered Einion. "We must have sailed eighty miles since last night."

Madoc sighed. "God grant we find something soon or the men will become restive. It is worse to have been given false hope than to have had none at all."

As if to answer his prayer, there was a shout from the man straddled across the yard, clinging to the mast with one arm.

"*Arglwydd*, I see . . . something!"

He sounded so doubtful, that Madoc's natural desire to yell with joy was muted.

"Something? What something? Is it land?"

"No land, Lord Madoc . . . but I see breakers. Yes, white water, not far ahead."

Svein came dashing to the mast and shinned up the knotted

130

ropes that dangled down the trunk.

"What do you see, Svein?" called Madoc urgently. Svein had beaten him to the mast, or he would have been up there himself.

Svein stared intently at a point to the west of the direction in which they were headed. Then his head slowly scanned the whole horizon in front of them.

"The lad is right," he called. "There are long rollers, but no land."

Einion was beside himself with frustration at not being able to see far enough.

"Breakers . . . is it shoal water?" he yelled.

"Too early to say, but I can think of no other reason, called Svein.

The *Gwennan Gorn* rapidly closed with the mysterious waves and within the hour, Madoc, now up on the yard himself, was able to decide on the explanation. "I see sand beyond them," he called down. "There is a line of sand stretching almost as far as the eye can see, with surf rolling up to them."

He clambered down and came to Einion and Svein on the stern decking. "It is land of a sort, but a bare few inches above the sea."

The Norseman ran a hand through his touslod hair. "Then there is better land not far beyond them, I suspect. Can we pass through?"

Madoc nodded. "I think so . . . there are several gaps, where there is no white water and no sand. It is probably shallow, but we can grope our way through."

Again the tacking boom was jammed against the yard and the *Gwennan Gorn* sluggishly came around to the west.

The vessel cautiously approached the line of breakers that now ran from horizon to horizon in a north-west direction. But as they drew level with the sandbanks, there was still ample water for the *Gwennan Gorn* to get through.

"The tide race running through the gap must scour the sand out to form a deep channel," commented Madoc, as he followed Svein's signals from the masthead. The gap was at least a mile wide, but they prudently kept to the centre in case there was shallow water on either side.

The breakers and the sand were now easily visible from the deck and all the crew stared curiously at the first land they had seen for so many weeks—if it could be called land. Featureless yellow sand, blasted into rounded ridges by the wind, stood at most a few feet from the level of the sea.

There was a silence on the ship as they slipped through the gap. No wild cheering at the first sight of a New World. More interesting than the bare sand was the sight of scores of birds parading at the water's edge, strutting and pecking in the surf. They were not the familiar birds of home, but generally resembled gulls and oyster-catchers.

"At least, they must have a better home than these heaps of grit," said Einion hopefully, as the ship slid through the opening and began to reach the open sea beyond.

"Pray we reach it soon!" said Madoc. This seemed to be his only prayer these past few days.

Alun the linesman now called that he could no longer reach the bottom with his stone. The water was still the milk blue, but there was no definite current now.

"What do we do now?" Madoc asked of Svein, when he had climbed down.

"If the sandbanks run true to others, there will be land marching in line with them. Let us keep on this course, straight across to the west."

For the rest of the day, they travelled across calm waters, there being little wind now. Towards evening, they were cheered by the sight of birds, not like the great one they saw the previous evening, but birds resembling gulls and cormorants, flying singly and in small groups. They went in several directions, crossing each other's path; most of them appearing to be headed for the sand keys that the ship had just passed.

Night fell with nothing new to see, but this time Madoc slept soundly with a fatalistic resignation to whatever the morrow might bring.

THIRTEEN

JUNE 1170

There was no doubt about finding land the next day, for the *Gwennan Gorn* almost ran aground upon it.

Some hours before dawn, the crew were curled up on their blankets and cloaks, with the few men at their sailing posts dozing off at the hour when life was at its lowest ebb. The ship was doing little more than drift along, with the sail hardly drawing at all.

The steersman kept looking up at the star pattern overhead, but there was little he could do to influence the ship's direction with so little way upon her.

Even though the ship moved so slightly relative to the water under her keel, that same water was moving faster than it had done during the last few days and the vessel's sluggishness was deceptive—in fact, they were moving at some four or five knots.

The look-out in the eye of the ship came back for a beaker of water, now a brackish fluid low in the big leather containers. As he returned along the deck, his tired brain was slow to grasp the significance of a new sound, but as he reached the stem post and looked ahead, he dropped his cup in consternation and let out a great yell.

"Breakers! Drop the sail, for God's sake! Put the ship about . . . breakers!"

His yell was as effective as if a thunderbolt had dropped amongst the sleeping men. With a flurry of arms and legs, cursing and thrashing, a dozen of the crew staggered to their feet. The two men looking after the sail let go the halliards and brought the heavy yard crashing down to the deck to add to the confusion.

Madoc and Einion were sleeping together under the stern-deck and took longer to be affected by the din and to pull themselves together. But Svein, sleeping on top of the cargo cover in the hold, was alert within seconds. He raced down the side of the deck to the bow and stared over the side. The ship was sheering

133

away already to the steer-board side, as the oars-man desperately tried to bring the ship about. But right under the nose of the *Gwennan Gorn*, long white rollers were beginning to break on their journey up a beach, dimly visible in the starlight.

Svein saw immediately that if the ship kept turning, they would come broadside into the surf and would be rolled over.

"Anchor, you fools . . . throw the anchors out!" he roared. "And bring her back on course . . . steersman, do you hear, bring her back on course." His voice was like the crack of doom, bellowing out over the sea.

Immediately, the steersman twisted his oar and the *Gwennan Gorn* swung back to point her bow directly through the waves.

Now the surf was catching at her and the ship started to pitch up and down like a large and stately horse.

"What's happening, Svein . . . where are we?" Madoc, still half asleep, staggered up to the Norseman on the heaving deck.

"We're almost aground," yelled the Viking, as he helped a crewman heave the big stone of the steerboard anchor over the bulwark. "Is the stern one out yet?" he shouted, and was answered by a splash that matched that of his own anchor going over the side. Now the vessel was held fore and aft by the heavy perforated rocks. As the surf hissed by her sides, she pitched and pranced, but the anchors held.

Madoc, now fully awake, was the first to get to the mast and shin up the tangle of walrus-hide ropes that dangled down to the deck.

"There is a beach . . . about three hundred paces ahead, by the shimmer of the surf," he called down. "But I can see nothing else in this light, only a dark line cutting off the sky above it."

Svein groaned. "Let God grant that it's not another sand dune."

But when the first flush of dawn appeared in the sky, an hour or so later, they saw something better than sand.

As the light reddened, the black line across the sky developed fuzzy outlines and soon they could see the upper fronds of trees.

There was a ragged cheer as the first man, with the keenest eyesight, spotted this vegetation, the first they had seen for over six weeks.

The surf was no deeper than a man's chest and with yells like children, a dozen men flung themselves over the side, with the big Norseman in the lead.

Madoc shouted a warning. "Careful . . . there may be strange beasts or fish in these waters." This stopped the more prudent from following, but as the light rapidly increased, they saw the adventurers struggling safely through the warm waters towards a great curving beach.

As the sky lightened minute by minute, Svein's party reached the beach and did a maniacal dance on the firm yellow sand. A few more men jumped over the side to follow them, but Madoc stopped any more.

They lifted the stone from the foredeck and hauled her backwards by sheer muscle power until the stern anchor was tight underneath. They were still in a heavy swell, so the other one was paddled out between two of the coracles and dropped at a distance, then the process was repeated until the *Gwennan Gorn* rode steadily on the calm blue sea, well beyond the breaking waves.

"Six men stay with the ship, you will have your turn later," he ordered. The rest of them, including Madoc and Einion, took the coracles and paddled ashore, hopefully carrying a water container in each fragile craft.

On the beach, they found Svein and the other men gambolling like children, falling down in the unmarked sand and running wildly in circles. They all felt unsteady on the dry land, after so long on the twisting, heaving deck of the little ship.

"Trees and grass . . . all manner of plants. Where they are, so must there be water," said Einion.

"Careful then, we know nothing of what manner of beasts there may be in this new world," advised Madoc.

They sobered a little as they approached the treeline, but nothing seemed to stir and they plunged into the gloom of the high vegetation. The sky was now a glorious pink and green, but the sun was not yet over the horizon. As they stepped into the tight mass of unfamiliar trees, there was a rustle of branches and several birds flew protestingly away. Underfoot was soft vegetation and patches of sandy soil.

"This is a sand island, like the others, but one that trees have had a chance to bind together," observed Svein.

"Is it a continent, a new world in truth?" wondered Einion. But in less than five minutes walking, he found a swift answer. Within a few hundred yards of leaving the beach, they saw the

135

light of the sky ahead of them and almost immediately broke out of the trees onto an almost identical beach.

"That's the narrowest continent I ever heard tell of!" grunted Svein.

As the slight haziness of dawn cleared, they saw that they were on the beach of a great bay, with open sea before them again.

"We must be on an island . . . a long narrow island," decided Madoc.

Einion stared at the horizon—"More islands . . . way out there." He pointed and as if growing straight out of the water, they saw several masses of green trees, just like those where they stood.

"We need food and water," said the practical Madoc. "Let's get back to the other beach where we can see the *Gwennan Gorn*. I feel safe with her in view—and one beach looks much the same as another."

They retraced their steps and began walking along the first beach towards the north. After half an hour's walk, Maldwyn, one of the steersmen, came up to Madoc after an expedition into the vegetation. "*Arglwydd*, I have seen some trees just as they had on the Fortunate Isles . . . the ones with the great nuts with milk and white flesh."

They all followed him into the trees and sure enough, there were fronded trees with huge nuts clustered at the tops.

"The first man to spy food in the New World, Maldwyn," shouted Einion, for these trees, similar to some that grew in Spain and France, were used in the Fortunate Isles for food and there the *Gwennan Gorn* had sampled some on her two visits.

One of the men had brought a plaited leather rope with him in his coracle and after much good-natured scrambling and climbing, they managed to get a dozen nuts down to the ground.

With knives and stones, they attacked the strange fruit and lying on the soft grass, drank the white milk and chewed the crisp pulp. Some of the men were violently sick, because their stomachs, tightened by weeks of foul water, fish and coarse grain, could not deal with such a sudden change in diet.

"We need water more than anything," commanded Madoc, prodding the party onward through the trees. "The ground is not so flat now, these must be old sandhills."

True enough, the dead flat ground of the narrow isthmus where

136

they landed was now undulating into hillocks of twenty feet or more, still completely covered by scrub and low trees, with occasional higher nut palms.

For two hours they searched, until one man, a brother of Alun Crookeye, began yelling with excitement. "Water . . . I've found water!" Soon they were all standing around a large pool of crystal-clear water that lay in particularly green vegetation at the foot of a large mound.

The man who had found it was lying on his stomach, joyously splashing water into his face and swallowing it greedily. The other crewmen flung themselves down and began following suit.

"We have no way of knowing if it is safe," shouted Madoc, but no one heeded him.

"There is little choice, Madoc. We have to have water and this seems to have been put before us by the Almighty," said Einion.

Alun's brother heard them and rolled over on to his back. "I saw a bird drinking . . . as I came up, it flew away, but there are small animal tracks at the edge, *arglwydd*."

Sure enough, on a patch of wet earth at one end there were a number of paw-marks, little bigger than those of a rabbit.

"We'll have meat before long, too," exulted Einion, "when we get back to the *Gwennan Gorn* to find some bows and arrows."

The day wore on as they filled the water vessels and collected more nuts. Two of the younger lads, probably adept at poaching in Gwynedd, managed to knock down five medium-sized birds by means of sticks . . . for there was apparently not a single stone on that sandy island. These they cooked after a fire had been started with flint and steel.

"Keep something for the men on the ship," commanded Svein. "Their mouths will be watering already, though they be a half mile out to sea."

Later in the day, they sent the coracles back to the ship, to let the men there have a chance ashore.

That night, as twenty of the thirty-two men sat around a great fire of dead wood on the beach, the three leaders conferred on what was to be done.

"We owe the men a few days here, to get their colour back and some decent water and fruit inside them," decided Madoc.

Einion and Svein agreed. "Though I am sure that this is

merely some island and not the great world that everyone expects," added the Viking.

"Why not sail or row the ship around it, just outside the surf," suggested Einion. "We could discover all there is to be found and still stay within reach of our water supply."

Next day, half the crew went aboard with Madoc, whilst Svein and Einion walked along the beach and foraged in the bush, keeping level with the *Gwennan Gorn*, as she was slowly rowed along parallel with the shore.

Some bows and arrows had been recovered from the hold of the *Gwennan Gorn* and with these, the unsuspecting birds of the new land fell easy prey to the skilled hunters from Wales. Several small animals, like large squirrels with ringed bushy tails, were also shot and together with coconuts and some smaller berries that resembled Welsh blackberries, a mixed diet was slowly gathered together.

Several more water-holes were found, almost always at the foot of higher rises in the ground. All the water vessels were full now and by the third day, everyone was feeling well-fed and contented with this latter-day Garden of Eden on the other side of the world.

It took them four and a half days to confirm that they were indeed upon an island. They were then on the western side of the island, at the place where they had crossed in the first hours of exploration.

Here they camped and Madoc took further counsel of his lieutenants.

"What do we do now?" he asked, as they sat on the sand in the glory of a multi-coloured sunset. He nodded towards the score of men, sitting around the fire. "They would be content to stay here until the crack of doom, by the looks of them."

"And who can blame them after those weeks of lying on a hard deck, with food and drink that we would be ashamed to give to pigs at home," said Einion.

Svein stretched his great arms luxuriously. "The itch to move is already upon you, Madoc, I can see that."

Madoc grinned sheepishly. "I came to find a great land . . . or some marvellous place like the Fountain of Youth," he answered truthfully. "This island, strange though it is, is not much different from the Fortunate Isles, which we have all seen twice before."

138

"Let's hope it is not the Fortunate Isles," chuckled Einion, "and that we have not gone in a great circle in the Western Ocean."

"Where are we, Madoc?" asked Svein, suddenly. "I know that we have gone south to about twice the distance from Spain to the Fortunate Isles . . . but how far west have we come?"

Madoc pulled out the leather wallet from inside his clothing and carefully unrolled the parchment.

"We have been away seventy-two days, Svein. Not counting the time we have been here, I have made a rough reckoning each day on the pace of the wind and current."

They looked expectantly at him.

"Between two and three thousand miles from the coast of Spain . . . that's where we are."

Einion gulped and the Norseman whistled between his teeth.

"I never knew such distances could exist," muttered Einion. "Surely the world cannot be that big."

"Then where are we, Welshman?" gibed Svein. "This island and the surrounding sea look very real to me, however far we are from home."

Madoc pulled his chart away. "I have marked each day's progress and the course by sun, stars and lode-stone, when we used it. It cannot be too far from the truth. Svein, how distant would you think those ancestors of yours sailed, when they found this Vinland in the north?"

Svein shrugged. "There are no good records, Madoc. It was done in separate steps, from Island to Grônland and then across to the barren ice islands."

Einion got up from the sand. "What are we to do next, that is the thing."

"Simple, lad . . . we go on, for we cannot go back," answered the Norseman.

Madoc looked towards the group of seamen at the fire. "It might come hard to some of them. But the winds blow always from the east and the current sets that way too . . . so we have no choice, the *Gwennan Gorn* cannot breast that river in the sea, with the wind as it is."

"It is already June . . . a few months and the sailing season will be over. We have to get somewhere to winter or find a way to re-cross the ocean before the autumn storms set in," worried Einion.

139

Madoc stood up alongside his brother. "Then we had better get on with it," he said firmly. He called to the crew.

"We sail the *Gwennan Gorn* onwards the day after tomorrow," he told them. "In the morning, we will hunt as many birds and small animals as we can and fill every water butt to the brim. I think there will be many other islands from now on, but it is best to take no chances."

There was an ominous silence.

"Where do we go from here?" muttered one of the crew.

"To find the place we set out from Gwynedd to find," said Madoc, easily.

"We know nothing of what we hoped to find," growled Alun, the man whom Svein had feared would cause trouble before they made a landfall.

"Every group of islands is near a mainland," persuaded Madoc. "The isles off Menevia, the Caledonian isles, the Fortunate Isles off Africa, Anglesey off Gwynedd itself. We shall find the great land in the west that the Vikings discovered many years ago."

"And if we don't?" asked Alun, with a suspicion of a sneer.

"Then do you wish to stay on a deserted island, ten miles long, and live on squirrels and great nuts for the rest of your life?" snapped Svein. He had little time for Alun Crookeye.

The man with the squint took a step forward. "Well, I for one won't set foot in that damned cockleshell for quite a time yet. We've had the better part of a quarter of a year huddled in that thing, living like rats, squeezed together, half-starved and drinking slime. If I'd known what it was to be like, I'd never have set foot off that quayside at the Afon Ganol."

Several of the other men mumbled half-voiced agreement.

Madoc felt pained at this sudden outburst. He thought that the few days' rest and good food would have restored the men to their original zest for adventure.

"We can't leave you here, Alun, nor any others. We have no means of finding the island again, even if the wind and sea would allow us to retrace our path."

"Leave us here! No, you certainly will not leave us here," snapped Alun. "The ship does not sail until we agree. And that may be a long time. Why exchange the known, solid land for empty wastes on the edge of the world? The world must end somewhere . . . and I don't intend to be one of those who finds

140

out where."

He said this with an air of smug finality, then looked knowingly at his supporters, to get confirmation of their approval of his ultimatum.

Madoc would have continued to argue and persuade, but Svein solved the immediate problem in a typically forthright way.

Stepping forward, he said, "Alun, look!"

The wall-eyed sailor turned his head to the Viking, and received a blow in the face that would have stunned a bull. He fell to the ground, bleeding from the nose and lay still.

"You've killed him, Svein," snapped Madoc, dropping to his knees and lifting up the seaman's head.

The Norseman was unconcerned. "His head is too hard for that. Leave him alone, he'll survive. Tell him that I'll repeat the dose every time he talks mutinous nonsense . . . that should cure his wayward tongue."

Next morning, Alun was conscious and able to walk, though he was lacking several of his front teeth and had a broken nose. He was unable to speak, but the look in his eyes as he glared at the Viking made Madoc fear that Svein should be on the watch for a dagger in the back from now on.

The day was spent in provisioning the *Gwennan Gorn* and that night they all slept on board, ready for a start at dawn. They had decided that they would set off again towards the setting sun, until they met a wind or tide that set them on a different path.

At dawn, they watched the island slowly slide behind them and vanish over the horizon.

The wind was weak and the current set them slightly to the north of west, but they kept going all day and the next without incident. Several times they saw sandbanks and islands, then on the third day, there was no land at all, nor on the fourth or fifth.

This worried Madoc slightly, as he felt sure they would have been in an archipelago of offshore islands. This empty sea made his heart sink.

"What do you think of this?" he murmured to Svein, as they stood on the stern deck, six days sailing from their last landfall.

"I think I should have punched Alun a lot harder, for he is already able to wag his tongue and disturb our other men," rumbled the huge fellow.

"Many more days of this, and we will hardly be able to blame him," replied Madoc anxiously.

Svein, looking around the sky, said nothing, but wondered if there was something brewing in the heavens that might do more than divert Alun Crookeye.

The vault of the heavens had taken on a deeper blue and the wind dropped almost to nothing.

By the next morning, it was apparent to everyone on the little ship that some change in the weather was imminent, unlike anything they had seen before. Towards evening, straggling white fingers of cloud appeared high in the sky and the sunset was a threatening yellowish colour.

During the night, the heat became oppressive, the first time that this had happened on the whole voyage. There was no wind and the sail hung limply, with an occasional forlorn slap against the mast. No one slept, every man huddled on his small area of deck or bilge boards, feeling the sweat run down his skin and the feeling of prickling fear of the unknown inside his brain.

Two hours after dawn, creeping over the southern horizon came a vast swirling mass of whitish-grey cloud, the under-belly of which turned blue-black as it climbed the sky towards the zenith. Before noon, it had blotted out the sun and the first gusts of wind began.

There was a sudden rippling of the sea as a little squall hit the vessel and bounced her gently up and down. Ten minutes later, a longer and harder blow came, then all was quiet again.

"I fear this, Madoc," grunted Svein. "I have been on the sea since I was seven years old, in every sea known to the Irish and a few unknown to them. But I have never seen the likes of this."

Einion was frankly frightened at the great pall of cloud that crept inexorably across the sky. "Is it the end of the world?" he asked Madoc quietly. "Perhaps this was the trap that nature has lured us into."

"It is a storm, Einion. Maybe the worst storm we have ever known. But it is only a storm and will die down, just as it started."

Another gust hit them, more violently this time and the vessel heeled sharply as it hit her high sides.

"We had better take that sail right down," advised Svein. "Stretch it across the hold on top of the coracles and tie it as firmly as we can."

142

"But leave room for bailing in one corner," added Madoc, looking with apprehension at the swirls of white in the grey mass that now hung almost from horizon to horizon.

"Bring the bow round to face the wind when it comes," shouted Svein to the men, who were now working frantically with the sail and anything movable above deck. "Put out two oars, just one each side, so that we have a chance to keep her prow to the storm."

Five minutes later, with no further warning, the hurricane hit them.

The crew of the *Gwennan Gorn* must have had many thousands of days sea-faring experience between them, but none of them had ever even had nightmares about a storm as bad as that one.

Within half an hour, Svein's oars had been snapped off, the steering oar had vanished and with it Gwilym, the steersman. The little vessel became nothing more than an ungainly raft, tossed and rolled in the waves.

Every man was driven off the deck and crouched terror-struck beneath the pitifully inadequate decking or under the edge of the leather sheets and sail that was lashed over the stores in the hold.

Waves like mountains careered under the ship, lifting her high towards the black sky.

Only the buoyancy of the light little vessel and the high bulwarks saved her, as the storm rushed her northwards at a speed that was treble that of a galloping horse.

Any thought of baling was pointless. Gradually, the hull filled with water, until each man was in up to his chest. Only the floating power of the wooden hull kept the *Gwennan Gorn* on the surface, though she settled lower and lower in the water. Even so, she would probably have foundered, but for twenty empty provision casks—all the food long exhausted—which were trapped under the bow and stern decking, unable to float away because of the hatch covers lashed across the hold. These gave that little extra buoyancy that saved all their lives.

All that day and all that night the storm went on unabated. One of the crew died when one of the wild lurches of the ship caused him to strike his head on a beam. He fell under the surface of the water inside the hull and in the dark, no one knew of it, until he was found swirling about against their feet, drowned.

Daylight brought no relief and by then, many of the wet,

exhausted and terrified men were praying for death to end their suffering.

Suddenly, the wind dropped and within an hour, the sea abated to a long swell. The *Gwennan Gorn* rolled uneasily, almost awash, her oar ports level with the surface.

"Has it finished, Madoc?" croaked Einion, his mouth crusted with salt and his tongue swollen from thirst.

Svein dragged himself up over the edge of the hold and unsteadily stood on the deck. There were hazy clouds overhead, but all around the horizon were masses of black, menacing and waiting.

"I think it is but a respite. We seem to be in the centre of a whirlwind," he muttered.

The crew crawled on deck and their first task was to quickly, but reverently slide the body of their dead comrade over the side into the grey depths. Gwilym had been taken earlier, but nothing marked his passing but memories in the minds of his comrades.

"Now bale, for our lives," called Madoc. He jumped down into the hold and set the pace by handing up buckets of water to Einion above him. The crew furiously lifted water from the hull, using any and every container that would hold fluid.

Cramped for space and afraid to unlash the covers too widely, the process was slow and inefficient, but gradually the level in the little ship went down until it was around their ankles, instead of their chests.

Madoc clambered out at this stage and stood and looked at the menacing sky and the threatening black water around them.

"We have had almost four hours respite, Svein. But I think we are going to be stricken again, very soon."

On the southern horizon, the junction of black sky and dark water was already hazy, as the storm began catching up with the *Gwennan Gorn* across the fifty miles of its calm eye.

The men looked fearfully at their officers.

Madoc raised a hand in a gesture that was almost a benediction. "We have survived one half of the tempest . . . so we can survive the other half. We will shelter as before and trust in God. Padraig, you can best occupy your time in prayer for us. I think you are better at that than struggling with a bucket."

Madoc's confidence rubbed off on the crew and there were even a few weak laughs at the skinny priest's discomfiture. Svein

144

walked across the gently rolling deck and laid a hand on the shattered pillar that had supported the steering oar. "A pity we lost Gwilym . . . he was a good sailor and a good steersman."

"Are we to rig the other steering oar?" asked Madoc. "We carry a spare below deck."

Svein shook his head. "Why lose another? It can do us no good and if we survive we shall need it."

Soon the wind began to hit them in irregular gusts. Having learned by experience, they hurried under the decks and crouched with the boards pressing on their necks again, clinging to the ship's ribs or the deck supports. They had to trust in the buoyancy of Welsh oak and empty casks to keep them on the surface of this terrifying ocean.

After a few preliminary gusts, the hurricane hit them as before, the wall of the eye slamming across the sea like a moving cliff of clouds, two miles high. Again they suffered for a day and a night, swamped, sick and in constant fear of death. The *Gwennan Gorn* raced northwest, covering untold hundreds of miles. Sometimes she sped bow first, sometimes stern first and quite often it seemed to be beam first. Rolling, pitching, almost somersaulting, the motion was so fearful that many men cried out in agony to die and escape the terror. Again the hold was flooded to nearly neck level, but no one died this time, in spite of the hellish conditions.

Padraig prayed aloud as much as he could, though his voice was almost drowned by the shrieking wind.

No one could eat or drink, they could hardly keep themselves above water, but the respite for a couple of hours when they were in the centre of the storm had given them the chance to drink a few mouthfuls and to swallow some dried meat and fruit from the island. More than that, they now knew that it was possible —if only just possible—to survive that tempest and this knowledge gave them the will to cling on until it passed.

Just as it had come, so the storm went.

Dawn came, so obscured that it was hardly noticed, but a few hours later, when the wind and the sea were at their worst, it suddenly abated and the great vortex of wind and cloud that stretched for almost a thousand miles, raced away from them to the north, to fling itself on some unknown coast.

Within minutes, the sky lightened, the wind rapidly dropped, and the sea moderated, changing from a white inferno to a long

145

green swell.

Like animals emerging from a winter's hibernation, the seamen crawled out onto the deck and lay trembling, almost afraid to believe that the worst was over.

But as the cloud thinned and the sun peered through, they scrambled to their feet and staggered about, clasping each other and muttering and crying almost like a boatload of drunks.

"Bale . . . then a prayer for salvation!" ordered Madoc, through cracked lips. They laboriously drained the hold right to the bottom, taking off the sail and cargo-cover, pulling the coracles aside and lifting out the remaining stores to dry in the sun that was by now back to its full strength in a blue sky.

As the day wore on, order was restored. They had no means of kindling a fire, as there was nothing dry on board for the flint to ignite, so any soup or cooked meal was out of the question. But they had some cooked birds from the island that were not yet too corrupt to eat and together with fresh water and fruit, noon saw them almost back to normal. The spare steering oar was unlashed from the inside of the hull and rigged to a make-shift pillar. Alun, the potential rebel, was the best steersman now and he took the oar on Madoc's orders. He was quiet, but not sullen, as far as Madoc could see. The perils of the sea over-rode any quarrels for the moment and Alun's bruised face and gums were forgotten for the moment, at least by everyone except Alun himself.

"The Almighty knows where we are," muttered Svein, "for I'm sure that I don't."

Madoc and Einion peered at their sun-board. "The shadow is longer," murmured Einion.

"We must have come an incredible distance in two days," said Madoc, tilting the bowl in time with the ship's roll to get the best reading. "Not only in northing. The speed that the tempest took us, for two nights and a day, must surely have sent us far to the west, as this northerly direction cannot account for anything but the smallest part of the distance."

"Would that some genius could invent a device for measuring east-west voyaging, as well as movements to the north and south," grumbled Svein, "for we now have no idea where we are."

"We did not know that before," pointed out Einion, "so we are no worse off."

146

Madoc dismantled the sun-board and stood up. "Wherever we are, it is a great distance from our islands. Let's hope that something turns up soon on the horizon, or friend Alun will be up to his tricks again."

They had raised the sail again and were under way in the same direction as the hurricane, following it at a leisurely pace in the winds that it left behind.

There were still masses of black cloud sinking rapidly far ahead of them and the horizon was too dark for anything to be seen clearly. The *Gwennan Gorn* sailed on uneasily across this totally unknown sea into the gloom of yet another night.

The wind dropped and in the morning they were almost becalmed, but Svein began to get excited because the dawn showed him that something was happening to the sea.

"Mud . . . look at that colour," he exclaimed, leaning over the side to point down into the water.

The blue of the great ocean had a definitely brownish tint. From the mast-head, it became apparent that far off to the right there was still some azure water, but the sea immediately around them was a discoloured stream, pouring past them to the south.

With almost no movement, they felt frustrated at being trapped at a time when the signs were the most hopeful of having land within reach, for every man knew the significance of muddy water. "A great river, this must be," declared Svein, "with brown water, yet too far from shore for birds to come out to us."

But then the wind came from the south-west and took them away from the muddy stream. In a few hours, the *Gwennan Gorn* was clipping along at almost her best pace, with the strong breeze dead on her stern. Madoc was tempted to try to steer her as far to the west as she would go, to get back to the origin of the coloured water, but Svein said that speed in any direction was the thing that mattered most. They would have halved the rate of their progress if they braced their yard to crawl due north. Madoc had great misgivings, but it seemed better to reach the unknown quickly, rather than slowly, with their food stocks so low again.

Nothing was seen for the rest of the day nor on the morrow.

The crew said nothing, but Madoc could feel their resentment growing again. Alun continued his sullen silence and did not appear to have been stirring up any trouble amongst the seamen,

147

but he threw some evil glances at Svein as he stood at the steering oar.

On the second night, Madoc slept uneasily wedged on his blanket against the bulwark as the little vessel pitched with the ever-following wind. Another man was clinging sleepily to the steering oar, it being Alun's turn to sleep. As ever, the Welsh prince's thoughts sped homeward across the great ocean. Whatever the cost, this voyage had been the best thing in the world for him, he thought—getting away from the turmoil of Aberffraw and the hatred of his brothers. Time to get over the loss of Annesta and to heal the wound by this almost monk-like solitude and penance of sailing in an empty world.

His reverie was abruptly shattered by a yell and a scream, mixed with a scuffling of bodies in the deck space below him. He leapt up and dashed to the edge of the hold, putting his head over the edge to try to see what was happening in the dim starlight.

"Svein . . . Einion . . . what's going on?" Madoc shouted into the hold. The scuffling still went on, mixed with the curses of sleeping men being rudely awakened.

"Whatever's happening down there, stop it," he yelled, suddenly alarmed by the struggling and moaning that came from below.

But the next second a pair of hands reached up and grabbed him by the throat. Helpless, he felt his breath being cut off and as flashing lights began to burst redly in front of his eyes, he was dragged further over the edge until, with a final explosion of stars inside his brain, he pitched forward into the hold and lost consciousness.

FOURTEEN

JUNE 1170

The first thing Madoc did when he awoke was to vomit violently. His head was throbbing like a drum and his main desire was to die and for an hour or so, he neither knew nor cared where he was.

Eventually, true consciousness came to him and he found himself squatting in the hold, his back against the curve of the hull. His hands were tied in front of him with leather thongs, but his feet were free—not that there was anywhere to go.

A grey light was filtering into the sky, which was clouded over again, though not with the ominous masses that had come with the storm.

He groaned and tried to identify the many aches and pains in his body. He managed to turn his face to the left and saw dimly that Einion was similarly trussed alongside him. There were a number of other men in the hold, all with their wrists lashed by the plaited leather. More serious, however, was the figure of Svein lying across the ox-hides that formed a mound over the cargo. He was not tied up and the reason was all too obvious. Though alive and breathing stertorously, his face was dead white and blood was seeping from under a crude bandage that was wrapped around his shoulder and chest.

Madoc found that his throat would not function. Pain and soreness in his voice-box prevented anything but a useless croak coming from it. But even this was enough to attract Einion's attention.

"Brother, are you all right?" he muttered. Madoc croaked back a noise that he hoped sounded reassuring. "Madoc, you sound like a goose with its throat cut. Your face is red and you have blood in your eyeballs, Madoc. Can you not speak?"

Madoc remembered being grabbed and throttled, presumably accounting for this damage to his throat and the sore puffiness of his face. He managed to make some noises which sounded near enough like "What's happened?" for Einion to understand him.

"Mutiny . . . that damned Alun Crookeye has raised a revolt against us. Svein is stabbed by him. I fear for his life."

Madoc tried to get up and crawl towards Svein. He reached him on his knees and touched his face with his manacled hands. It was cold and sweating, but the Viking groaned and opened his eyes.

"Treachery, old friend," he murmured.

"Where are you hurt?" Madoc tried to ask. It felt as if a razor was being drawn across his windpipe.

"He has a stab in the chest, on the right side under the armpit, thanks to Alun," growled Meirion, the man who had been steering.

"I will recover, never fear," said Svein, in a weak, but resolute voice. "I have to do so, in order to tear the limbs off that damned traitor."

Madoc gradually got the world into perspective.

"The crew . . . how many are on Alun's side?" He found that by whispering, instead of trying to talk, he could make himself understood to Einion.

"All except these nine men here, I think . . . though their attachment to Alun is probably one of expediency, not loyalty," murmured his brother.

"Call him . . . call that damned dog with the crossed eyes," hissed Madoc, unable to do so himself.

Einion struggled to his feet, his head just below the deck level. "Alun . . . Alun Gam, come here."

Into the dawn light of the square hold opening, Alun appeared.

"Don't shout orders at me, I'm the ship-master now," he snapped.

Svein grunted and tried to move when he saw his arch-enemy, but he was too weak and fell back onto the oxhides.

"What's the meaning of this Alun? What can you gain by so mistreating us and trying to kill Svein Olafsen?" grated Einion.

The skinny, wall-eyed sailor looked down grimly at them. "Sanity . . . that's what I shall gain. We have come on a devil's errand and you compound it, you and that barbarian Viking."

Madoc was genuinely puzzled. "What do you mean, compound it?" he croaked.

"As if coming into the unknown was not enough, you saw a sign of land two days ago . . . a muddy effluent . . . and you sailed away from it. *You* may court death, but the rest of us want to live."

"So what have you done, madman?" asked Einion boldly.

"Put our steering oar and tacking boom to take us back towards the source of that current," snapped Alun. "As you should have done in the first place. You madmen have not enough sense to run a boat across the Straits of Menai, let alone into evil waters so far from the Christian world as this."

"And have you reached this muddy current again, clever sailor?" snapped Einion.

"Not yet, but the wind is not in our favour, thanks to your madness in leaving the river water astern of us."

"What are you going to do with us?" croaked Madoc, managing to make himself heard, in spite of the pain. "Kill us, as you have tried to kill Svein?"

Alun's ugly face twisted in hate. "Kill him! What did he do to me . . . smash my face and injure me for advising some other course. No, I'll not kill you, Prince Madoc, for you are still a king's son, bastard or not. We shall have to see what befalls us in these devilish waters."

Madoc struggled to his feet, to stand alongside his brother. "Then let us free. You are on your new course, it is pointless changing back again now. We have no cause for quarrel with you, apart from the need to have justice over your attack on Svein."

Alun shook his head emphatically. "Oh no! You shall stay there for the time being . . . and those stupid men who refused to see the sense of my actions. I have other men here who are sensible and who want to see their families again, not throw their lives away in this endless sea."

"Then you will need us to get you home, Crookeye," snapped Einion, "for none of you know anything about navigating a vessel out of sight of land."

Alun nodded. "For that reason, as well as my reluctance to lay a finger on the life of a royal man, you will be treated as well as the rest of us. You will share our food and water and share the thirst and hunger, if we do not see the shore soon."

One of the other sailors—sullen and uncommunicative—came down to hand round some water and a meagre ration of rotten meat, coconut flesh and some dried fish.

Madoc tried to make Svein as comfortable as he could. He managed to unwrap the wound coverings with his tied hands. There was no more bleeding from the knife slash, though it was red and angry-looking.

Alun refused to untie their hands and without this they had no hope of climbing up out of the hold. They tried unpicking each other's knots, but the water slopping about the bottom of the vessel had tightened up the leather until it chafed cruelly into their skin.

Though weak and feverish, Svein watched their struggles, then beckoned Madoc near him with jerks of his head.

"I have a knife inside my jerkin," he murmured. "They forgot to take it away when they searched you others."

Cautiously, Madoc slid down beside Svein on the cargo cover, propping his back against the casks and boxes under the oxhides. He slid his bound hands under the rough cloth of the Norseman's jacket and closed his fingers on the hilt of a seaman's knife. Svein's eyes watched the deck edges above them. "Now!" he muttered and Madoc slid the knife out and held it close to his own stomach as he rolled back to his place opposite.

He slumped across his neighbour, just in time, covering the knife with his body, as Alun stared suspiciously down at them.

As soon as he had gone, Madoc put the keen edge of the knife to the bonds of Meirion, the man alongside him. Meirion twisted his wrists to meet the knife and the leather parted easily.

They worked fast after that, but always with eyes turned to the deck above, stopping when anyone approached. Soon the eleven men with Svein were free, though they sat with the cut bonds draped around their wrists as camouflage.

"What now?" asked Einion, in a low voice.

"Wait till dusk . . . that cannot be far off," replied Madoc. He was sore in his heart as well as his hands, to think that so many of the men had gone over to Alun. He sensed all along that the crook-eyed seaman had a strange power over lesser men.

"What do we do then?" persisted Einion. "Rush them without weapons? They are more numerous than us and we have the disadvantage of being below their level in this damned hold."

Madoc shrugged. "Let the inspiration of the moment tell us what to do—I am sure that once the others see that we are free, they will desert Alun and come back to their senses."

They sat for some time, waiting for the first signs of the rapid sunset, when their dilemma was solved in a most dramatic way.

There was a sudden shout from one of the seamen standing in the bow. "Birds! Many birds . . . look." He pointed upwards and sure enough, a whole formation of dark-coloured birds were steadily winging their way high overhead.

Another man sprang up the rigging to stand on the main spar. His eyes followed them as the steady beat of their wings took them towards the horizon. Then his face took on a look of incredulity. He pointed away to the steer-board side.

"Land . . . land!" he yelled hoarsely. "Land all along the sky-line."

Alun and most of the crew ran to the steer-board bulwark, some jumping up and holding the rigging.

In the hold, the captives heard the cry themselves staggered to their feet. They dropped their severed bonds, but the crew above were too intent on looking into the distance to worry about them.

Madoc grabbed some broken wood from old crates that was intended for fire kindling and with the other ten at his heels, scrambled up the heap of cargo and leapt for the edge of the decking.

Surprise had its effect. Alun kicked Madoc in the face as he tried to get to his feet, but Einion smashed a baulk of timber at his shoulder and knocked him down. Madoc scrambled up, oblivious of the blood running down his cheek from a large gash. He threw himself on to Alun, while the other men advanced threateningly on the rest of the crew.

As soon as the half-hearted rebels saw that Alun had been felled, they capitulated. Madoc's half-score, incensed and seeking revenge for the hours of indignity and discomfort in the hold, advanced on them and laid about them with fists to relieve their feelings.

Alun was trussed up and dumped unceremoniously into the hold, where his prisoners had so lately been kept. Svein was carefully brought up and laid on blankets on the deck.

The rebels sheepishly made their apologies to Madoc, saying that they would not have continued long with Alun's madness. After the blows had been flung and honour satisfied all round, Madoc was inclined to forget the whole affair, apart from Alun

153

Gam himself. There were more pressing problems and excitements, as the land was now clearly visible from the deck.

"We must cease all this idiocy and join together as we always have done!" shouted Madoc, as he paused at the foot of the standing rigging. "We are the crew that found the Fortunate Isles and conquered the currents of Gwennan's Bane. I know your endurance has been sorely tried, but the end is in sight . . . I feel it in my bones."

With that, he swung up the walrus-hide ropes and clambered to the main spar, with the sail billowing below him. The journey was over, at least for the time being. Low, flat land stretched as far as the eye could see, all along the horizon. If this was not a continent, it was an immense island, he thought, with thanks and gladness in his heart.

The coast seemed featureless, with trees and scrub growing down to the water's edge, as far as he could see from this ten mile distance. Sand dunes began pointing like a great finger far towards the west, where there seemed to be an opening in the coast-line.

He came down and told the news to the others, who took it in turns to climb the mast and gaze on this new land.

Madoc went to Svein and for the first time his wound was cleansed and properly bandaged. He still had a fever and the margins of the stab were even redder and more angry-looking than before, but his mind was clear and he listened eagerly to the news of the land-fall.

"Find some safe anchorage away from the main coast, Madoc," he urged. "We are on a lee shore and if one of those storms from the very depths of hell should come along again, we would surely be wrecked."

"There seems to be an inlet or river mouth some miles ahead," reassured Madoc. "We are making for that and will get inside by morning."

Madoc turned the ship's bow inshore until they could reach bottom with their line. The anchors were dropped and with fervent hopes that no wind would blow up in the night, they sat out the darkness in anticipation of land under their feet and new water and food in their bellies in the morning.

"What do we do with that dog in the hold?" asked Einion, as they squatted on the deck in the dark.

154

Madoc sighed, "I don't know, brother. He has been nothing but trouble since we entered the waters of the new world."

"We would do best to throw him over the side and be done with it. We have a just right to do so, by any law."

"I cannot do it, Einion. If we were home, perhaps. But here, where no Welshman has ever breathed the air before, I cannot bring myself to do such a thing in cold blood."

Einion shrugged. "We store up more trouble for ourselves if we let him live," he said.

Madoc put off the decision. "Let us see what we can see when our feet touch this new land. Maybe some answer will be given to us."

In the morning, the wind had shifted around to the south-west and they had difficulty in getting the *Gwennan Gorn* along the coast as they desired. For a time, they managed to coax her along by dint of hard work on the steering oar, combined with the use of the tacking boom to prod the sail around the mast.

But by mid-day, the wind was in front of their beam and reluctantly, the sail came down and the oars came out.

All that day, they pulled the bluff shape of the little vessel through the water by means of human muscle alone. After weeks of poor diet and the days of physical exhaustion in the storm, they had little enough muscle to spare. It was almost evening when at last they brought the ship round the point of the long sand-bar that they had been following for most of the day. This low tongue of land ran for more than twenty miles.

"Bring her round into the gap," ordered Madoc, again at the mast-head. The opening was about ten miles wide, a small island being visible on the far side. As they laboriously crept around the corner, they moved into the wind again and the sail was hoisted, to the relief of the sweating crew. A smell of vegetation drifted to them, even though the nearby land seemed mainly sand-dunes and grass.

As they sailed into the channel, Madoc was astonished to see how it widened out again. It was a river mouth without doubt, but its size was enormous. It must have been thirty miles wide just inside the entrance, going back a long distance behind the sand spit that they had been following.

Inland, the estuary was lost in the distance, though the low

155

lands on either side seemed to gradually approach each other as the river mouth funnelled its way deep into the interior.

"Where shall we land, Svein?" asked Madoc.

The Norseman rolled his feverish eyes at his friend. "The nearest bit of earth, Madoc," he muttered hoarsely through his cracked lips. "Much as I love the sea, in my present state I would love to lie on some solid ground for a time."

As one piece of land was the same as another for the moment, Madoc readily agreed.

They dropped the sail and, pulling with renewed strength, brought the *Gwennan Gorn* around the point of the sand bar and up as close as possible to the beach.

"Almost touching the bottom, we can walk ashore from here," yelled the man in the bow with his line and sinker.

The water was very shallow, even the couple of feet that the little vessel drew was too much to get them closer than a hundred yards from the water's edge.

"The tide is about half risen," observed Einion, looking at the rim of seaweed further up the beach. "We could get in closer in a few hours."

Madoc shook his head. "God knows what sort of wild creatures or even wild men may be here. I have no wish to be beached at a dangerous moment. As it is, we will be left high and dry at low tide, by the looks of it."

At last the *Gwennan Gorn* came to rest in the peaceful waters of a great and distant land, for this was no island, unless it was the size of Britain itself. There was a feel about the horizon that told of an immense country-side. The size of the muddy river current was proof enough of some gigantic drainage area. In the far distance, hazy blue hills could be seen. They all felt in their bones that this really was the New World.

"You must be the first to set foot on the land, Madoc . . . to claim it for Wales," said Einion.

Madoc smiled at him. "I'll set foot on it with pleasure, but I'll not claim it for anyone, even Wales. I have a feeling that this country has the strength to look after itself . . . no one will claim it and survive the claim for long."

With Meirion, he clambered into one of the coracles that was rapidly dropped over the side and paddled off easily towards the beach. They were sheltered from the ocean by a couple of miles

156

of grass-covered sand and the waves on the beach were merely little ripples.

A few yards from the water's edge, Madoc hopped over the side of the frail cockle-shell and found that the water was barely up to his knees. He waded ashore ahead of Meirion and as he came up out of the water, he felt a strange sense of exultation.

Striding up a few more yards, he turned and looked back. Like a toy ship, the *Gwennan Gorn* sat placidly at anchor, the great expanse of the landlocked bay behind her. He marvelled at the fact that that little pile of wood and leather had come untold thousands of miles from the Afon Ganol in Gwynedd, guided only by the wind, the sea and the skill of her crew.

He raised his hands to the sky, partly in worship of the powers that had guided them and partly to convey his joy to the ship. Then he collapsed onto the warm dry sand and felt the odd vertigo that solid land caused after so long on the pitching deck of a ship.

Meirion dragged the coracle to the edge of the wavelets, then lifted it clear of the water altogether. He flopped down alongside Madoc and dug his hands gleefully into the sand.

"No dragons or devils of hell here, *arglwydd*," he said happily. "Just a beach and yellow sand, as if we were on the shore at Aberffraw."

"The new world looks much the same as the old, friend," agreed Madoc, lying back and staring up at the blue sky. "Old wives' tales and the brooding melancholies of the wise men are as false as the minds that decide facts without any evidence, Meirion."

"This is a great land . . . I feel it to be so. What are we to do with it all, there are only a score or so of us?"

Madoc sat up with a laugh. "We may not be the sole owners, Meirion. For all we know, there may be castles and kings and princes here, just as at home. They may take exception to our arrival. Think what would happen in Wales if some strange vessel arrived in the Menai Straits and the crew stepped ashore and claimed the country for some distant prince !"

Meirion nodded. "Your royal father would cut their heads off for their audacity . . . but I see no signs of life here, no castles nor roads or habitations."

Madoc looked around them. "It's a wild place, true enough.

157

But there are many such in Wales looking as desolate."

They got up and walked up the beach into the grassy wasteland that stretched infinitely before them.

"Little hopes of fresh water here, prince," scowled Meirion. "The rain would sink into this sand like going into a sponge."

Madoc agreed. "I do not think that we will stay long here . . . but we have some water left in our casks, enough for a few days. Let the crew come ashore for today and tonight, at least, just to give them a respite from the cramps of the vessel. Svein can be brought ashore in a coracle."

Within an hour, everyone except a watchman was on the beach, running around like children on a holiday, except poor Svein, who lay on the sand, his head propped on a bundle of cloaks.

"What think you of this land, Norseman?" asked Madoc gently.

"I'll tell you better when I can see it from six feet above my shoes, when I am able to stand," gibed Svein weakly. "This fever and the raging ache in my shoulder make it hard for me to give deep thoughts to the scenery. But it seems a fair country."

Madoc held a cup of water to his lips. "When you are recovered, we will press on up the river and see what is to be seen."

"How long will we stay?" asked his brother.

"In this spot or this land?" asked Madoc, watching Einion's face with amusement.

The younger man rubbed his jaw. "I have never thought of it until now . . . getting here was job enough, without worrying about why we came."

Madoc yelled with laughter and even Svein managed a grin. "Why did we come?" asked Einion, defiantly.

Madoc laid a hand on his shoulder. "For me, it was an escape . . . but for all of us, it was an adventure, Einion. The urge that all men have to climb the nearest hill, see what is in the next valley."

With that, his brother had to be content.

They stayed for two days on the grassy upper beach, rigging crude tents with hides from the ship and living off what was left from the stores. Foraging parties found many birds' eggs in the grass and hunted a number of large sea birds. They also caught a few of the rabbit-like creatures that were the only animals that

158

appeared to live there.

When the tide went out, the *Gwennan Gorn* was left high and dry. Madoc took the opportunity to inspect the hull beneath the waterline. To his gratification, there was not the slightest sign of any damage or loosening-up of the timbers. The stag-horns had done their job perfectly and in spite of the battering the vessel had suffered during the hurricane, she was as sound as the day they left Aber Cerrig Gwynion. There was a great deal of water-weed and barnacle on the planking and for a whole day, the crew were busy scraping this off with knives and other tools.

Svein's wound began to suppurate, with evil-smelling pus running from the slash on his arm-pit. He became paler and more feverish, but thankfully showed no sign of delirium. The cause of the trouble, Alun of the Crooked Eye, remained manacled and ostracised.

"What are we to do with this damned fellow?" snapped Einion, who had the least love and the least patience with the trouble-maker.

Madoc sighed. "I wish I knew . . . we cannot keep him tied up for ever. The other men seem to have rejected his notions of mutiny, but maybe this is because they have their feet on solid ground and fried hare and eggs in their bellies. Once the going becomes hard again, then the rebellious whispers of Alun Gam might take root in their minds."

But he again put off the hour of decision, leaving Einion to keep a sharp eye on Alun. There seemed nowhere for him to run to, so on the third day, the leather thongs on his wrists and ankles were taken off and he was allowed to roam as he would, though a sharp lookout was kept by Madoc and Meirion at night-time . . . they had no desire to see him finish the work that he had begun on Svein, who was too weak to defend himself.

It was now early July and the sun was just beginning to sink lower from the zenith at each noon-tide. Their water began to run low after a few days on the sandy peninsula and with no means of replenishing it, they reluctantly waded out to the *Gwennan Gorn* on the third morning and hauled up the anchor stones.

Early in the day, they had enough wind to take them gently up the great estuary. For some hours there was little to see, except the flat wooded land many miles away on each side. In the afternoon, the wind died away and the crew had to use the long oars. They pulled against a sluggish stream, slightly brown with mud. Occasionally, a branch or log floated past, on its journey to the sea from some unknown distance inland.

Towards evening, the land began to close in on them and Madoc, looked out for a suitable place to get ashore for the night.

"The banks are still tidal and the water is getting more shallow as we move inland," he commented. The line-man was getting bottom in progressively shorter casts of his weight.

"The banks all look the same . . . trees everywhere. We may as well land at the nearest point, there's little to choose anywhere," suggested Einion.

They crept in until the line showed that they would soon be aground, then dropped their anchors. The muddy beach was about two hundreds yards distant and they used the coracles to ferry an advance party of eight men ashore, Madoc amongst them.

They found plenty of grassy clearings when they scrambled up the banks above the shore. The ground was firm and well drained, with no swamps. The trees were fairly low and though a number were quite unknown to the Welshmen, there were some familiar types.

"Just like home . . . maybe we will see sheep and cattle in the next clearing," joked Meirion, as he dumped his coracle on the grass.

Within half an hour, they had discovered a stream of clear water running down to the estuary, a number of bushes with very edible-looking fruit upon them and—best of all—a number of small deer racing away through the trees.

"We have everything here to survive for ever," rejoiced Meirion. "Build a few dwellings and we can relax for the rest of our lives."

Madoc felt equally at ease in these pleasant surroundings.

"Take the coracles back empty," he ordered Meirion. "Bring another seven men, but tell Einion to stay with the rest until morning. We can beach the *Gwennan Gorn* then and bring everything ashore to make a more permanent settlement."

By noon next day, the vessel was high on the mud of the shore and everyone was busy in the clearing alongside the small stream. Svein lay under a rough shelter of branches and thatch, whilst a party of men laboured to put up a rude hut of poles and branches, big enough to shelter all of them for the night.

Another group had gone off with bows and arrows to hunt deer, while the remainder, including the silent Alun, collected firewood and carried up the remaining stores and empty boxes from the ship.

That night, they ate the best meal since leaving Wales, three months before. There was venison, trout from the pools higher up the stream, fish caught on lines off the beach and fruit that looked sufficiently like wild strawberries to risk being used as a dessert.

After the meal, the thirty men sat around the blazing fire, with full stomachs and contented hearts. Even Alun could find little to complain about under his breath.

There was singing and joke-telling, almost as if they were back on the slopes of Snowdonia. Madoc took out his precious *crwth* —a small stringed instrument, part-harp, part-zither. Another man had a *pibgorn*, a type of flute with a cow's horn at the end and between them, they made sweet music that put the finishing touches to the celebration.

"We are in a far land, Madoc," said Einion nostalgically. "This seems a paradise second only to our native Cymru."

Madoc nodded in the firelight. "More of a paradise, for so far, it has not been marred by the presence of men," he said rather bitterly. "I fled not from Wales, Einion, but from those who make her hell to live in."

Einion nodded. "But they seem a long way off now, brother,"

"They are a long way off . . . no man has ever been farther from the shores of Gwynedd than we. By my calculations, we must have travelled some four or five thousand miles to get here."

"And still have not fallen off the edge of the earth!" chuckled Meirion, who sat near them.

The evening moved into deep night, as they talked out their experiences and expurgated their past fears on the great ocean.

The fire crackled and glowed and the talk, stories and low singing carried on for hours until one by one, they pillowed their heads on the soil of this new land and went back to Wales in their dreams.

FIFTEEN

JULY 1170

Two weeks later, the whole party moved camp to a place some miles higher up the river. As soon as they had settled in the clearing, Madoc sent foraging and exploring parties out, to find the lie of the land and obtain a good stock of game.

He went with one of the groups on an expedition up the bank of the river. They took two of the four coracles and made their way up the western side of the estuary for about twelve miles. Here the two banks began to close in on each other, though the land was still fairly flat. The river started to divide, with large islands dividing it up into a number of separate channels. They began to explore one of these, but they became uneasy at being so far from the ship and the camp. The trip was worth the effort, as they came across a perfect camp site a few miles downstream from the place where the channels began to diverge. This was a low spur sticking out from the otherwise regular line of the shore. There was a flat, grassy top to it and a sizeable river running down on one side to join the main estuary. It was well above any possible flood level and was elevated enough to give a good view in all directions. Moreover, because of the promontory running a few hundred yards out into the river, the water was deeper and the *Gwennan Gorn* could be anchored literally within a stone's throw of the camp.

Perhaps subconsciously, the site reminded the Welshmen of the typical hill-top fortification in their native land, where since early Celtic times, the tops of mountains and hillocks had been ringed with palisades against both human and animal marauders.

The day following their expedition, the ship was loaded up again and everyone clambered aboard. Svein, slowly mending, was able to walk to a coracle and be hauled up by willing hands onto the deck for the short journey up river.

When the tide began to flow, the *Gwennan Gorn* came off the mud and caught the remnants of the morning breeze to start her upstream. The incoming flood tide took her much of the way and by mid-afternoon, she was snugly anchored under the spur of the land, which the men already jokingly called *Castell Newydd* —the new castle.

Once more, everything was off-loaded, this time into the coracles, as the water was too deep to wade, even at low tide.

On the top of the ridge they cut down a few stray saplings that were dotted across the grassy top of the ridge and began making a more permanent camp than they had at the other site.

Within three weeks, they had a palisade of posts and brush-wood encircling an area some fifty yards across, with a large thatched hut in the centre. Around this were a few smaller shelters, some little more than a sloping roof of branches with a weather-proof covering of turf, stones and inter-laced twigs. There was a gap in their fence, which was closed at night by dragging a hurdle of branches lashed together into a crude gate.

On the evening that the construction work was finished, Madoc ordered a specially lavish meal, with as much meat as every man could eat. Afterwards, around the usual great fire on the stone hearth outside the "hall", there was no music or story-telling but a more solemn occasion.

Madoc stood up, the red light flickered on his tall, spare figure as he looked around at the circle of expectant faces.

"Friends, we have been on this new soil for almost five weeks. We have done well, we have built soundly and we are well set for survival. But we have said nothing, whatever we have thought in our hearts, about what is to happen next."

There was a low mutter of agreement. The men recognised that Madoc was at last bringing into the open the thoughts and fears that they had been pushing into the backs of their minds. They wanted to be led, to be invited to loosen their tongues, so that they could see themselves what secret feelings they possessed.

"The *Gwennan Gorn*, the best ship in the world, brought us here safely. This is an immense land—though we have but scratched its skin with our explorations, I know we all feel in our deepest souls that here is no island, but some vast country. Perhaps it is another part of that country which Svein Olafsen's countrymen found in the north, many years ago. Perhaps we shall never know how huge this land really is. But we have

163

to decide what we are to do about this new-found land."

He saw Svein listening intently, lying propped on a heap of dry grass. On the other side of the fire, behind all the other men, was Alun, as silent and withdrawn as ever.

Meirion, by now tacitly acknowledged as the leader of the crew, under the more aristocratic trio of Madoc, Einion and Svein, spoke up. "What choices have we, *arglwydd*?" he asked.

"I see three things we can do," replied Madoc. "We can all stay here indefinitely or we can all get aboard the *Gwennan Gorn* and sail away hoping to find Wales once more."

"And the third?" asked someone.

"Some can stay here, some can go home."

There was a silence whilst they all digested these alternatives.

"We are thirty men, sitting on this hill-top," came the voice of Svein. It had regained a little of the old strong rumble, Madoc was pleased to hear. "Thirty men, I repeat . . . not many to start a new nation."

"It could be ten-thousand and thirty, Svein, and still not be enough to start a new nation," said Einion crisply. "We have been at sea for a long time, but my memory has not decayed so much that I forget that one needs women to produce children."

There was a general guffaw around the camp at this pert reply.

Madoc grinned at his brother. "You were ever one for the girls, Einion. You should have got yourself a wife before leaving. But I take your point, brother. Are we to stay in this land? Do we want to establish a New Wales here? Or do we want to take ship and sail home, content to be hailed as the world's greatest voyagers? If they can tear themselves away from their petty intrigues to give us a second's thought," he added bitterly.

This provoked a flurry of talk, some men being for the first plan, others wishing to stay.

"Meirion, you are usually the spokesman, what do you think should be done?"

The burly seaman, older and tougher than the rest, scratched his leathery cheek. "We are divided, Lord Madoc, but it seems to me that part of the answer is beyond question. If we wish to stay in this land—we need both more men, for we are too few . . . and we need women. Men cannot and will not spend the rest of their mortal lives without the comforts of women. And some of these men—myself included—already have a wife whom we cannot abandon in Gwynedd, while we spend our lives here in the New Land."

He sat down again and Madoc took up his suggestions.

"This follows my own reasoning, Meirion. I think that either we should all return home and those who wish it should come back with a bigger expedition with wives and even some of the children—or some should return, leaving the rest to wait upon our coming back."

The matter was argued back and forth until it became obvious that some men wished to go home and stay there, though there were only five or six of these. Another half-score wished to return home for their wives, sweethearts or any other comely woman and return here with them. The remainder, another dozen or so, were content to stay in the New World indefinitely. Of these Einion was an enthusiastic member, declaring that if he never saw Wales and his damned family again, it would be too soon!

"And what of you, Alun Gam?" asked Madoc. "We have heard nothing from you. You are entitled to speak, though you have lost much of the respect that you had when we sailed from the Afon Ganol."

As he had been the leading trouble-maker of those who wished to turn back earlier in the voyage, Madoc had little doubt that he wished to return home as speedily as possible. But Alun said quite the opposite. "I'll not risk my life in that damned ship again! What chance have you got of ever finding Wales again, when you do not even know where we are now? And if you ever found it, how could you ever return to this spot again? No, I'll stay here and live my life out on dry land."

"So be it," Madoc answered. "It is a free society, this fellow-ship of the *Gwennan Gorn*. None of you need ever have come with me and each of you can do what he likes in the future."

He asked for a firm show of hands on who wanted to return. There were fifteen who wished to take the ship home. Svein was one of them.

"So with myself, there will be sixteen men to crew the *Gwennan Gorn*," he announced. "That should be enough . . . it will *have* to be enough. Half the party will go, the other half will stay here in *Castell Newydd*, growing fat and idle in the sun, until we return!"

Svein painfully pulled himself up on to an elbow. "You had

better not delay much longer, Madoc. It is almost midsummer now and God knows how long it will take you to find your way home. Come the autumn gales and any chance you have of finding Europe, let alone Wales, will vanish."

Padraig, the sailor-monk, was amongst those who volunteered to stay. "I have no wife . . . it would be a strange monk who did —and this pack of heathens here needs a man of God to get them to pray now and then," he declared.

For several days, they made determined efforts to catch as many deer, hares and birds as they could. Within a week all the provisions that the *Gwennan Gorn* could carry were packed below her two small decks. The water vessels were filled on the last day and all was ready for the departure.

Three of the coracles were left behind, though the settlers now had plenty of material to make more.

To take advantage of the ebb tide and the river flow, the *Gwennan Gorn* raised her anchors in the afternoon of an August day, the slight offshore breeze behind them to speed them down towards the sea, twenty-five miles away.

Madoc clasped his brother Einion to him, before he clambered over the side of the ship. "Keep to the castle, Einion . . . take no chances until we return. And keep that record of the days . . . I have given Padraig a deer-skin and charcoal to write with. You can tell when Christ Mass and the New Year comes. We should be back here some time in the late spring, if God shows us the way."

He sounded more confident than he felt about either getting home again or finding their way back to this unknown spot. He was fairly confident of his north-south position to within a few hundred miles. It was almost exactly the same as that of the Fortunate Isles, but the east-west point was anyone's guess within a range of a couple of thousand miles, as only the crudest reckoning of distance had been possible on the journey out.

They hauled up the sail and Meirion, who was going home to fetch his wife, twisted the steering oar. With a few pulls of the sweeps, they got themselves out of the lee of the headland and caught the breeze.

The men on the shore waved madly as they glided away. Voices came through the clear air as their gentle wake curved round and pointed back at *Castell Newydd*. "Bring us back some comely girls . . . fetch some yeast to make beer . . . seed corn . . . women . . . mead. . . . "

The voices became fainter and faded. Looking back, Madoc could see the dots of men waving on the beach and a couple of coracles bobbing on the water.

"God preserve them," he murmured.

"Keep your prayers for ourselves," said Svein. "We need them more than they."

SIXTEEN

NOVEMBER 1170

"Come near, Madoc. Tell me more about how you returned."
A hand made gaunt by age and illness beckoned feebly across the
bed-chamber.

Madoc, his sun-bleached hair contrasting even more with his
weather-beaten face, moved across to the great bed and sat on a
three-legged stool close to his father's side.

"I will never move from this couch again, my son, so tell me
of these far places and strange sights, so that I may travel with
you at least in imagination."

Madoc looked up at the figures at the other side of the bed.
The *meddyg*, whose knowledge of herbs and potions was the best
the court could provide as a healer, shrugged helplessly, as if to
say "Carry on, it can make no difference." Dafydd and Rhodri
were there ostentatiously looking through the window slit, their
backs to Madoc. Elsewhere in the room were the Chancellor, the
Bishop of Bangor, the chief judge, Llywarch and Gwalchmai the
bards and a few palace retainers. At the foot of the bed sat Cristin,
Owain Gwynedd's faithful wife, still unrecognised by Rome.

Behind Madoc stood Svein, looking sadly down on the dying
Prince of Gwynedd.

Owain had been in this state for some weeks, getting slowly
weaker from no particular disease—just old age and the weakness
of a dozen battle wounds of previous years.

Madoc had been home for a week and had seen his father
several times, giving him parts of the story of the great voyage
on each occasion. Now he was coming to the last episode, the
return.

"It took us much longer than we thought, sire. We left our
camp and my brother Einion in the last week of August—I found
on returning here that my rough calendar was two days in error,
but it was near enough to the end of the summer month that we
took leave of our brave friends."

"God allow them to be safe still," murmured Owain, the words having a depth of meaning, rather than a pious prayer.

"The *Gwennan Gorn* was in calm waters for the first week or so. We sailed east from the mouth of that great river, but the winds were not helpful, blowing either off the land or straight from the south. Sometimes we made some progress with the tacking boom helping us to cross the southerly wind, other times we rowed."

He held up his hands, palms towards his father, to show the great callouses from the looms of the oars. "With only sixteen crew, all took their turns. Then we saw land again, straight before us in the east. We had hoped that the coast would curve away northwards and maybe become the Vinland of the old Norsemen who had voyaged from Grônland. But this land blocked our path. We sailed northwards, hoping that it was some large island, but it went on for ever, so we turned and re-traced our path. This wasted many more days and Svein was becoming worried about the lateness of the season."

Svein spoke up from behind him. "It was September and we still were on the same coast as when we left."

"We landed several times, but it was a fearful land, all swamp and strange trees with legs that supported them in the mire."

There was a snort from the two at the window, making their disbelief evident. They took every opportunity to pour scorn on this returning hero. Madoc had tried to avoid them since he returned. The sight of the pair of evil schemers still filled him with sickness.

He carried on, trying to ignore them. "We managed to find some drinkable water, though our stock was still good, then sailed on down the coast for another week. The winds were still contrary, but some miles off shore, there was a brisk current that helped us greatly."

"Yet a day's sailing further from the coast, the current was in the opposite direction," put in Svein. "There are some curious seas in those parts, I feel it is because the water is warm and somehow swirls across the earth under the influence of the sun."

Dafydd swung round to the doctor. "Why you allow our royal father, who is sick unto death, to be plagued by these liars, is strange logic to me, physician."

The Chancellor, a powerful man, even to prince's sons, held up

169

an admonishing hand, but Owain was fit enough to look after his own interests. "I am well enough to choose what I wish to hear," he said in a fitful return of his old voice. "And it is not the jealous whimperings of men who have never set foot beyond Ireland. Continue, Madoc, these tales will give me pleasant dreams tonight."

"Well, sire, the *Gwennan Gorn* continued south, always in sight of the coast. Sometimes we were tricked into thinking that the shoreline had turned east, but they were but huge land-locked bays and we had to come out again. But one day, now in mid-September, we came upon a chain of flat islands, mere sand-bars, with some trees and water that stretched far across the horizon east to west."

Owain nodded, his blue eyes staring into the imagined horizons of the new world that he would never see.

"We sailed the *Gwennan Gorn* through this line of banks and isles out into the open sea beyond. Within a few miles, we felt a new current under our keel and the wind began to blow directly behind us, from the south-west. We had filled up with fresh water and fruit on one end of the islands, but within a few days, going north and east, we came upon more islands, a pair of small ones set in a sea that seemed like paradise. Again we landed and found a crystal spring there that some of the crew said must be the true Fountain of Youth. I know not if it was or whether this was wishful thinking, but I drank from it, along with the rest of them."

"It was like the Garden of Eden that the priests spoke of when the world was young," put in Svein, who had been so impressed with the little island that he had been almost reluctant to leave it.

Ignoring the covert sneers from his half-brothers, Madoc leaned nearer the gaunt figure in the bed.

"Whereas we were so hard pressed for land, water and food on the outward voyage, we seemed to have an endless succession of idyllic stopping places on the way home . . . at least for the middle period of the journey. A week after leaving this paradise island, we came to yet another great group of low islands, stretched across our north-easterly path. Again we watered and filled our casks with small game and birds. This was the end of the New Lands and there was only open ocean in front of us. We sailed out from the last island at the end of September, by my record, again riding easily before the prevailing wind."

Owain Gwynedd's bony face, the skin stretched tightly across his cheekbones, turned to Madoc. "You are a brave son, a true member of the blood of your grandfather. He was half-Norseman, was Gruffydd son of Cynan. No wonder you have such a bond of friendship with that great Viking standing behind you."

Madoc smiled gently at his father. "I only wish I had been around you during all those years of my youth. I would have liked to have heard your tales of my forebears, sire."

Madoc went on with the saga of the *Gwennan Gorn*, which was now nearly at an end.

"Some days after sailing out into the ocean, we came upon a most unearthly area of sea. At first, there were merely wisps of drifting sea weed, but as the days went by, it thickened to form a matted area as far as the eye could see. The men became uneasy and some remembered legends of sea monsters and evil serpents who lived in such places. We had to use all our powers of sailing across what breeze there was to take us back to the west out of that weird and frightening ocean."

"Some days, we even resorted to the oars, so keen were we not to be driven deeper into the weed, for surely it must have thickened enough to eventually stop our passage," put in Svein.

This brought a derisive guffaw from the pair at the window. "God's teeth, these charlatans are telling a pack of lies! They have probably been no further than the coasts of France and have deserted the rest of the crew or allowed them to drown through some criminal negligence."

"Be still, you mouths of spite!" said Owain, with as much spirit as he could muster. "Finish your tale, Madoc."

"There is little more to tell—except that we sailed free of the weed and carried on northward until one day another extraordinary marvel was seen. There was a wide river in the sea, more obvious than that which we had seen on the outward trip. It was of a deeper blue and ran from horizon to horizon for weeks on end. The water was moving faster than we could row the *Gwennan Gorn*, even with a full crew. It was warm and moist and there was a wind following it in the north-easterly direction. We hardly needed the sail, as the current took us without effort. Though the season was advancing fast, we knew that our northing was most rapid. After a week, the current began drifting eastwards. The skies became grey and we met much fog, but the sea was calm for another week. Soon we knew that we must be approaching the levels of Europe, though we had no idea how far to the east they were."

"Then the weather broke and we knew we must be nearing home!" Svein spoke feelingly of the western sea storms that had given them such a rough time on the last part of the journey.

"Our water was easily replenished from the rain . . . God, how it rained! And blew! And the waves were like mountains, though not as dangerous as that terrible storm on the westerly voyage. The wind and the current raced us across the ocean. We had little food left, no bread or meal and all that remained was fish . . . dried fish, fresh fish, any sort of fish."

"I thought I would begin to grow gills," grumbled Svein.

"It grew greyer and colder and we began to despair, though the lode-stone told us that we were running north and east all the time. Then one day, when our food had all gone, except for damned fish, out of the rain clouds we saw mountains! They could have been Wales, but no one recognised them. We went ashore and found that we were on one of those barren western isles in the north of Caledonia. We crept down the coast, reluctant to lose sight of Britain after all the trouble we had taken to get back here. Finding Aberffraw was a child's task after the miles that had slid under the keel of the *Gwennan Gorn* these past seven months."

The dying prince asked a few questions of his wandering son, then pleaded fatigue. "I am tired unto death, Madoc. Leave me now, though I hope to live long enough to see you and hear more wonders in the days to come."

Madoc and Svein knelt to give their homage to Owain then quietly moved to the door.

"A last question, my son." The weak, but firm voice stopped them. "What do you do next? What of those brave men left on that hillock on the other side of the world?"

Madoc stepped back towards the bed. "They will not be deserted, *arglwydd*. I am going back, along with Svein and some of the other men on the vessel. I hope to find more men willing to venture with me in other ships, and to take women and seeds and other things necessary to begin a new Wales beyond the ocean. I hope that my brother Riryd will come with me, at least to see it, if not to stay."

Owain's head dropped wearily back onto the pillow.

As Madoc and his friends left the bedchamber, Dafydd and Rhodri waylaid them in the sunlight outside the wooden building.

Madoc looked at them warily and Svein's hand slipped stealthily towards the dagger at his belt.

"We care little for that pack of lies you spun our father," snapped Dafydd. "But what of this scheme for taking Welsh men and ships off to this fabulous land of yours?"

Madoc looked from one to the other of his half-brothers. He was at a loss to understand them.

"What is it to you, brothers? I shall not trouble you more. Once we leave in the spring I doubt you'll ever see my face again."

Rhodri, a fleshy, small-eyed man, spat on the ground. "A fine tale, a land three thousand sea miles away. I'll wager you've set up camp on some remote part of the Irish coast—or maybe Cornwall or Brittany. You're taking men and supplies there, to build up an army against us, eh?"

Madoc's jaw dropped. It was beyond the wildest bounds of his imagination to think that the ordeals of the past months could be so misconstrued. He was at a loss for words for a moment and the brothers seized on this as evidence of his guilt.

"You'll take no ships and no men from Gwynedd, you lying schemer!" snapped Dafydd. "This land is the rightful property of legitimate seed of Owain, not his bastards."

Madoc's slow temper began to burn inside him. "For God's sake, brothers, are you so besotted and obsessed with your claim to this damp landscape that you can see no other aims in life? For the last time, I have no interest in the politics of Gwynedd. . . . I have no desire to usurp your selfish greeds. . . . I came home to seek out those like myself who are disillusioned with feuding and intrigues. As soon as I have found them, I shall leave these shores for ever."

He turned on his heel and strode away from the glowering pair, with Svein grinning covertly at this outburst from his usually placid comrade.

A week later, on the twenty-third of November, 1170, Owain Gwynedd died and with him passed the stability of North Wales for which he had so painstakingly worked during the previous thirty-three years of his reign. His funeral was a grand and solemn affair, attended by nobles from all over Wales, Caledonia, Ireland, and even from France. In spite of the excommunication of Canterbury and Rome, the clergy of Bangor placed his body in a fine arched tomb near the high altar of the cathedral. But even as he was being laid to rest, turmoil was breaking out in many places. Henry II had just authorised the invasion of Ireland by his mercenary barons and that island was in a state of near-panic and confusion. But near at hand, Dafydd and Rhodri could hardly wait for the burial service to finish before setting about their long-awaited vendetta and began hustling about Gwynedd raising support for their personal causes.

"We would be well advised to shake the dust—or rather mud—of this place from our feet as soon as we can," growled Madoc's Norse companion, as they sat in the hall one evening, eating the evening meal. Madoc had just returned from one of his frequent visits to little Gwenllian, who was happily settled at the court of Menai.

Dafydd and Rhodri had been away from Aberffraw since the funeral, two weeks before, but this evening had come swaggering back, together with Hywel, the poet brother, and Cynan, yet another contender for part of the lands of Gwynedd.

"Llywarch the bard has been whispering the same thing to me," commented Madoc. "He had a bad time here after I escaped him. He was accused of killing me, poor chap, and almost was brought to trial. It was only the discovery that the *Gwennan Gorn* had slipped out of the Afon Ganol that saved his neck."

"You have no father now to protect you, Madoc. Those apes there would dearly like to see their rivals reduced in number—slitting your throat would be an easy answer." He nodded across the hall at the roistering group on the high table.

"We can do little until the spring. It will be Easter before we dare venture out even as far as the Fortunate Isles. That means three months hanging about this unfriendly place."

"We'd never survive it, Madoc," muttered the Viking. "There would be another fire, or a knife in the night . . . something. We have to wait, but for God's sake, do not let it be here."

After the meal, they walked out in the frosty December air to the river and stood looking at the *Gwennan Gorn* as she sat on the sand of the little river. Their minds were both far away,

174

remembering her sitting on another beach, just inside the sand bar of the river, on their first arrival on the mainland of the New World.

"I wonder how our brave friends are?" rumbled Svein. "How severe is the winter there . . . we have no means of telling."

"Much less hard than here, I think," replied Madoc. "The place is far to the south of Wales, there may be no snow or even frost. That vegetation there was not of a tropical kind but neither was it the sort that you have in your harsh northern lands."

"The time must hang heavy for them . . . what can they do, perched on that little headland?"

"Explore . . . Einion told me before we left that he intended to build more coracles and maybe a longer curragh out of withies and deer hides, so that they could make a long expedition up the various mouths of the river, where we saw those islands in the stream."

They stood looking at the little ship again, marvelling that such a frail-looking craft could ever have gone that distance.

"I think we should leave here as soon as we can get a crew together," said Svein decisively. "I feel a great evil brewing with your brothers. They have no brake to their ambitions now that their father has gone. They have a score to settle with you."

Madoc was inclined to agree with him. "We could go to Riryd in Clochran. The English are reported to be fighting their way up from Wexford to Dublin, but we could land on the coast above the Liffey and make our way across country to Clochran. We need a crew first, though."

Svein slapped his hands together in the frosty air. "We crossed the great western ocean with only half a crew. We could cross the Irish Sea with two men, my friend."

Madoc pondered this. "We would have to return eventually, to pick up those who wish to return with us and those who want to bring their wives and children. That cannot be until the spring."

"Then come back at Easter . . . better that than wait to be murdered in our beds by your dear brothers," advised the Norseman.

Two days later, they got together a scratch crew and took the *Gwennan Gorn* across to the Irish coast.

They found Riryd, the Lord of Clochran, more than a little disturbed by the events in Ireland. "Last year, some Norman adventurers from Pembroke landed in Wexford and again this year we have more of them. They have established themselves in Dublin—with the hearty co-operation of your Norse kinsfolk," he said to Svein. "Now we hear that Henry, King of England, is worried about the rival power of these barons of his who have set up veritable kingdoms of their own here in Ireland. It seems likely that next season, he will bring an army to settle the matter."

The prospects at the manor of Clochran were uneasy, to say the least. When Riryd heard the full story of the Great Voyage and the colony of Welshmen left at *Castell Newydd*, he took no persuading at all to fit out a ship and join them on the next expedition in the spring.

"I do not say that I will stay in your new land for ever, brother. But I cannot miss the chance to see it and the situation here is so gloomy that I would be glad to leave it until peace returns again."

His wife had died two years before and his daughters were either married or betrothed, so Riryd had no compunction about uprooting himself and voyaging off into the unknown.

"But this is three months ahead of us," said Madoc.

"I need that to find a good vessel. I think I can find a number of men from the Welsh settlement here who will be willing to join us. The prospect of having Norman overlords here within the next year is enough to make most men want to flee the country."

Riryd found a ship which suited his purpose and the two experienced ocean navigators helped him to direct refitting and equipping. The manor of Clochran had been a rich one and there was no lack of funds to fit new sails, strengthen the decking and add a tacking boom, coracles and all extras that the explorers had found so necessary on their epic trip.

The vessel was another Norse *knarr*, very much like the *Gwennan Gorn*, though slightly longer and higher. It had no stag horn nails, but the usual wooden dowel pins. However, it was a well-found craft and with a good crew, Madoc felt sure that it could survive the journey. With luck, they would miss another terrible storm like the one that hit them beyond the islands.

"What shall we call her?" asked Madoc, as they stood on the banks of the river and looked at the vessel gently swaying at her moorings.

"She has an outlandish Viking name now," said Riryd, with a

wink at Svein . "So I'll choose a good Christian Welsh name . . . what about *Pedr Sant* . . . the sacred Saint Peter was a seaman, even if it was only on Galilee."

So *Pedr Sant* it was and the name was carefully carved on the bow.

Some days later, Madoc returned in the *Gwennan Gorn* to Gwynedd, leaving Svein with his friends and relatives in Dublin. The Norseman was now contemplating finding a strong nordic blonde to take back to the new country, in case he decided to stay there for good.

Madoc and his skeleton crew ran into dirty weather as they rounded the north of Anglesey, as he was bound for the creek of the Gele, where he wanted the vessel to be overhauled by the craftsmen who had built her.

Wet and exhausted, they reached the little river and with difficulty got the *Gwennan Gorn* inside.

Meirion, his chief seaman, promised to be back at the Gele within a month, together with all those who had promised to sail west a second time. Each man had promised to find at least one other man who was willing to come with them, preferably with a wife but no children. The rigours of the voyage were not really suitable for children—it would be hard enough on the women.

Madoc spent a couple of days with the ship-wrights, then took a horse and cautiously travelled westwards towards the mountains of Snowdonia.

He came to the little castle of Dolwyddelan, where he had been born and where his later life had really begun. None of the sons of Owain was there, but he learned from the castle residents that Iorwerth had been fobbed off with the estates of Nanconwy and Ardudwy, whilst Dafydd and Rhodri had divided up the whole of Owain's domains between them. Hywel, the soldier-poet, was in Ireland and Maelgwyn, yet another brother, had established himself in part of Anglesey.

It was obvious to Madoc that it would not be long before all the brothers would be at each other's throats.

He recruited a few of the castle staff for the expedition, after spending a whole evening regaling a spell-bound audience about the Great Voyage and the attractions of the new land. They were not seamen, but it would be farmers and craftsmen that would be needed once they returned. In spite of Madoc's frank warnings of the dangers and hardships of the voyage, he left Dolwyddelan with a firm promise of nine emigrants, who would be at Abergele by the end of February.

Madoc made his way down the Llyn peninsula to Aberdaron, the little port to which the *Gwennan Gorn* had limped after its battle with the terrors of Bardsey Sound. He came away after two weeks with another ten recruits for the new voyage, most of them expert seamen.

By the time he made his way back to the Gele, via Conwy and Deganwy, he had mustered thirty more souls for the second expedition back to the New World. Sometimes at night, when he tossed and turned on his bed in some tavern or friendly court, he had guilty dreams about his ability to find the estuary beyond the sand spit or to even get within a few hundred miles of it. He had his precious map always in his pouch, with the sun-board readings and the reckoning of days sailed. In his saddle bag he had the magical lode-stone carefully wrapped up and he hoped that with all this, his experience and a leavening of both luck and God's will, he would be able to find the coast of the mainland.

It was late February and still deep winter when he got back to the *Gwennan Gorn*. There was snow on the ground and ice on the streams and ponds.

Meirion was already back there, with his wife and child. During the next weeks, the crew—both old and new—began drifting back, some with wives and a few with children of all ages.

By the early days of March, there were forty-two souls assembled on the banks of the Gele. The vessel was as ready for sea as the skilled craftsmen could make her and all that was needed now was improvement in the weather. Taught by the experience of the last trip, Madoc took much more grain and meal aboard, as this was the shortest commodity on the first voyage. Sheep, goats and fowls were bought, some for food on the voyage, but others to establish breeding pairs when they reached the settlement.

"We'll be like Noah's Ark," muttered Meirion, as he watched the animals being herded into their pitifully cramped pens in the hold. The overcrowding was going to be acute, especially with women and children aboard, thought Madoc. He got the shipwrights to add some extra boards along the edges of the two decks, to make the cargo hold smaller and to give more shelter beneath.

Madoc's anxiety to be off at the first sign of a break in the weather turned out to be a fortunate precaution.

Three weeks before Easter, one of the younger members of the new crew came hurrying back to the camp, after a visit to his family in Conwy. "Prince Dafydd is on the march, they say. He is seeking out all who will not support him in his claim to be his father's sole successor."

"Does he know that I am here, with the *Gwennan Gorn* and this camp of hopeful travellers?" asked Madoc, worrying for the safety of those under his care.

"I do not know, but I suspect that he will hear of it before he comes within ten miles. It is no secret and our efforts to recruit members have broadcast the news all over the district."

Madoc made up his mind in an instant.

"We will sail for Dublin on tomorrow's tide . . . it is not worth risking the whole venture for the sake of a few weeks. The weather is moderately good, it will see us across the small seas, even with a cargo of women, children and sheep."

Next day, they were hull-down on the horizon, well out of reach of Dafydd or any other interference. After two uncomfortable nights at sea, they anchored in the Dublin river.

Madoc found the town in a state of unrest, with many Normans mingled with the Irish and Danes. There was uneasiness at the intentions of the King Henry of England and the town was preparing for siege as soon as the season for war came upon them.

Svein was not there; he had taken ship to the Isles of Orkney, north of Caledonia, to visit some relatives and say farewell before his second trip into the unknown.

Madoc took a horse to Clochran to see Riryd. His brother was not expecting him so soon.

"The *Pedr Sant* is by no means ready yet, Madoc. I have promises of a crew of thirty-eight men, women and children, but provisioning and all the work of making ready is not nearly completed. I thought you would be another month yet."

Madoc explained the dangerous position in Gwynedd, but Riryd had similar worries. "Things are in a dangerous state here . . . the Normans are all along the coast and still coming in from Pembroke. Ironically, some are our own kinsmen, Madoc. They are part-Norman, part-Welsh, the progeny of the Fitz-

179

geralds, whose mother was Nest,* daughter of Rhys, King of South Wales. Our father's sister, Gwenllian, married her brother Gruffydd, so we are related to those who now invade us."

"What's to be done, then?" asked Madoc, anxious for his ship-load of women and children, lying in the Liffey.

"I'd not stay there for a month or more . . . and you need that time until the weather breaks. Find a safer place."

Madoc sighed. "We have already run from Wales for the same reason. We are hounded now from Ireland. Where can we go next?"

"What about France?"

This pricked Madoc's senses. "No need to go so far . . . *Ynys Wair*, the island they now call Lundy. We can be safe there; de Marisco is well known to me and we would be cut off by the sea from any foe. Henry of England has eyes on it, but I think his worries with Ireland will keep him off Lundy for more than the time we need."

A week later, all the crew and families from the *Gwennan Gorn* were safely camped in the outbuildings of Marisco Castle, perched on the lofty rock stuck in the entrance to the Severn Sea. De Marisco had welcomed Madoc warmly.

A week after Easter, a balmy spring suddenly appeared. Riryd had promised to come as soon as the weather improved bringing Svein with him and true to his word, one blue-skied morning saw the *Pedr Sant* sail into the cove and anchor alongside the *Gwennan Gorn*.

It was a Sunday the next day and all the eighty-two souls that were going on the great adventure assembled in the courtyard of the castle for De Marisco's priest to say Mass and bless them on their journey.

At noon, they trooped down to the two boats and set sail. The two tiny vessels, laden low in the water, slowly vanished over the western horizon.

Jordan de Marisco watched them from his eyrie, instinctively conscious that something had happened this day on his island, that would become a legend that would last long after he had returned to the dust.

* Whose story is told in the book *Lion Rampant*.

HISTORICAL POSTSCRIPT

The argument about the Madoc story has gone on since Tudor times, with a considerable revival in interest in the past few years, both in Europe and America. The notable investigation by Richard Deacon, published in 1967, has turned a legend into a distinct possibility. This, together with the discovery by Helge Ingstad in 1960–68 of Norse settlements in Newfoundland, forms an important part of the evidence that Europeans reached the New World long before Columbus, whose motives and methods are currently undergoing much unfavourable historical examination.

Some of the main points of the vindication of the Madoc legend are summarised below :

1. Willem the Minstrel was a Flemish writer, possibly from the Abbey of Drongen, near Ghent. He spent a long time on the Welsh border, where he knew Walter Map, another writer, who establishes the date of Willem's active period. Willem wrote the famous *Reynard the Fox* about 1250 and the prologue to this mentions that he was also the author of *The Romance of Madoc*, an earlier work thought to have been lost. Part of it was found at Poitiers in the seventeenth century and a modern expert on the chronicles of the troubadours says that this must have been translated not later than 1300, possibly much earlier. Though only an incomplete precis, it states that "Madoc was the scion of a noble family, driven into exile".

Willem had the story from bards and sailors, who told him to keep it secret from the English, who would seek out Madoc if they knew of it. This was written within fifty years of the voyages, probably much less. Willem lived for a time on an island called "Ely", which is more likely to have been Lundy than in the Fenland, as Ely was another name given to Lundy by the Norsemen, from the Welsh dedication of the church there to

181

Elen. The Pipe Rolls for 1197 say that "Walensian" mercenaries were on Lundy and Willem might have been with them.

The book mentions Madoc's fame as a sailor, his grandfather's Viking blood (though it does not actually name Owain Gwynedd), the belief of Madoc in the Fountain of Youth and the fact that he went to the court of Louis as an envoy, disguised as a monk.

There is then a gap, the Manuscript being incomplete. It recommences by saying that Madoc's voyage was a penance inflicted on him by a conscience-stricken bard (possibly Llywarch). Willem states that Madoc found a "paradise under the sea" and how he returned to Lundy for two new ships. He mentions that the expedition was equipped with "ten painted pearls to probe the rivers"—perhaps a reference to coracles. The "seaman's magic stone" is also mentioned, confirming the knowledge of Western sailors of the magnetic compass at that early date : it is interesting to note that Willem's friend, the Welsh Walter Map, was educated in Paris until 1161, in the place and around the period when Guiot de Provins and Alexander Neckham were writing about the magnetic compass.

Willem says that the magic stone would ensure the safe return of a sailor to his home port, provided he ensured the safety of his ship with nails of horn—a striking agreement with the Welsh tales of the construction of the *Gwennan Gorn*.

Willem says that the "paradise" was not Madoc's ultimate goal, but that this lay six days distance from the "treacherous garden in the sea—*la mere degringolade*" . . . again, extraordinary in that it described the Sargasso Sea, almost three centuries before Columbus. Willem must have known Walter Map between 1161 and 1200 and it seems certain that this story must have been written within fifty years of Madoc's departure.

2. A French chart of the 1600's has "St. Brendan? Matec?" written alongside the Azores, with the word "Matec" again in the corner, followed by the words "voyez Guillaume P-B et Jacob van Maerlant".

The first name must refer to Willem (PB = Pays Bas), the other to a Dutchman who had written several romantic epics around the year 1260. In his *Spiegal Historiaal*, van Maerlant refers to "Madoc's Dream". Again these facts point to very early references to Madoc, untainted by post-Columbus influences or Tudor anti-Spanish propaganda.

3. Meredudd ap Rhys, a clergyman-poet living at Ruabon about 1450, wrote several odes to Madoc, saying that he was the son of Owain Gwynedd and was tall, of comely face, mild manners, pleasing countenance and fond of sea-roaming.

4. In a ship-load of granite which arrived at Barnstaple in 1865 from Lundy, a partly-defaced stone tablet was found. On it was carved, in old-style Welsh, an inscription reading: "IT IS AN ESTABLISHED FACT, KNOWN FAR AND WIDE, THAT MADOC VENTURED FAR OUT INTO THE WESTERN OCEAN, NEVER TO RETURN."

The tablet was undated, but experts who examined the script said that it could not be more recent than 1300. The fact that the words were in the Welsh language suggests that it was carved before 1242, as in that year William de Marisco was taken prisoner to London, ending the era of alliance with the Welsh in defiance of the English king.

5. Devonshire records of 1893 quote archives of Lundy stating that in 1163, "an emissarie of the Prince of Gwynet (Gwynedd) landed at Lundy to seek aid against Henrie of England".

6. G. D. Burtchaell, an Irish antiquarian, mentions some Gaelic verses from an Old Irish song which indicate that Madoc was a Welsh sailor-prince and friend of Dermot McMurrough, King of Leinster. He was "learned in the ways of the sea, creator of a ship harder than the curragh and who praised the beauties of the seas as he sang to the music of his harp".

7. Cynfric ap Gronow, a pre-Tudor Welsh bard, wrote in a poem—"Horn Gwennan, brought to the Gele to be given a square mast / Was turned back from Afon Ganol's quay, for Madoc's famous voyage".

He also testified to Madoc having discovered "a wondrous new lande of strange and delectable fruits, surrounded by a warm sea in which plantes do grow . . . this last is interpreted as referring to the Sargasso Sea. Cynfric also agrees with another bard, Ieuan Brechfa, in stating that the oak for the *Gwennan Gorn* came from the forests of Nant Gwynant in North Wales.

8. This Ieuan Brechfa, a bard from the Carmarthen area who wrote around 1450, has much to say about Madoc, some repeated from earlier sources. One poem included the verse "Madoc, alive in truth, but slain in name / A name that would be whispered on the waves, but never uttered on the land".

This again confirmed the fact that was some mystery about

183

Madoc's disappearance from Wales, fitting in with the poem "Ode to the Hot Iron" by Llywarch Prydydd y Moch, who wrote in 1169–70 (the date of Madoc's emigration) :

"From having with my hand and blade slain the blessed one,
From having been accessory to a murderous deed,
Good Iron exonerate me; that when the assassin
Slew Madoc, he received not the blow from my hand".

This is obviously a plea—possibly allegorical—to the ordeal of the hot iron as a judicial test of truthfulness.

Another of Brechfa's poems says "Hail to thee, Winetland, fabled country of the Norsemen". Written about 1450, this is a remarkable allusion to Vinland, the Newfoundland settlements of the Vikings, established about the year 1000, showing that these Norse tales were well-known in Wales before the Columbus era.
9. Meirion, an eighteenth century bard, quotes currently unknown poems of Llywarch, which tell of Owain Gwynedd's wrath with Brenda of Carno and his suspicion that a youth was having an affair with her. This was only rectified on her death-bed. He also quotes that "Madoc, the lonely one, was forced to find consolation on the great ocean after being robbed of his love."

The same bard states that Madoc sailed with Riryd from Lundy. In 1634, Sir Thomas Herbert wrote that Madoc sailed with his brothers Edwall and Einion from Abergele—the reference to Edwall is wrong, as he had been killed before 1170.
10. Another Cardiganshire poet, Deio ab Ieuan Ddu, writing about 1450, makes Madoc a legendary figure, the patron of fishermen and renowned as a sailor.
11. In the Cottonian Manuscripts in the British Museum, a Latin text of 1477—before Columbus again—says "Filius Oweni Gwynet et eius navigatione terras incognitas; Wallice".
12. An old parchment, not later than the 1400's, was found among the papers of a Heaven family, previous owners of Lundy. This was in Welsh (again suggesting a latest date of the thirteenth century) and was an adaptation of the Moses story of a baby cast adrift, this time applied to the infant Madoc in a coracle. It went on to say that he was a skilled handler of ships, having learned this from exile in Ireland. It later describes him as "the sailor-magician of Bardsey", creator of a ship that could not sink.
13. Roger Morris of Coed y Talwrn, writing in 1582, explained

the name "Ffrydiau Caswennan" from old stories. He says that Madoc, son of Owain Gwynedd, was a real sailor, having voyaged far and wide, but was baffled by the Vortex of Bardsey Race. He built a ship fastened with stag-horns, which he called *Horn Gwennan*, so that the sea would not swallow it. With this ship he visited many lands, but even so, the Bardsey Race severely damaged it on his return from a voyage.

14. John Dee, the Elizabethan mathematician and astrologer, confidant of Queen Elizabeth, based arguments in support of the Madoc story on several sources, including the "Inventio Fortunata" map by Nicholas of Lynne, a Carmelite Monk who made arctic voyages about 1300. Dee also quoted James Cnoyen, a Dutch explorer, saying that Cnoyen possessed a pre-1400 map based on information from Nicholas of Lynne and Willem of Ghent. It showed the track of Madoc's and Nicholas's voyages and indicated an island far out in the western ocean called "Gwerddonau Llion", discovered by Madoc. Dee thought that this was somewhere near the Sea of Weed and could be either "Bermoothes", (mentioned by Shakespeare in *The Tempest*), now called Bermuda or possibly the Bahamas.

15. Sir George Peckam wrote the first Tudor account in a book *A True Reporte* (1583), laying claim to English rights in the New World. He claimed to have a source in David Ingram who had sailed with Sir John Hawkins and who had heard Welsh words spoken in America.

16. In 1584, David Powel's *Historie of Cambria* was published, claiming many ancient sources, including Caradoc of Llancarfan, Gutyn Owen and Cynfric ap Gronow. On Madoc, it says: "He was one of Owain Gwynedd's sons by diverse women. Loved by many, but caring nothing for power, he left the land in contention between his brothers and prepared certain ships with men and munition. He sought adventure by sea, sailing west, leaving the coast of Ireland so farre north, that he came to a lande unknown, where he saw manie strange things. This lande must be part of Nova Hispania or Florida (at that time, Florida meant any part of America) and he returned home and prepared a number of ships and got such men and women who were desirous to live in quietness and taking his leave of his friends, took his journey thitherward again. This Madoc, arriving in the countrie in the year 1170, left most of his people there and returned back

for more of his nation."

17. Richard Hakluyt, who wrote a survey of voyages of discovery in his "Principall Navigations" of 1589, researched deeply into Welsh and continental sources and definitely avers that Madoc reached the New World, probably the West Indies.

18. Peter the Martyr was a scholar at the Spanish court of Ferdinand V, where he wrote a series of "Decades". The first was published on 6th November 1493, only a few months after the return of Columbus. Peter says in it : "Some of the inhabitants of the land honoreth the memory of one Matec, when Columbus arrived on the coast . . . and that the nations of Virginia and Guatemala celebrate the memory of one of their ancient heroes, whom they call Matec."

He also asserted later that Columbus had marked one of his maps in the area of the West Indies with the comment "Questo he mar de Cambrio" (These are Welsh waters).

19. The Dutch writer, Hornius, states in his *De Originibus Americanis* of 1652, that "Madoc, a Prince of Cambria, with some of his nation, discovered and inhabited some lands in the west and that his name and memory are still retained amongst the people living there, scarcely any doubt remains".

Hornius refers to Peter Martyr's "Decades" : he thought that Madoc made two landings, one in Mexico and the other in Chicimecca Indian country.

20. Aber Cerrig Gwynion is no longer on maps of Wales, but in the Welsh Ports Books of 1550–1603, "Aber Kerrik Gwynon" was listed under Caernarvon and Denbighshire.

In a Rye sale-room a few years ago, a damaged manuscript was bought by the late Rev. E. F. Synott; this was part of a list of lost ships from the twelfth and thirteenth centuries. One entry read : "Aber Kerrik Guignon; non sunt Guignon Gorn, Maduac . . . Pedr Sant, Riryd, filius Oueni Gueneti. An 1171."

Against the name of the ship belonging to Riryd, son of Owain Gwynedd, was the sign of the Cross, possibly indicating that it was known that the ship had foundered.

The site of Aber Cerrig Gwynion was established by the presence of an old stone pier, still used as rockery in the garden of a house called "Odstone", at Rhos-on-Sea, Colwyn Bay. This now has a memorial plaque upon it, stating that it was from there that Prince Madoc sailed for America in 1170. The cement in the quay has been examined and declared to be as least as old as that used in Conway Castle.

The old creek which used to run past the quay to the sea, a few yards distant, was called the "Afon Ganol" (the middle river), but the name was lost until recent researches rediscovered it. It is the same name as that mentioned in the poem of Cynfric ap Gronow.

21. The Spaniards were concerned with suggestions that other Europeans had ante-dated Columbus in his discovery of America. Even some of his own nation were sceptical of his claims, including Peter the Martyr. It was suspected that Columbus knew of the existence and location of the West Indies before he set sail. In 1959, a Russian historian, Professor Isypernick of the Uzbek Academy, discovered a secret letter written by Columbus to Queen Isabella, revealing that he had a map of the new islands provided by earlier explorers. This was confirmed by the Map Curator of the Royal Geographical Society, who said there had been secret communications between Columbus and Isabella : there are other maps in the U.S. Library of Congress and one discovered forty years ago in Turkey, which bear this out.

In 1526, the Spaniards sent out three expeditions to look for the "gento blanco", the white people, which included searches in the West Indies for traces of Madoc. Between 1624 and 1627, letters passed between the King of Spain and Luis de Rojas, Governor of Florida, indicating that searches were still being made in Alabama, Florida, Georgia and Mexico.

Hernando de Soto, the Spanish explorer, found traces of ancient fortifications in the neighbourhood of Mobile Bay and in the Chatanooga area, which he considered could not be the work of Indians.

22. A manuscript bought in London in 1947 was found to be a translation of 1599 of a work of the previous year in Spanish, by Buid de Haro, entitled "Anatomie of Spayne". Now in the United States, the manuscript reads "Presumcions to prove ye Spaniardes not to be ye first discoverers of ye Indes" . . . "Francisco Lopez de Gomara wrighteth that the inhabitants of Acumazil and other places, long before the Spaniardes ever arrived, honored the Cross. A sonne of the Prince of Wales called Madoc in the year 1170, sayled into the West Indies and inhabited the country of Mexico. When Fernando Cortes conquered it, Montezume made an oration

to his people, in which he led them to understand how they were descended from a white nation, come from afar off. And how their prophets had often told them how they were again to become subjects to another nation of the same qualities."

23. This speech of Montezuma is recorded elsewhere, by Cortes himself and also in a Spanish manuscript found in Mexico in 1748. Montezuma is recorded as saying : "We came from a generation very far off, in a little island in the north." Another version from Spanish records says : "The ancient tradition that the Great Being had declared on his departure that he should return some day. The white men had come from the quarter where the sun rose beyond the ocean."

24. The tales of pale-skinned, blue-eyed, Welsh-speaking Indian tribes in the south-eastern United States are legion and cannot be touched upon here.

Suffice it to say that for much of the seventeenth to nineteenth centuries, repeated claims and assertions have been made, many of them spurious. The consensus of opinion is that there are fortifications of medieval type and date (certainly not Indian) spread through Alabama, Tennessee and Kentucky, following the rivers that join Mobile Bay to the Missouri. One tribe, the Mandans, last heard of on the upper Missouri, have atypical characteristics that mark them as different from other Amerinds. They were studied by George Catlin in the early part of the last century and he records their destruction as a tribe in 1838, from small-pox introduced by fur-traders.

The American end of the Madoc story has no historical or literary evidence to back it up, but even so, could occupy another book for its full exploration.

25. Lastly, on the 10th November 1953 a tablet was erected on the shore of Fort Morgan, Mobile Bay, Alabama, by the Virginia Cavalier Chapter of the Daughters of the American Revolution. Under the Red Dragon emblem, stand these words :

"In memory of Prince Madoc, a Welsh explorer, who landed on the shores of Mobile Bay in 1170 and left behind with the Indians, the Welsh language".

Even more recently, the Welsh community in New York commissioned a bronze likeness of Madoc, to be placed in 1975 in the museum at Mobile.

In spite of the denials of many centuries, the thin thread connecting the old quay at Aber Cerrig Gwynion and the shores of Mobile Bay, still holds firm; recent interest has strengthened it appreciably.